I0740894

Serpent Point

by

Caleb Clarke

This e-book edition of *Serpent Point* is an original publication. It has been published by arrangement with the author.

THIS IS A WORK OF FICTION. All of the events, characters, names and places depicted in the novel are entirely fictitious or are used fictiously. No representation that any statement made in this novel is true or that any incident depicted in this novel actually occurred is intended or should be inferred by the reader.

No part of this book may be used or reproduced in any manner whatsoever without written permission except in the case of brief quotations embodied in critical articles or reviews. For information, please contact the publisher at:

Yeoman House Books
10 Old Bulgarmarsh Road
Tiverton, RI 02878
E-mail at yeomanhouse@cox.net.

ISBN: 978-0-9822659-1-8

Library of Congress Control Number: 2015954373

Prologue

EDITH SCOGGINS WAS IN A HURRY. Her day had started out on the wrong foot when her 14-year-old son overslept, missed the bus and needed a ride to the junior high school. Then, she had a long list of errands to run: the dry cleaners, the grocery store, the drug store and the bakery; so she was now late to meet her mother for their regular Thursday lunch.

Normally, with time to spare, Edith would have taken her usual route down to Dorchester: Boylston and Huntington streets to Mass. Ave. and then out to her mother's neighborhood. But today, she decided to visit the Trader Joe's store in Cambridge—they always had great deals on good wine—and so she decided to continue down Memorial Drive along the Charles River and then take the new central tunnel through downtown Boston and pick up Mass. Ave on the far side.

Edith was somewhat claustrophobic, which was why she usually avoided the tunnel. Even though the new facility was brighter and cleaner and roomier than the old exhaust-stained highway that first rode high on a rusting steel platform through the downtown area before dipping briefly underneath the harbor at Chinatown, she always felt a bit clammy driving through the tunnel.

The new tunnel, popularly termed the "Big Dig," had been one of the most expensive public works projects in the history of the United States. The project took down the old green-girder elevated highway, built in the post-World War II days, which had cut off Boston's North End and waterfront from downtown Boston, and buried the interstate highway beneath the mud and shale of the old Colonial town. Originally projected to cost just $2.8 billion, the final price tag had climbed and climbed to well over $15 billion, and while the federal government had paid most of the tab, the state was going to be paying interest on the damn thing for generations to come.

But Edith wasn't thinking about dollars as she nervously guided her Toyota Camry down into the tunnel. She kept her eyes forward as she moved into the right-hand lane, next to the shiny white-tiled walls, letting cars, trucks and taxis whiz past in the other two lanes. Almost immediately, traffic slowed to a crawl, a stop-and-go holdup that wasn't supposed to happen in the new, wider tunnel. Edith took in a deep breath and told herself to remain calm. The line of cars would begin to flow again, she told herself hopefully.

The roadway beneath the streets of Old Boston was curved, so it wasn't until they passed the Government Center exit that Edith could see the reason for the traffic holdup: two geysers of dirty water were pouring out of the ceiling into the right-hand lane just ahead, and the cars were stopping and crowding into the two faster lanes on the left to get around the waterfall. Edith remembered hearing on the news that there had been several leaks in the walls and ceilings of the new tunnel, and some Beacon Hill politicians, always ready to pounce on any potential scandal, had been asking for a major safety audit of the tunnel to make sure the work had been done properly.

That would probably not be a bad idea, Edith thought to herself as she waited patiently for the line of cars to reach the area where the water was cascading down from the ceiling and disappearing down a drain at the side of the road. Everyone knew that in in a state like Massachusetts a huge public works project like the Big Dig was an open invitation for graft, corruption and corner-cutting for the usual players of politicians, labor unions and the Mob. Whenever huge sums of money were involved, those three groups were usually first in line, hands out and pockets gaping.

Finally, after several minutes of snail-like, stop-and-go progress, Edith's car approached the wet area beneath the waterfall. But just as she got to the leaky ceiling, the water stopped flowing out, as if someone had turned off a tap. The car in front of her, taking advantage of the end of the waterfall, splashed straight ahead in the now open lane, instead of waiting for a gap in the line of cars merging to the left. Edith decided to do the same and pressed on her accelerator.

It was a fatal decision, and the last Edith Scoggins would ever make. For just as her car leaped forward, the ceiling above her lane collapsed with a huge roar. A large reddish steel beam and several panels of concrete ceiling dropped downward and crushed the little Toyota like a bug. Thankfully, Edith Scoggins never knew what hit her—she died instantly under the weight of the heavy steel and concrete.

A truck driver jumped out of his rig and ran to the crushed wreckage. He peered inside, saw Edith's body and shook his head. Cars behind in the tunnel began honking impatiently, not knowing what had happened. Two or three other people, who had seen the accident, also got out of their cars and came over to see if they could help. One of them pulled out a cell phone and called in a report to 911.

"Gonna be a while," the truck driver said to no one in particular. "But I tell ya something…I sure as hell wouldn't wanna be those people." He nodded at the logo imprinted on the dripping steel beam that now rested atop the crushed car. PYLE INDUSTRIES. "They're in for a shit storm of historic proportions."

JACK DUNNE STRODE INTO THE EXPANSIVE LOBBY SPACE of One International Place, crossed to the express elevators and rode in ear-popping silence up to the 40th floor. He emerged in the elegant reception area for Pyle Industries, decorated in mahogany paneling, deep tufted leather chairs and what looked like real oil paintings of Yankee clipper ships beating their way around the Horn to China. A window wall to the right presented the stunning view of Boston Harbor, spread out below the building, a view that today extended all the way out to Provincetown, clinging to the sand dunes at the very end of Cape Cod.

Dunne walked over to the reception desk, where a striking red-haired woman presided over an empty granite-topped desk, a small, white-plastic microphone extending down the line of her right jawline the only hint that she was in communication with the outside world.

"Good morning, Mr. Dunne," she said with a bright smile. "Mr. Pyle is waiting for you in the conference suite. Is the rest of your party on the way?"

Dunne shook his head. "I'm the only one coming," he said.

A look of confusion briefly clouded the woman's face—this was not what she had been told—but she quickly recovered and within seconds another well-dressed and perfectly coiffed young woman appeared and beckoned Dunne to follow.

"May I bring you a cup of our fresh-roasted coffee?" the escort asked as she led him down a paneled hallway. "Mr. Pyle has his own special blend flown in weekly from his farm in the highlands of Colombia. It's really quite remarkable."

"I'm sure it is," Dunne said. "Thank you. I take it black."

"Certainly, sir," she said. "Here we are." She opened a large, double-panel mahogany door and ushered Dunne inside.

He stopped inside the door and took in the scene. The conference room was easily sixty feet long, and the center of it contained a massive pedestal table, around which were set high-backed black leather upholstered armchairs. Most of the chairs were occupied by what looked like a small army of lawyers and accountants. Each one of them had a laptop open and several were whispering into cell phones. All around the room, large rectangular video screens displayed charts, graphs, and tables of figures. At the head of the table at the far left of the room, sitting is a throne-like red leather chair, was Thomas Pyle, the CEO and chairman of Pyle Industries, probably the largest public works construction company in the world.

Dunne stood there quietly as he studied Pyle. The Old Man, as he was known in the industry, both with and without affection, was now in his mid-60's, with leonine white hair swept back dramatically on his head, thick white eyebrows, a flattish nose and a square chin. Although he was sitting, deep in conversation with the man to his right, Dunne knew that Pyle was well over six feet tall and had a stocky build that he kept in rock-hard shape. Pyle was wearing a light-gray suit, a shirt of the faintest cranberry hue and a colorful summer necktie and matching pocket square. At his wrist a gleaming gold Rolex and the diamonds in his cufflinks winked in the overhead lighting of the room.

Pyle looked up and saw Dunne and stood up with a broad, welcoming smile.

"Jack! Great to see you again! Come in, come in!" The Old Man's voice was gruff and deep, born of a thousand tough negotiations over the forty years he had taken a company with one bulldozer and one dump truck and turned it into the worldwide powerhouse that was Pyle Industries. Thanks to Pyle's combination of street smarts, bravado and ability to bust some heads to get a job done, he had taken his company to the pinnacle. Everywhere in the world, from China to Russia to Boston, Pyle Industries was involved in almost every major infrastructure construction project. Tom Pyle was a personal friend of tyrants, dictators and back-slapping politicians in a dozen countries, including the United States.

Pyle waved Dunne into the leather chair at the other end of the conference table. Dunne felt like he needed binoculars to see the group gathered at the far end. As soon as he sat down, a beautiful Limoge china cup and saucer were placed soundlessly at his left elbow, the dark ebony liquid inside releasing a heavenly aroma of deep, richly roasted coffee.

Pyle glanced at the door to the conference room. "Where's the rest of your team, Jack?" he asked. "They get lost in the parking garage?" He boomed out a hearty chuckle.

"It's only me, Tom," Dunne said. "I am the team."

Silence fell over the room, as Pyle's legion of bean counters stopped what they were doing to stare at Dunne.

The tall, thin, elegantly dressed and patrician-looking lawyer at Pyle's elbow cocked his head and raised his eyebrows.

"I beg your pardon?" the man said.

"Pardon granted," Dunne said. "Who the fuck are you?" He fixed the man with an unwavering stare.

The man sat back as if he had been slapped. He recovered quickly and stood up, shooting his cuffs and straightening his Brooks Brothers suit.

"I am Marshall Cabot," the man said, his disdain undisguised. "I am a senior partner in the firm of Ropes and Gray and we are representing Pyle Industries in this proposed merger transaction. Am I to understand that you alone will be conducting the negotiations here today? We were led to understand that you would be providing your corporate data today that would help us arrive at a transaction price that would be acceptable to all parties in the agreement, subject, of course to further due diligence and …"

"Marsh, old boy," Dunne said. "I'm starting to get a headache. I don't do 'due diligence' and all that other bullshit. I pay people to do that shit for me. If I'm going to sell my company to Mr. Pyle here, then Mr. Pyle and I are gonna talk about it, arrive at a price and then we'll either shake on it, or decide not to do it and shake on that. Pretty simple, don't ya think?"

Marshall Cabot, scion of the Cabot family, the ones from the 'land of the bean and the cod who spoke only to God' as the old toast had it, graduate of Harvard College and Harvard Law, chairman of the board of Mass General Hospital, member in good standing of The Country Club, Myopia Hunt Club and the Agawam Hunt Club, patron to both the Boston Symphony Orchestra and the Boston Civic Opera, and owner of residences in Lewisburg Square on Beacon Hill, the Jupiter Island Club in Hobe Sound, Florida, St. John's in the U.S. Virgin Islands and the Yellowstone Club in Montana, sat back in his black leather chair as if he had just been slapped with a dead mackerel.

"My dear sir," he said, ice dripping from every word, "This is most irregular. There are literally hundreds of issues that we have identified as unresolved in this proposed transaction, and to resolve them will require hundreds of hours of negotiations between the parties. If you insist on being the sole negotiating party, then I am afraid …"

He left the rest of the sentence dangling in the air, but it was clear from the shake of his head that he believed only the worst of possible outcomes would result.

Dunne sat there for several moments.

"Marsh old boy," he said finally. "You may have identified hundreds of issues which you think need resolving. You may have even convinced Tom here that there are hundreds of issues to discuss for which he can't possibly go on without you. I don't give a rat's ass. I'm here to negotiate with Tom Pyle about merging our two companies. That's the only issue I've come here today to discuss. If you're telling me that I can't discuss that with Tom today without paying for a busload of $500-an-hour comma checkers in the room, then I guess I've come to the wrong place."

He waited. Marshall Cabot stared across the table at Dunne, who stared back calmly, his hands folded in his lap, the coffee untouched beside him. Cabot had, of course, been briefed at length by his staff about Jack Dunne prior to this morning's meeting. "He's a little rough around the edges," his associate had told him in the cab coming over. Cabot recalled the biography on Dunne that had been included in the preparatory documents. He had been born to a single mother in the Beverley neighborhood on Chicago's South Side. His mother, a heroin addict, had died shortly thereafter. There was no information about his father at all. He had been raised by the State of Illinois in a series of foster homes and reform schools, the latter required after Dunne began breaking the law at about the age of 10. Once he hit age 18, the state had offered Edward "Jack" Dunne a choice: ten years in the state prison at Joliet, or three in the U.S. Army. Dunne chose the latter.

He had actually liked the Army, and volunteered for the Rangers. He passed through all the training with flying colors: Dunne was a tough, street-hardened kid, but was smart enough to know when to keep his trap shut. In return, the Rangers let him do what he liked the best: sneaking up on the enemy behind their lines and killing as many of them as he possibly could. After two tours in the killing fields, the Army highly recommended Dunne for a transfer to a private, CIA-run company where he could continue to operate behind the lines on secret missions. Once again, he loved his work, while his employers, learning just how much discipline from above Dunne would accept, pretty much let him operate as he wanted. He went from the Mideast to Afghanistan, where he helped the mujahedeen fight the Russians, and, on the side, accepted a couple of wet jobs in Europe, taking out the leaders of certain radical groups, like the Red Army Faction and the Baader-Meinhof Gang.

Then, suddenly, the Company had unceremoniously retired him. It was not clear exactly why. But they gave him $2.5 million, tax-free, to start over with back in the States. He bided his time, explored a few options here and there, and eventually used some of his nest egg to purchase a small but growing construction firm located just outside Philadelphia named Burke Construction. He had paid off the eponymous Burke, sent him down to his Florida retirement condo in Sarasota, rolled up his sleeves and went to work. Dunne had determined that large-scale public works projects offered the best chance for big profits: the money came from the never-ending fount of government appropriations, and with politicians always trying to get reelected by bringing home new and exciting projects like highways, bridges, tunnels, new courthouses, university dorms and post offices. The supply of money was large, liquid and constant.

Cabot remembered reading that Dunne and his company had broken in to the otherwise tightly-knit world of public construction quickly. Dunne had hired a few of his former Company mercenaries and the result had been an almost instantaneous flow of work for the small but growing company. Instead of picking off enemy leaders in the jungles of Southeast Asia, Cabot had thought, Dunne was now picking off favors, promises and contracts from numerous state and federal governmental agencies. Hopefully, this new career was not as "wet" as the last had been, Cabot mused.

Dunne and his Burke Construction had become something of a problem for Pyle Industries as it began to encroach on what Tom Pyle had thought of as his business, including the Big Dig project here in Boston. Despite the best efforts of both Pyle and the phalanx of lawyers at Ropes and Gray, Burke Construction had managed to get a foot in the door of the massive Boston project. And, once inside, he had been a pain in the posterior. Assigned to handle the excavation and construction of an offshoot of the main artery tunnel, one that ran out to East Boston and Logan Airport, Dunne had immediately imported some designers from Europe with an entirely new tunnel-building technology that dropped pre-fabricated sections of tunnel into prepared sections of the seabed, bolted them together and created an instant tunnel. This new method was faster and cheaper than the method used by Pyle Industries by about forty percent, and after Dunne had described his technology to reporters from the Globe and the New York Times, the state legislature had quickly passed resolutions demanding that this technology be used on the main sections of the Big Dig Tunnel.

That change had cost Pyle several billion dollars of projected revenue, and made Jack Dunne a nice chunk of change, even though the lawyers and accountants had been able to recoup much of that money through change orders and other accounting sleights of hand. Tom Pyle had first been furious. Then, after thinking about it for a while, he had been envious. Jack Dunne reminded Thomas Pyle of himself, thirty-five years ago.

"Marshall," Pyle had said to his lawyer, "We can either spend the rest of our lives fighting with this sumbitch, or bring him inside and make him part of our team. I think it might be cheaper to have him inside the tent pissing out rather than the other way around. Go make him an offer."

Which was why this highly insulting man was now staring at Cabot across the long mahogany conference table at Pyle Industries. Cabot took a good look at Dunne, who was somewhere between 45 and 55 years old—difficult to tell. His black hair was full and glistening, his eyes dark and guarded. He had the ruddy complexion of his Irish background, broad shoulders and a hint of stubble on his chin. He wore a nice, but not overly expensive suit, and Cabot noted he wore no watch or jewelry of any kind. Cabot looked at Dunne's hands, and saw that the knuckles on the man's huge hands were squashed and white—not from anxiety, but as if they had been smashed repeatedly into a brick wall. He wondered what other scars there were in the man, both physical and emotional.

"Mr. Dunne," Cabot started again, "I appreciate your desire to simplify the transaction as much as possible. But Ropes and Gray has a fiduciary duty to our client to provide him with the best legal advice possible. I am afraid we cannot let this deal go forward on the strength of a simple handshake agreement. The potential complications are too important to both sides."

Dunne stood up. "In that case, I guess there's nothing more to discuss," he said. "Too bad. Marsh, you may think you crap $100 bills, but it still smells an awful lot like shit to me. Tom, if you ever want to talk man to man, I'm ready. Good luck with that involuntary manslaughter thing on the ceiling collapse. If you're lucky, the DA will make a deal with you for, what? ... ten years in the slammer? By the time you get out, I'll have all your business anyway. By the way, you guys bidding on that new bridge in Copenhagen? You might as well save the time…we've got about six guys from the European Parliament in our back pocket."

He turned to go. The sound of hands clapping stopped him.

Tom Pyle had been sitting in his big red chair watching and listening, his eyes never leaving Jack Dunne's face. Now he was applauding, exaggerating the motion, with a big smile creasing his face.

"That, my friend, was brilliant!" he said, standing up and walking over to shake Jack Dunne's large hand. "Fuckin'-A performance of the year! 'Crappin' hundred dollar bills!' My God!"

Marshall Cabot also rose, his face red with anger.

"Thomas, I recommend that you say nothing more. I recommend that we cancel this proposed transaction at once and move on. I further recommend …"

"Oh, can it Marshall," Pyle said, clapping Dunne on the back. "Me an' Jack here are gonna go and do some talkin'," he said. "When we're done, I'll let you and your $500-an-hour comma checkers take a looksee."

He was still laughing as he led Dunne down the hall towards his office.

Tom Pyle's office was, as one might expect, large and lavish, yet it had the feel of a space where work was actually done. The corner office had the best views of Boston Harbor, where one could stare across the way at the planes landing and taking off at Logan, or look down and watch the fishing boats and pleasure craft skimming back and forth across the harbor like water bugs. His desk was large and crowded with flatscreen computer monitors—three of them, each containing flickering banks of data.

Pyle waved Dunne into one of the plush visitor's chairs in front of his desk and went to a credenza on the side of the room.

"Need something to drink, Jack?" he asked. "Coffee? Water? Whiskey?"

"Nothing, thanks," Dunne said. He folded his hands and waited.

Pyle poured himself a Diet Coke, taken from a small refrigerator, and came back to his desk, sitting down heavily. He took a sip and glanced across the desk.

Dunne spoke first.

"Why do you want to buy Burke Construction?" he asked.

"Because you are a royal pain in my ass," Pyle answered promptly. "You've been chipping away at my business, reducing my profit margins, hiring away some of my best people. As I told Marshall—" he smiled again at the memory of the conference room scene—"I'd rather have you inside my tent working for, er, *with* me."

He paused and sipped again. "To tell you the truth, Dunne, you remind me of someone. Someone who started off in this business with nothing, fought for every dollar he ever made and who likes nothing better than to win. In other words, a real tough guy."

"And who is that?" Dunne asked.

"Me," Pyle said. Dunne nodded in acknowledgment of the compliment.

"What's in it for me?" Dunne asked next.

"Hell, what do you want?" Pyle said, spreading his hands out wide. "Big salary? Company jet? Stock options? I figure with the business you can bring inside, plus our normal on-going work, we can grow this baby three, four times what we are today. Be win-win for everyone. You got high energy and street smarts; I got resources. Sounds like a no-brainer to me."

"What if I want this office?" Dunne spoke quietly, knowing this was the crux of the deal.

"Can't have it as long as I'm still here," Pyle said. A smile played counterpoint to the narrowing of his eyes.

"We all gotta go sometime," Dunne said. "Then what?"

"You know I've got two boys," Pyle said, "Michael and Jason. They work with me here."

"I know that Michael spends most of his time in Washington wining and dining members of Congress," Dunne said. "And I know that Jason spends most of his time waterskiing and playing golf. You really think either one of them can run Pyle Industries?"

Pyle was silent, but his face grew red. He struggled to maintain control of himself, and took another sip from his glass.

"That's a cruel thing to ask a man," he said, finally, managing to keep the tone of his voice level.

Dunne shrugged.

"The truth hurts, sometimes," he said. "Listen, I'm sure both of your boys are nice fellows, but face it, they're soft. They've never had to work hard for anything in their lives. You think they'd stand up against the bastards you and I deal with every day? The sheiks…the politicians…the Mob guys? You know as well as I do, Tom, that they don't have what it takes. You leave Pyle Industries to one of those two, and it'll be out of business in six months, a year tops."

"Whereas, if I agree to leave my company to you, it will thrive," Pyle said.

"You said it yourself," Dunne said. "We're a lot alike. Look, I know it hurts. I have a son, too, a little boy I'm crazy about. And if someone told me something like I just told you, I'd probably feel like killing him. But business isn't personal, you know that. You also know I'm right."

The two men were silent. Pyle stood up and went to the window wall and stared out at Boston Harbor. Dunne knew what he was thinking. Pyle knew that Dunne's evaluation of his sons was correct—they were good boys, but they couldn't run an empire like Pyle Industries. Yet they were his sons, blood of his blood. How could he toss them overboard in favor of a stranger, a ruthless, take-no-prisoners bastard? And that's what it all comes down to, Dunne thought. In the end, despite all the warm fuzzy family feelings and bonds of love between fathers and sons, in the end it all came down to who could do the job. Predator or prey. Eat or be eaten. With either of the Pyle boys in charge, Pyle Industries would be like a big, fat, slow wildebeest trying to outrun a hungry lion. With Dunne at the helm, there was a better than even chance the wildebeest would turn on the lion and kick its ass.

"And how are you planning to handle the tunnel cave-in problem?" Dunne continued. "The vultures are already beginning to circle, and it hasn't been two weeks yet. The morons here on Beacon Hill want to gin up a lynching party to come down here and string you up. Your Congressional friends are running for cover. There are bound to be hearings, all on TV, where you can explain why your beams weren't supported well enough and how sorry you are that that poor woman got her brains smeared all over her upholstery. They'll start measuring out a striped suit for you in Leavenworth. You're one of those super rich guys that we're all supposed to hate these days."

Pyle turned away from the window, came back to his desk and sat down. "My boys think we should admit our culpability, settle with the woman's family and move on," he said wearily. They think that's the best way for it to blow over."

Dunne was silent. "And what do you think?"

Pyle shook his head. "We didn't do anything wrong!" he said, trying to keep a slight tone of whining out of his voice. "That's the hell of it. This thing wasn't our fault."

"And whose fault was it?" Dunne asked, his voice low.

"My engineers say the concrete poured for the support beams wasn't up to the specifications," Pyle said. "Somebody cut corners."

"And who poured the concrete?"

"Subcontractor. Company called Benito Concrete and Paving," Pyle said. "On a special, no-bid contract arranged by our beloved senator, Malcolm O'Malley."

"And who owns Benito?"

"Well, there's some guy's name on the papers down at the State House, but the company is totally controlled by Jerry Bruno."

"The Mob guy Bruno?" Dunne asked.

Pyle nodded.

"That's your answer," Dunne said. "Giving in shows weakness. It will be remembered. Instead, you fight back. Let the press find out about Benito, its owners and its sponsor, that corrupt Irish bastard."

"There's only a couple of things I can see wrong with that idea," Pyle said, a smile playing at the corner of his lips. "One is that Jerry Bruno would have me wrapped in a cement suit and dropped into the Mystic River before the sun set. Two is that Malcolm O'Malley is the last beloved member of the most famous political family in the state, has approval ratings of 80 percent or more, and is planning to announce his run for President this fall. He's not a real good guy to piss off."

"Fuck 'em both," Dunne said. "Once you start the press in on the case, they'll both be too busy ducking the shitburgers being tossed at them from every direction to think about you. If O'Malley is as powerful as everyone says, he'll be able to ride it out, or have the whole thing buried. And as for Bruno, well, you let me worry about him."

Pyle sat back and smiled. "Does that mean we've come to an agreement?" he asked.

"Not until you decide about the boys," Dunne said. "I want to be president and when you die or retire, I want to have controlling interest in Pyle Industries. The rest is just filler to me. You can have your boy Marshall call my legal beagle, Isaac Finkelstein. They can work out the montetary details. Isaac knows what I want. You can afford it."

"What firm is this Finkelstein with?" Pyle asked, writing on a memo pad.

Dunne laughed as he stood to go. "Isaac doesn't have a firm," he said. "He works for me. 24/7. Used to be in the Israeli Special Forces before he became a lawyer. You'd better tell your boy Marshall not to piss him off too much. Isaac knows about seventy-seven ways to kill a man, and I think I taught him about sixty of them."

Pyle laughed. "I will," he said. "Listen, how would you like to come down to the island this weekend? I've got a little summer place down on the Cape at a place called Serpent Point, just outside Winter Cove. It's private, it's peaceful and we can talk some more. I'll invite the boys down and you can meet them."

"Serpent Point?" Dunne said. "I'm guessing Saint Patrick hasn't been there yet."

Pyle chuckled. "Yeah, the name is a little off-putting," he said. "But there aren't any snakes there, at least I've never seen any. The name goes back to Colonial times. I've heard some say that 'serpent' is some old Indian name that got Anglicized. I've heard others claim that some old Puritan preacher of the fire and brimstone variety named it. It's a private little piece of land and my neighbors and I like the name. We think it helps keep some of the summer riff-raff away."

Dunne thought for a moment. "I have my son Tiger this weekend," he said. "Is it all right if I bring him along? He's just five years old, but he's a good kid."

"Sure, sure," Pyle said, walking Dunne to the door. "That will be nice. I'll have Margaret my housekeeper get the cottage ready. It's right on the beach. You guys will love it."

"Sounds great, thanks," Dunne said. They shook hands. "See you Friday afternoon."

JACK DUNNE GUIDED HIS BLACK SAAB CONVERTIBLE over the
Sagamore Bridge that spanned the Cape Cod Canal and down
the central highway that split the arm-shaped peninsula in
two. He took the exit for Winter Cove and soon was driving
through the center of that small, quaint New England village,
one of several in a row that clung to the pebbly beaches of the
Cape's southern shore. It was not yet the prime summer season—that would come near the Fourth of July—but the sidewalks of the old fishing village were still busy as pedestrians
browsed through the gift shops, ice cream stores, art galler-
ies and other businesses whose main purpose was to separate
tourists from their dollars.

Following the directions that Tom Pyle had sent him,
Dunne crossed over Route 28, followed Ocean Avenue to the
shore and turned west for a mile or two. He passed a sign saying "Private Neighborhood—Please Turn Around" which he
ignored and continued on until he came to a gray cedar-shake
and white-trimmed building sitting on a bluff overlooking the
ocean. Several rows of floating docks extended out behind the

building into Nantucket Sound, and Dunne guessed that the gold-embossed sign, "W.C.Y.C." stood for "Winter Cove Yacht Club," which he knew was a bastion of Old Yankee money and privilege. He was amused to note that the parking attendant waiting patiently at a guard shack for members to arrive was a young black man.

"Bet they don't let him into the main dining room," Dunne said to himself. Or maybe he said it aloud, because suddenly the tousle-haired bundle of boy, who had been soundly sleeping on the seat next to Dunne, stirred and said "Wha-?"

Dunne looked over at his son Tiger and smiled. Five years old and fearless, the boy meant the world to Dunne. He had named him Anthony after one of his Special Operations buddies who had bought the farm on a mission deep into Laos; but the boy had been known as Tiger ever since, as he was first beginning to learn language, he began to imitate the growls of the tiger on one of his pull'n'play nursery toys. Since it always amused people when he did so, Tiger had growled at every opportunity he could.

"We're almost there, pal," he told the boy, who had been fast asleep in the warm sun streaming in from above. Tiger nodded and closed his eyes again.

Dunne followed a narrow road around the yacht club and down a long causeway. The ocean sparkled in the sunlight off to the left, while a pretty estuarian bay spread out to the right, the tidal creek snaking through hundreds of acres of marsh grass and mud. At the end of the causeway, the land rose into a large bluff of land covered with pin oaks and pine, on which Dunne could see at least two large houses.

The causeway ended at two stone pillars, each ten feet high, topped with polished granite orbs. One pillar's carved granite sign read "SERPENT" and the other, "POINT." There was also a rectangular white metal sign that warned drivers that they were entering private property and that trespassing would be treated with dire results. Dunne flipped the bird at the sign. "Fuck you," he said. "We're invited."

"Fwuck you," came the high-pitched little voice from the boy. Dunne blanched. He had to remember that Tiger was at that age where he repeated everything he heard, bad language included.

"Hey kiddo," Dunne said, "We're here! The beach!"

Tiger sat up and peered over the top of the Saab's dashboard.

"I don' see the beach, Daddy," he said. "Where is it?"

"It's over this way, behind this house…look! Across that lawn!"

Dunne pointed to a wide green lawn that bordered the side yard of an expansive beachfront mansion. The home had a large central section and two wings in either direction, like arms opening to the warmth of the sunshine beaming in across the Sound. The entire house was covered in the same grey cedar-shake shingles as the yacht club, but on this home, the trim was in British racing green. A circular drive ran from the small dusty road up to an impressive front portico that looked strangely familiar to Dunne. But Tiger had finally spotted the beach and was squealing in delight.

"Swimmin,' Daddy, swimmin'! Can we go? Can we? Huh?"

Dunne laughed. "Sure, boy. We can go for a swim. First we have to go meet a nice man. Remember to be polite, OK?"

"Daddy," Tiger was suddenly serious and, it seemed to Dunne, sounded slightly offended. "Mommy already tole me that."

Dunne laughed again and continued down the curving narrow lane. Across from the large beachfront house, tucked away on the side of a hill overlooking the marshes, were two more large Cape Cod homes, connected by a garage. Around another curve and up a rise, and the Dunne's passed a magnificent white clapboarded house with wraparound porches overlooking the bay and another rolling sward of green lawn, neatly trimmed, that ran down to the shock of wild rose bushes at the edge of the bay. Dunne noted the beautiful swimming pool, a wire-enclosed tennis court and what looked like a large putting green.

"This guy looks like he has all the toys," Dunne said.

"Can we play at his house?" Tiger asked hopefully.

Dunne laughed again, something he found himself doing a lot when he had Tiger. "Sure, kiddo," he said, reaching out and brushing the golden hair back from his son's eyes and sweaty forehead.

The last house on Serpent Point belonged to Tom Pyle. It was situated atop a high bluff at the edge of the ocean. A thicket of trees blocked off the house from the roadway, but a curved drive ran up to the front. The house was two stories high, covered in aged grey cedar shake shingles, and the windows were all framed with white-painted shutters. It seemed rather plain from the front, but Dunne could tell the back side had the killer views of Nantucket Sound and its own private beach below.

Dunne pulled the Saab up in front of the entryway and killed the engine. He got out and helped his little boy clamber out of the car. The front door of the house opened and a grandmotherly woman of about sixty years came outside. She dressed casually in shorts and a T-shirt, her graying hair pulled back off her face which was creased with a welcoming smile.

"Welcome to Serpent Point!" the woman said as she came out to greet them. "What a lovely day! I'm Margaret Andrews, Mr. Pyle's housekeeper. He's had to go into town on some errands, but should be back soon. This young man must be Tiger! I'll bet he'd like to go for a swim!"

Tiger's little face lit up in delight and he gave the woman a big hug. She smiled down at him, and then shook Dunne's hand. "Welcome Mr. Dunne," she said. "Come on in and we'll find some iced tea and maybe a little apple juice for this young man."

"How did you know I like apple juice?" Tiger asked in his high-pitched little voice.

"Well, I just guessed," Margaret said. "Most little boys I know do."

"Do you know a lot of little boys?" Tiger asked seriously.

Margaret laughed and took Tiger's hand. "Only good little boys like you," she said. "Come in, come in."

They walked inside the house. The floorboards were wide pine, obviously very old, and the walls were covered in tongue-and-groove paneling, all painted bright white. The wide foyer extended the length of the house, and the double doors on both ends were thrown open to allow the sea breeze to blow through, creating a delightful cooling effect. To the left of the foyer, facing the front of the house, was an office-like den and overlooking the ocean side was the dining room, with a dark-stained mahogany table and elegant Louis XIV chairs.

To the right, large picture windows in the comfortable living room allowed the bright sun to pour into the whitewashed room, whose walls were hung with colorful paintings and nautical-themed sconces of brass. Outside, a large screened porch opened onto another broad wooden deck, scattered with colorful Adirondack chairs and wooden tables. There was a narrow patch of grass and wooden stairs that led down to the private beach below. The view out the windows was, indeed, spectacular, a horizon-to-horizon view of the ocean.

"Nice place," Dunne said approvingly.

"Thank you, Mr. Dunne," Margaret said. "It has been in the Pyle family for three generations now. Mr. Pyle is very proud of it. I'll take Tiger here off to the kitchen. There's a powder room back here if you need one. Otherwise, make yourself at home. I'm sure Tom will be back shortly."

She led Tiger off to the kitchen. Dunne heard his little voice asking "Is the water very cold here? Mommy said the water might be too cold for swimming."

Dunne looked around the bright sitting room. It had the feeling of being well lived in and comfortable, the perfect atmosphere for a beach house. The chairs were covered with soft chintz fabrics, a round table in one corner had a work-in-progress jigsaw puzzle with pieces scattered across the top, and there were piles of books and magazines all around the room. He sat down on one of the sofas, picked up a copy of *Forbes* and idly leafed through, scanning a story analyzing the prospective field for next year's Presidential campaign. One of the leading Democratic candidates was Senator Martin O'Malley of Massachusetts, the article said. "O'Malley hopes to finally fulfill the destiny long expected of his family," it said.

The O'Malley name was a famous one in American politics, but not so much for anything any of the large Irish Catholic clan had been able to accomplish, but rather, for the heartache and tragedy the family had endured through the years.

Senator O'Malley's grandfather had been one of Franklin Roosevelt's top diplomats, roaming the world trying to keep the alliance together. At least until the Nazis had managed to shoot his plane out of the sky as he was flying from London down to Morocco. Some years later, the Old Man's son had been elected to the Senate from Massachusetts, and was heavily favored to win the Presidential nomination back in the 1960's, when he fell off his horse while jumping over the hedgerows in his expansive estate in the Virginia countryside. Hitting his head, he had never regained consciousness and finally the family had taken him off life support. Now Malcolm O'Malley, the third generation of the family to enter public service, had won back his father's old Senate seat, held it for a decade or more, and was now getting ready to launch his own campaign for the White House. And all the pundits had him at better than even money to pull it off.

Dunne heard the front screen door bang open and Tom Pyle walked in with a brown paper bag under his arm. "You made it!" he said, a wide smile creasing his face. "Great! You brought the boy?"

"Margaret has him under control in the kitchen," Dunne said, standing up and shaking hands with Pyle. He tossed the magazine down. Pyle noticed what he was reading.

"They say my neighbor is planning to run," Pyle said.

"Your neighbor?" Dunne asked.

Pyle smiled. "That first house you passed coming in? The big one on the beach? That's O'Malley's place. The senior senator from the Commonwealth of Massachusetts. The rest of his clan lives over in Winter Cove."

"Are you supporting him?" Dunne asked.

Pyle laughed, a bitter-sounding laugh. "You mean, 'Am I giving him money?' Absolutely yes," he said. "He wins the White House and Pyle Industries can get an inside track into American construction projects all over the world. That's worth all the campaign donations I can make or collect. But will I vote for him? Never in a hundred million years."

"How come?"

"Let me count the ways," Pyle said. "He's a crook, a bastard, a drunk, he'll fuck anything that walks and half the things that don't, his family is shit, he'll steal the country blind and sell us out to the first group that asks for it."

Dunne laughed. "He must have one redeeming character-istic," he said.

"Yeah," Pyle said, "One day he'll die and we'll all be the better for it."

Margaret and the little boy came back in from the kitch-en, Tiger munching on a chocolate chip cookie. He stopped to shake hands gravely with Pyle as his father introduced him, and then smiled up at the adult faces.

"Can we go swimming now, Daddy?" he asked.

The three adults laughed. "I'm afraid the time has come," Margaret chuckled, running her fingers through the boy's hair. "He's been as patient as he can be."

"Okay," Tom Pyle said. "I'll show you fellows the Boat House. It's nice and quiet down there and right next to the beach. You can swim, play on the beach or whatever you want. Meet back here around six, six-thirty. I've invited my boys down for dinner, and we can catch up on things then."

"Are we gonna sleep on the boats in the boat house?" Ti-ger wanted to know.

"No sir, young fella," Pyle said with a smile. "There hav-en't been any real boats in the boat house for years. We turned it into a nice place for boys and their Daddies to stay when they come to visit us. I think you'll like it."

"Okay," Tiger said. "That's good 'cause I might get seasick sleeping in a boat."

"You and me both, kiddo," Dunne said.

Both Tiger and his dad were slightly sunburned when they appeared on the deck of Tom Pyle's home at six that evening. Pyle had put some steaks on the grill and Margaret was tossing a green salad. The sun was setting, giving the sky a rosy glow.

"Hi guys," Pyle greeted the two. "How's the water?"

"It's freezing!" Tiger said.

"But not so cold that we couldn't spend most of the afternoon in it," Dunne laughed.

Pyle motioned to a side table that had been set up with liquor bottles and mixers. "Jack, make yourself a drink," he said. "We've also got wine and beer in the fridge. And for you, Mr. Tiger, I've made a hamburger and Margaret baked up a batch of her world-famous macaroni and cheese this afternoon. And Angel should be here soon. You guys can watch a movie upstairs while the grown-ups have dinner and talk a little business. Okay?"

"Yumm," Tiger said. "Thank you!" He hesitated a moment. "Is she really an angel?"

Pyle laughed. "Well, I don't know about that, but Angel is a sweetheart, that's for sure," he said. "Her real name is Angela.

She's almost sixteen I think, and lives across the street. Lovely child. We've watched her grow up all these years."

Dunne made himself a gin and tonic at the table. "Are your sons here?" he asked.

"They're driving down from Boston," Pyle replied. "Should be here soon."

Margaret came outside with some bowls of nuts and plates of crackers and cheese. She also brought a glass of juice for the boy. Setting the snacks down, she stopped and sniffed the air. "Don't you just love the smell of the ocean this time of year?" she said.

"Smells like fishies," Tiger piped up.

"Indeed it does, Tiger," she agreed, smiling down at him.

The sound of the front screen door slamming was followed by a "Hoo-ooo!" Margaret called "We're out here, dear," and Angel stepped out onto the deck. The teenager was fresh-faced and tanned, her long dark hair pulled back in a pony tail tied with a pink ribbon. She was wearing short shorts, a tee shirt and flip flops. She ran over and hugged Tom Pyle, and then Margaret. She then turned to look at the two others on the deck.

"I'm Jack Dunne," he said, shaking her hand. "And this young man is my son Tiger."

"Pleased to meet you," Angel said. "Wow, Tiger…they told me you were a handsome little guy, but they didn't say you were so cute!"

Tiger beamed with pride and gravely shook Angel's hand.

"I've put your dinner on a tray in the kitchen," Margaret said. "You can take it upstairs to the den and pop in a movie."

"Okay," Angel said. She took Tiger's hand. "You hungry, Tiger?"

He nodded, and they went off.

"He is adorable," Margaret said. She poured herself a glass of white wine and sat down. "Are you married, Jack?"

Dunne paused before he answered. "Officially, I guess yes, I am," he said. "Kathryn and I are working out some issues at the moment. We've separated while we try to figure things out."

"Oh, that's too bad," she replied. "I hope you can. Such an adorable little boy should have both his parents around."

"Now Margaret, don't be butting in," Tom Pyle interjected, as he pushed the steaks around on the grill. "I'm sure they are doing the best they can. A good marriage is tough … tougher than running a business. Takes more energy, too."

"How long were you married?" Dunne asked.

"Thirty years," Pyle said. "Jenny died twelve years ago this summer. Cancer. It was tough. Tough on the boys and tough on me. But we fought through it."

Dunne turned to Margaret. "Did you know Mrs. Pyle?" he asked.

She nodded. "Tom hired me as a nurse and housekeeper when she got sick," she said. "I was there for the end, poor dear. At least it happened fairly quickly." She shook her head. "But enough about sad things. Where are those boys? Dinner's almost ready."

Almost on cue, the front door slammed and someone yelled "We're home! And hungry!"

Two young men came out onto the backyard deck. Jason Pyle, the oldest son, was about thirty-five years old. He was six feet tall, had a barrel chest and a head full of curly blond hair. He was wearing blue shorts and a white tennis sweater over a t-shirt. With a big, happy grin, he bounced across the deck, leaned over and gave Margaret a big hug and a kiss while his brother shook hands with his father. Michael was a few years the younger, but had a much more serious outlook. He was tall and thin with mousy brown hair and wore round wire-rim glasses that gave him a studious look. He wore tight black jeans and a white oxford dress shirt, open at the neck. He was blinking rapidly in the soft descending light of the sunset.

"Aren't there a lot of bugs out here this time of year?" he asked his father.

Tom Pyle laughed and clapped Michael on the back. "Naw, the breeze blows most of them away. Get a beer, take your shoes off and relax!"

Jason Pyle was already at the mini-refrigerator and tossed his brother a cold can. "Anyone else need one?" he said and looked around the deck. He saw Jack Dunne and locked eyes with him. His body stiffened and something of his boyishness disappeared.

"Hey, Jack," he said, nodding slightly. "You OK?"

"I'm good, Jason, thanks," Dunne said. "How you doing, Mike?" he said to the other Pyle son. Michael nodded back.

"Right," Tom Pyle said, breaking the suddenly awkward silence. "I think these steaks are done. Margaret? Everything else ready?"

"It's all right here," Margaret said, standing up. "Everyone, sit down. Pass your plates over to Tom for a steak." She retrieved the bowls of cold salads as well as a basket of rolls and brought them over to the picnic table, which she had laid earlier with brightly colored dishes.

Dunne and the two Pyles bustled around, loading up their plates and sitting around the table to eat. Margaret poured wine from a crystal decanter and Tom Pyle dished out the grilled steaks. When everyone was seated, the elder Pyle raised his wine glass in a toast.

"To family, friends and the future," he said. Everyone clinked glasses except Michael Pyle, who just took a quick sip of his wine and put his glass back on the table. Dunne caught a quick frowning glance of disapproval from Tom toward his son, whose face colored a bit.

"So, guys," Tom Pyle said as they all began to eat. "What's the latest news from the salt mine?"

"Not good," said Jason, wolfing down a big piece of steak. "I had a meeting this morning to discuss the tunnel thing. The attorney general told Cabot that he's gonna subpoena all records concerning the I-beam collapse. Plans on going public with it in three weeks unless we hand it over to him at once."

"Oh, screw him," Tom Pyle said, shaking his head. "He's just a publicity hound. Wants to run for governor next year, and thinks we're his meal ticket."

"I dunno, Dad," Michael said, his face serious and frowning. "I think we ought to cooperate. We don't want to get into a public pissing contest with the state. That can't be good for business, long-term. There are a lot of projects in the pipeline."

Tom Pyle glanced over at Dunne, who had been quietly eating and watching the interaction. "Jack?" he said. "Comment?"

Dunne took a sip of his wine, a nice red Bordeaux.

"I wouldn't worry too much about the AG," he said, fingering the stem of his wine glass. "Word is, he's having an affair with one of his staffers, who is also the wife of the head of the senate tax committee."

Michael Pyle swung his head around to stare at Dunne. "What? What's that got to do with our problem?" he asked, his voice rising.

"Right now, everything," Dunne said, his voice calm. "As Tom said, he's getting ready to run for governor. Last thing he wants is for his little fling to become public. Wouldn't sit well with all the Catholic voters."

"Wait a minute," Michael Pyle's face was now red. "Are you proposing that we blackmail the Attorney General of the Commonwealth of Massachusetts? Are you crazy? We could all end up in jail for a stunt like that." He turned back to his father and looked at him. "I mean, c'mon Dad, you can't seriously be considering something like that. It's…it's …"

"Effective?" Dunne said, a small smile playing at the corner of his lips.

"Illegal!" the younger Pyle almost shouted.

Jack Dunne laughed out loud. "What's that got to do with anything?" he shot back at the young man. "Business is business."

"Dad," Michael turned again to his father and couldn't keep a note of pleading out of his voice. "Pyle Industries has a clean record. As an officer of this company, I cannot countenance approving any illegal actions. And if you're really going to listen to this … this …hooligan … I'll … I'm … I just don't know what I'll do."

"Resign," Jack Dunne said softly, almost to himself.

"I beg your pardon?" Michael Pyle said, his face splotched with anger.

"Pardon granted," Dunne said. "I said you can resign. If you don't agree with the direction I'm taking this company, then you are free to resign."

"Now, Jack…" Tom Pyle started to interrupt.

Michael Pyle stood up. His face was now beet red and his eyes were hot and angry. "You have no right to tell me what to do," he said. "This is our company, not yours. I do not understand why my father has brought you into it, but I can tell you that I will fight you every step of the way. This is our company, damn you!"

"Michael Pyle—you sit right down and apologize to our guest!" Margaret Anderson's voice had a no-nonsense edge. "You will not be disrespectful in this house, I won't allow it!"

The young man looked for a moment as if he was going to obey. But instead, he blinked and, pushing back his chair, stalked into the house.

There was another awkward silence around the table.

Jason Pyle looked up at Dunne. "Do you think you can keep the state, and the AG, off our backs?" he asked, a slight smile playing at the corner of his lips.

Dunne smiled back. "Absolutely," he said. "The first instinct of any politician is self-preservation. The guy wants to be governor, and he thinks he can get there by keeping this case before the public, pretending to battle the bad old construction company that killed some little old lady."

"How do you convince him to back off?" Jason asked.

"Oh, that's easy," Jack said. "We just slip him half a million bucks or so and the problem goes away."

"Just like that?" Jason sounded dubious.

"Well, maybe we deliver some photos along with the check," Jack said. "Shots of the guy coming out of the love motel with his honey-bun. He'll go find some other windmill to tilt against on his way to the corner office at the State House."

Jason Pyle took a sip of wine and shook his head. "That's pretty raw stuff," he said.

His father laughed out loud. "Welcome to the big leagues, kid," he said.

THE RED SOX GAME WAS ON THE TELEVISION, but Joe Bruno kept getting distracted as he tried to watch. His wife Rosa kept getting up from her chair to go look out the window. After the fourth time, he growled at her.

"Wassamatta?" he said. "You keep jumpin' up and down, I can't watch the goddam game."

"It's almost ten," Rosa said. "Angela should be home by now."

Joe sighed. "You want me to send Peter over to get her?" he asked.

Rosa hesitated. She knew she was being overprotective. Their daughter Angel was almost sixteen years old, a dangerous age, even though she was a well-behaved child for the most part. Besides, she had just gone across the street to the Pyle's house to babysit. Rosa knew she shouldn't worry about Angel's safety so close to home, especially here on Serpent Point. If her daughter wasn't safe here, there was no place on earth where she would be. Still, she was just a girl ...

Joe Bruno watched through hooded eyes as his wife fretted, her hands jumping nervously in her lap. He knew his wife worried continually about the kids, both Angela and her older sister, Isabelle, who now lived by herself in Boston. He knew that women always worried. It was the one thing they did very well. But he also knew that his two daughters were probably the least endangered children in the state. Everyone knew that if anything … anything … ever happened to Isabelle or Angela, Joe Bruno would unleash the full fury of the crime family he controlled in revenge. And his organization was the largest in eastern Massachusetts, Rhode Island and southern Maine. Joe Bruno controlled the rackets, the drugs, the loan sharking, the prostitution … all of it. He had the muscle and the political pull to back it up. No, no one would dare touch a hair on his daughter's head.

But he rose from his couch with a sigh. "I'll have Peter go get her," he said to his wife. She smiled at him in gratitude. Women, he thought, If they couldn't worry about something they'd probably explode.

Joe Bruno walked into the kitchen. Fat Peter LaGuista sat at the table, the day's Boston Herald spread out in front of him, the radio on the counter blaring the ballgame. At well over six and a half feet tall, and tipping the scales at more than 300 pounds, Fat Peter took up one entire side of the square maple table, his massive thighs spilling out over the sides of his chair. But from his vantage point, he could see out the window that overlooked the street and the garage to the side of the house, so he could see anyone coming up the drive. And Joe Bruno knew that Fat Peter, when he had to, could move with light-ning speed. Bruno had seen him in action countless times over the last four decades.

"Fuckin' bullpen's gonna blow another one," Fat Peter said as Joe walked in. "That fuckin' Epstein kid better hire some better arms or I may have to go down to Fenway and slap some sense into his Jewish ass."

"Never mind about the goddam Red Sox," Bruno rasped. "Rosa is worried about Angel. Maybe you should send Joey over to walk her home."

Fat Peter frowned. "It's only ten after ten," he said, looking at the clock over the stove. "She said she'd be back no later than ten-thirty. You know how she gets when she thinks you're checking up on her. Give her some space. I'll send Joey across the street in fifteen minutes."

Joe Bruno glared at his lieutenant. "Whose fuckin' kid are we talking about?" he growled. "Rosa wants her home. Get her home." He turned on his heel and stalked out.

Fat Peter sighed to himself and folded up the newspaper. He loved Angel as if she was his own daughter, and protecting her was as important to him as it was to Joe and Rosa. Still, he always tried to go easy on the kid. He knew it must be hard to be the child of a powerful crime boss. How many hours had be spent in his life listening to her ranting and raving about her father and his absurd ideas about safety? About how she just wanted to be like other kids, to live her life on her own terms, not those of her parents?

He sighed again. Truth was, she wasn't like other kids and never would be. She was Angela Bruno, daughter of a crime boss. A powerful crime boss. And that came with both benefits and responsibilities. And realities. Like never being truly alone. Ever.

Fat Peter heaved his girth out of the chair and was about to lurch out to the garage office where Joey LaCava and Mario Scatuzzi were on duty, when he caught a flash of white coming down the drive. He looked. It was Angel, walking home from her babysitting job. He sat back down and opened the paper again.

The door flew open and the girl came in.

"*Buona notte*, Petronus," Angel said, coming over and planting a kiss on the top of the fat man's outsized head.

"Angelina," he nodded back, secretly pleased at her affection. "Your momma has been worried about you. Better go check in."

She sighed. "You mean the Warden?" She opened the refrigerator door and began rooting around for something to eat. She found a piece of pound cake and took it out.

"They just want the best for you," Fat Peter said as the girl plopped down opposite him. "They have your best interests at heart."

"Yeah, yeah," the girl had heard it all many times before. But she jumped up and ran into the living room, kissing her mother and telling them both about little Tiger and his nice daddy, a Mister Dunne.

"Mister Pyle said that Mister Dunne is going to spend some time this summer living in the boat house," she said. "And since Tiger visits his dad a lot—he said his parents are 'corrugated,' I think he meant 'separated,' isn't that the cutest??—that means he'll be here a lot and I can sit for him," she said. "Isn't that great? He's a nice little kid and his dad is …"

Joe Bruno waved his hand at the TV. Angel understood… he wanted to watch the game. Rosa smiled at her daughter and nodded. They would talk about it later. Angel returned to the kitchen and her piece of cake.

In the kitchen, Angel poured herself a glass of milk and sat down across from Fat Peter. He folded up his newspaper again. Angel reached over and turned down the radio.

"So," Peter said as the girl ate her cake with the ravenous glee of a hungry teenager, "What did you learn tonight?"

Angel told Fat Peter about Tiger, the little boy and his Dad and how she expected to do quite a bit of sitting for him over the summer.

"Staying in the boathouse, huh?" Peter said, almost to himself when Angel relayed that bit of information. "There hasn't been anyone in that place for years."

"How do you know that?" Angel asked.

Peter smiled his enigmatic smile at the girl. "It's my business to know stuff, kiddo," he said. "What else did you learn?"

Angel told Peter that Jack Dunne was apparently separated from his wife, which was why he was going to camp out in Pyle's boat house during the summer. She said it sounded like Dunne and Pyle were working together on some business deal, and said she didn't think Pyle's sons were happy about it.

"What makes you say that?" Peter asked.

"I heard them arguing about it in the kitchen," she said, with a small, self-satisfied smile. "Mister Pyle's two sons think that Mister Dunne is trying to horn in on the business. At least that's what one of them said to the other. He was pretty angry about it."

Fat Peter nodded. It was his business to know everything about anything that was going on around Joe Bruno. That was his job as consigliore. He didn't care much about the family who lived across the street, but he kept up what went on with all the neighbors. Especially the O'Malleys. The more he knew, the more prepared he could be on his boss' behalf.

He smiled at the girl. "That's good, hon," he said. "You're getting good at keeping those big ears of yours open."

"My ears are not big." Angel said, pretending to be outraged. They both chuckled at the running joke they had shared since she could talk. She finished her snack, rinsed out her glass and yawned. "I'm beat," she said.

"What's cooking tomorrow?" Fat Peter asked.

"I've got piano lessons with Mister Regan in the morning," she said. "And hopefully I can get a little beach time in for the afternoon. It's time I got a little sunshine on this bod."

"Yeah, well, not too much," Peter said. "You know that more than fifteen minutes in the sun means skin cancer."

"Oh, you big ole bear," she said, giving him a kiss on top of his huge head. "Nitey night."

"Night, Angel," Peter said and watched as she flounced away, a pretty young girl without a care in the world. He poured himself a cup of coffee and returned to the table. He knew he should go out to the garage and make sure the two idiots out there were doing what they were supposed to do—calling every manager across the state to make sure the day's funds had been collected and accounted for. It was a nightly duty, and Fat Peter knew that Joe Bruno would want the night's numbers before he went to bed, which would be soon after the Red Sox game ended.

Fat Peter stared out the black window and thought about how far he and Bruno had come since those childhood days in the North End. They had started out stealing fruit from the vendors in Scollay Square and around Fanueil Hall and then began their rise through the ranks. Bruno had been the brains and Fat Peter the muscle, an arrangement that worked well for both. They had gotten their break when Fat Peter had overheard a couple of headknockers he knew talking about a planned hit on Raymond Patriarcha, the *capo di capi* down in Providence. Peter told Bruno what he had heard, and Bruno used the information to get noticed by Patriarcha. Fat Peter believed that Bruno and Patriarcha hit it off because they were both short men, neither one over five feet, five inches tall. In any case, one thing had led to another and after one long bloody weekend, Joe Bruno and his four brothers had ousted the Cambrelli family and taken over Boston. With Patriarcha's help, as well as the thick envelopes of cash delivered to the usual list of politicians, police captains and the sharp dressers in the Boston office of the FBI, Bruno had been able to gradually expand his scale of operations and area of influence. The Bruno family now collected protection money throughout Massachusetts, New Hampshire and Maine; ran the rackets and prostitution in every major New England city, and took a cut from the heroin trade, still a big money maker. The family enjoyed the benefits of a flood of cash—millions every year, all of it tax-free—and had turned a lot of that cash into rock-solid investments in legitimate businesses and downtown Boston real estate. Yes, it was a long, long way from stealing oranges from old man Verducci's street cart.

Fat Peter sipped some coffee. Yeah, it had been quite a ride. Fat Peter had never had any regrets. He had chosen this life, chosen to become Joe Bruno's loyal lieutenant, and had always followed orders without question. He had killed, he had maimed, he had knocked heads whenever Bruno told him to. That was his job. And always would be, he hoped. At least he had job security, as long as he was unswervingly loyal to Joe and managed to avoid taking a cap to the head. With a sigh, he finished his coffee and heaved his massive body up from the table. He went out the kitchen door, crossed over to the garage and let himself in the side door of the garage.

From the outside the building looked like a typical two-car garage, with twin roll-up doors in front and siding that matched the house on the outside. Inside, however, the space had been reconfigured as a mobile office and quarters for the two bodyguards who were always on duty. Both Joey and Scats were hard at work, telephones screwed to their ears as they made their nightly calls. Fat Peter glanced at the numbers they had scrawled on the report sheets and nodded with satisfaction. It had been a pretty good night.

Joey saw his boss's nod. "When the weather warms up, people start to get out more," he said. "Business is picking up." Fat Peter nodded in agreement. Joey LaCava had a brain for the business side of things, he knew, as well as being a crack shot and pretty damn good with a knife at close quarters. The other man, Mario Scatuzzi, known to all as "Scats," was pure muscle…big, tough and stupid as a rock. But he did what he was told without complaint, which made him invaluable to the organization.

When the last calls had been made and the numbers totaled, Fat Peter memorized the important data and Joey took the worksheets and burned them in a metal wastebasket next to his desk. No paper, no trace. The Feds were always lurking.

"OK boys, thanks," Fat Peter said. "See ya in the a.m." He went back to the house. Joey and Scats would keep watch on Joe Bruno's house throughout the night, even though the chances of anything happening out here on the point were remote. But that was no reason to let down the guard. In fact, it was an excellent reason for the bodyguards to remain alert. Joe Bruno did not get where he was by being lazy or by cutting corners.

Timothy Regan woke in his down-filled bed covered with the finest Egyptian cotton sheets and removed his velvet eye shade, blinking against the bright sun of the morning pouring into his windows. He lay there for a long time, looking out at the marshlands, where the estuarine creek wound its way through the muddy banks on its way into Nantucket Sound. He could see the gulls pecking at periwinkles and watched a blue heron near the grassy edge of his back yard stand motionless for long minutes, waiting for a tiny fish to swim near enough to spear with his long, narrow beak.

Eventually, his thoughts turned from the natural world outside to memories of the previous evening. The rough man at his door, extending a hand into which Regan had placed several hundred-dollar bills. And the first sight of the fresh-faced young boy who then was ushered into Regan's house. So young, so innocent, so …

Timothy Regan began to sob as he remembered that beautiful young boy, and all the things he had made the boy do. Of course, the boy had been neither as innocent nor as young as he looked. At the time, Regan had been ecstatic and alive and almost feverish in his desire. But now, the morning after, he felt desolate and empty and weighted with guilt. He glanced with sudden loathing around his bedroom, with its rich lime and black colors and the heavy furnishings that looked like those of the Roaring Twenties, but were really the work of a skilled modern decorator. What had, the night before, been a soft and alluring den of forbidden love, was transformed in the harsh light of morning into a hateful, awful place of pure sin. Timothy Regan wept until he felt he had no more tears left.

His manservant, Willie Johnson, had heard Regan stirring, and came into the room, regarding his boss with sad eyes. He knew that the morning after was always hard. Regan could go months without succumbing to his depravity, but would always give way to his implacable needs. And suffer for it the next day.

"Mornin', Mistah Regan," Willie drawled in the soft accent of his native Charleston. "Why'n't we run you a nice hot bath to start this day? I do declare that Ruby has made up a fine breakfast this morning. Your favorites—French toast, bacon and biscuits with your favorite huckleberry jam."

Regan nodded his assent, rose from the bed and began to peel off his pajamas. Willie took them and quickly whisked them away. It was important to remove all evidence of the previous night's activity. Once Regan was in the bath, Willie would strip the bed. Both bedclothes and pajamas would be burned. There would be no evidence or remnant of last night's sexual depravity.

The bathtub filled with hot water and Willie tossed in some aromatic oils. "Mmmm," Willie said, "Smells like Arabia. Just like in that movie with Errol Flynn, back in the day."

Regan stepped into the hot bath and sank thankfully into the warm, fragrant water. "Ahhh," he said in relief, his tears a forgotten memory. "That was quite a picture, wasn't it? Poor Errol, he was one of the most beautiful men in the world. Just couldn't keep his pecker to himself. Did I ever tell you where the phrase 'in like Flynn' came from?"

"Why no, Mistah Regan, I don' believe you ever did," Willie lied.

"Well, he was once charged with raping a young girl," Regan recalled, splashing water on his arms. "He beat the rap somehow, even though he was guilty as sin, but forever after 'in like Flynn' meant someone who did the deed, if you know what I mean."

"Shore do, Mister Regan, shore do," Willie said with a chuckle. He had finished stripping the bedsheets and was now digging through Regan's huge closet. "What you got doin' today?"

"I believe my young piano student is coming over this morning for a lesson," Regan said. "Then I'm supposed to meet Charles at the yacht club for a late lunch."

"Yassir," Willie said, nodding, and picked out the day's wardrobe.

Regan motioned that he was done, and stepped out of the bath, water pouring down his shriveled body and over the flaccid flesh of his sex. He toweled off, stepped into a thick, lime-green terry cloth robe held by Willie, and sat down at his dressing table. Willie flicked on the bank of bright lights that surrounded the round mirror and Timothy Regan started at his image. He saw an old man, face ravaged by eighty-plus years, skin sagging and white, a few slight wisps of hair clinging to his rough scalp. He poked at his eyes, a frown forming on his face.

"My God," he said, turning his head from side to side, "More baggage here than in my attic."

"Not to worry, Mistah Regan," Willie said cheerfully, "We'll get y'all fixed up in a jiffy." He reached over to a styrofoam figurine and picked up Regan's wig, which featuring carefully coiffed curls in a handsome if slightly unnatural shade of red-dish-brown. He brushed it carefully and then placed in onto Regan's mostly hairless head. Regan reached into a nearby glass and took out his dental plates, which he inserted carefully after squeezing out the Polident adhesive. He clacked his teeth together and nodded in approval.

"Just a few more adjustments and I won't even scare the cat," he said with a smile. Willie chuckled softly as he began to whip up some shaving lather in a small ivory bowl with the handmade shaving brush and its soft badger bristles. He applied the cream liberally around the old man's face and then began to strop an ivory-handle straight razor against a thick leather strap. While he shaved the man, he kept up a steady patter to keep Regan's mind from sliding back into melancholy.

"You got you a letter from Mistah Richmond," Willie said as he carefully but expertly shaved the old man's face. "He done sent you the final plans for your revival tour. Thinks that people is ready again for the Irish Nightingale to sing!"

"Well," Regan said, "Good music never goes out of style. They may think they like this modern stuff with its lyrics about rape and whores, but nothing can beat the old Irish ballads... nothing!"

"You may be right about that, yassah," Willie said, as he carefully carved around Regan's bulbous nose. "Why, you got 'most seventy years of success behin' you. Be good to make a little more money, too. You must be down to your last hundred million!"

Regan laughed at Willie's gentle gibe. "Not so long as the Coca-Cola Company continues to sell soft drinks," Regan said. "Smartest thing I ever did was put all my money in that company. Ole Robert Woodruff, back when he was in charge, told me I'd never regret it, and I never have."

Willie finished the shave, wiped off the remnants of the cream with a thick and soft towel, and, pouring some into his hands, splashed a biting after-shave onto the old man's cheeks.

"Yow!" Regan said, "That smarts, Willie!"

"Gots to wake you up, Mistah Regan," Willie replied.

"I'm awake already." Regan peered into his mirror again. "Willie, we've got to do something about my eyelashes," he said. "Why, they're so light they're almost invisible."

"Yassir," Willie said, "All in good time, all in good time." He pulled out a drawer filled with jars of makeup and dozens of brushes and pencils and selected a jar of pancake, which he applied to the old man's cheeks. He followed that with spots of blush high on the cheekbones, and then began to work on the singer's eyes, adding some mascara and just the tiniest bit of color to the lids. Finally, he sat back, satisfied.

Regan looked at himself in the mirror and nodded in satisfaction. "Hot biscuits and tea!" he exclaimed, "I sure look different from that old hog who was sitting here just a few minutes ago!"

As if on cue, Ruby Williams came into the dressing room. "Well jus' look at us this mornin'," she exclaimed, "Willie, where did you find this fine-lookin' man? His breakfast is ready." She was short and round, with huge buttocks and breasts that rolled out from both sides of her body. But she wore a bright white smile wreathed by her jowly black face.

Ruby left while Willie helped Regan into his clothes—crisp linen trousers, a white silk shirt and a maroon-and-black smoking jacket with velvet lapels. He slipped his feet into hand-built Moroccan leather slippers and, with a final glance into the mirror, pronounced himself ready to meet the day.

After his breakfast, Regan sat at his Steinway grand piano in the music room, with its bay windows looking out on the rolling green lawn, and played his usual repertoire of old Irish songs and ballads. He had started his career in show business as a young lad of 10, busking on the street corners in his native Kilkenny where his high-pitched contralto voice had been successful in attracting coins and the occasional folded note from passers-by. From those beginnings, he had graduated into singing in pubs and by the time his voice deepened into a richer tenor range, he was a sought-after talent. He joined a series of bands and made his way to Dublin. At a time when rock was king and musicians competed to see who could be more outrageous in looks and comportment, Regan stubbornly stayed with his genre of Irish folk music. It was really all he knew. His band, Lil Timmy and the Leprechauns, were a fixture on weekend television shows in Ireland, singing songs of times gone by, sweet girls pining for their handsome men, and somewhat militaristic songs about marching off to war against unnamed foes that everyone assumed were the British.

He was handsome, popular, talented and soon became quite rich, by Irish standards. Women, of course, threw themselves at him, but none, of course, were successful. Regan had an image to protect, and his sexuality was a threat to that image, and therefore was a closely guarded secret.

An American impresario saw his act on Irish television during a visit to Dublin, bedded him, signed him and brought him to the States. It was about the time of the Riverdance phenomenon, a time when all things Irish were big, and for a period of five years or so, Timmy Regan toured the concert halls and arenas, singing his sad ballads and stirring marches, now backed by full orchestras and flanked by lovely dancers.

Another lover became his business manager and made sure Regan's millions were well invested in real estate, blue chip stocks and inflation-proof bonds. He became fabulously wealthy, and without the usual parade of ex-wives that other singers and stars had to deal with, he managed to keep most of it for himself.

He was now over eighty years old, but with his wig and his make-up, he thought he still looked like the handsome Irishman he had once been.

It was around eleven when the lithe figure of Angela Bruno climbed the wooden stairs of the deck at the rear of Regan's mansion and waved through the window at the old man at the piano. She came bounding in the glass door and ran over to plant a big kiss on the top of his bewigged head. He immediately began to play the chords of "Angel Eyes," an old Sinatra song.

"Good morning, my little angel," Regan said. "How is your dear mother?"

"She's fine," Angel said, plopping down in an overstuffed chair next to the piano. She picked up a copy of one of the fan magazines from the glass-topped table and began leafing through the pages. "She said to say hello. Oooo, isn't that Leo just the cutest thing?"

"Leo?"

"Leonardo DiCaprio, silly," the girl giggled.

The old man harrumphed. "Sounds like an Italian tenor," he said. "Never heard of him."

"Oh, you old bear," she said. "He's a big star. And a fox and a half!"

Regan peered out the window. "Did you bring Peter with you this morning?" he asked. "That man is going to eat me out of house and home."

Angel laughed. "No, he said he was too busy to walk me over," she said. "But he did want me to ask Ruby to send a few pastries home."

Regan frowned. Fat Peter usually made sure he accompanied Angel everywhere she went, or sent one of her father's other henchmen in his place. Even though the distance between the two houses was less than a hundred yards, Regan wasn't sure he approved of Angel coming through the hedgerow unaccompanied.

She saw his frown and pouted. "I'm almost sixteen years old," she said. "I don't need a full time babysitter anymore."

He thought: *this is the time in your life when you need a babysitter more than ever.* But he didn't say it out loud.

Ruby came in to the music room with a tray: hot chocolate for her and a cup of tea for him, along with a plate of chocolate chip cookies. She, too, asked where Fat Peter was. Angel asked if she could take some cookies for him when she left. Ruby went off to pack some up.

Regan made Angel sit at the piano and go through some of the scales he had been teaching her. The music lessons were a secondary part of their meetings: they enjoyed each other's company more. She wanted to learn some of the songs she heard on the radio, but the modern music with its strange rhythms and power chords completely eluded the old man. And she, in turn, was not the least interested in old Irish ballads.

So they spent most of their time just talking. He was a good listener and she felt comfortable confiding in him. She enjoyed telling him the gossip from her girl friends, especially some of the more salacious things she had heard. There were stories about some of the things the mothers and fathers of her friends were up to—social events, infidelities, business deals. And there were stories about the boys that Angela and her friends were interested in. Those were mostly innocent—who "liked" whom and who saw whom at the mall and what they said and did. Timothy Regan was sure that if her father, Joe Bruno, knew of some of the things she relayed to her neighbor, he would not be happy, although she never, ever said anything about Joe Bruno's business. But Regan had never violated one of her confidences, not even to Willie or Ruby, and she trusted him. He had even reached something of an understanding with Fat Peter, having taken the time to get to know him a little when he had walked Angela over for her lessons. Fat Peter knew of Regan's homosexuality; indeed, it was the Bruno gang that provided the "boys" that he enjoyed from time to time.

Despite that, the two men understood that each of them treasured Angel and wanted nothing but the best for her. Fat Peter knew that Angela was safe with Regan; he would never harm a hair on her head. And Regan could see that Fat Peter loved her like his own child.

She told Regan of her job the previous evening babysitting for Jack Dunne's adorable young boy, Tiger, and how she expected to earn some more money during the summer doing more of the same. Regan filed away the information about Dunne and Pyle and the Pyle sons; and that Dunne would be spending time living in the Pyle's boat house. Regan liked to keep up with all the gossip on the island.

They both lost track of the time, and finally Willie came in and mentioned that Regan had made an appointment for lunch at the yacht club.

"You have a busier social life than anyone I know," Angela laughed, giving him a farewell kiss on the cheek.

"Maybe someday you will honor me with your presence at lunch," Regan said gallantly.

Her face clouded. "I don't think I can do that," she said.

"Why ever not?"

"Daddy says we're not welcome at the yacht club," she said, frowning. "I wanted to take sailing lessons there this summer, but Daddy says they don't allow our kind."

"And what kind is that, dear child?" Regan was upset.

"You know," she said. "Italians. They think we stink like garlic or something."

Regan was outraged. "I will speak to the manager myself," he said, his voice trembling. "If you wish to take sailing lessons or have lunch with an old man, then that is what you shall do and I defy any man alive to say that you can't."

Angel laughed ruefully. "Then you'd better go see Senator O'Malley," she said. "Daddy says he is the one who won't let us in."

"We'll see about that," the old man said darkly. "We'll just see about that."

THE VILLAGE OF WINTER COVE is just one of a string of towns along the shore on the southern edge of Cape Cod. All of them share the characteristics of tourism-oriented places: jam packed from June to October, virtually empty during the winter months. The only thing that makes Winter Cove slightly different from its neighbors to the east and west is its ferry dock, from whence some of its visitors depart for the nearby islands of Nantucket and Martha's Vineyard; and its historic association with the O'Malley name.

Winter Cove's one main road runs through about three blocks of what could be called its downtown: an area of shops, ice cream stores, T-shirt emporiums, and the requisite white-washed and steepled Congregational church, with aged gray-green headstones leaning as if into a headwind in the historic churchyard. There is also a small brick museum dedicated to all things O'Malley, one of America's most dynastic political families, which has given the nation three senators, two governors and an unending source of gossip and celebrity.

Jack Dunne had come to town to pick up a few supplies he needed for the cottage. He had come to enjoy living in

Tom Pyle's little boathouse, even when, as now, Tiger was back home with Kathryn in Needham. Dunne had been trying to get his wife to agree to come down for a weekend, promising her a separate bedroom and plenty of space. He thought that she might enjoy the beach and the peace and quiet, and hoped they might be able to talk without rancor in a new location where neither one could claim a territorial advantage.

The town was bustling now that the season was in full swing. Parking was next to impossible and the sidewalks were jammed with people: families with kids, couples holding hands, old people swept along in the crush of humanity. Dunne bought some batteries, a few spare light bulbs and some cleaning materials, and was heading back to the town parking lot, juggling his packages and thinking of nothing at all, when he very nearly ran headfirst into her.

The woman had come staggering around the corner from a side street. She was petite, no more than five feet in height, blond and almost painfully thin. If Dunne had collided with her, he would have sent her flying, but he managed to stop in time and put out one arm to catch her around her waist as she stumbled. She was wearing a pretty summer outfit of blues and greens and a pair of leather sandals. Her blond mane was pulled back from her face and tied in the back with a black leather bow.

"Whoa," he said as he set her back upright. "Where's the fire?"

He looked down into the face that he instantly recognized as Gillian O'Malley, the wife of the senior senator from the

Commonwealth of Massachusetts. She had that long flowing blond hair and leonine features that had been a favorite of the paparazzi for years. She looked back at him with unfocused eyes, a slack mouth and Dunne immediately caught the scent of cheap whiskey on her breath.

"Get your hands off me," the woman slurred at him and pushed to get past him. Out of the corner of his eyes, Dunne saw two women passersby whispering to each other and pointing.

"Sorry, Ms. O'Malley," he said. "I just didn't want you to fall. Is there anything I can do for you? "

She peered up at him, still a bit unsteady on her feet. "Do I know you?" she asked, trying to make her eyes focus.

"No ma'am," he said. "But I'm your neighbor out on the point. I'm staying in Tom Pyle's boathouse for the summer."

"Pyle...Pyle...yeah I know him. His wife died. Did ya know that? I liked her. She was always nice to me. Now he's sleeping with his housekeeper." A few more people began to gather on the sidewalk next to them. Gillian noticed them and turned to stare at them. "What the fuck are you lookin' at?" she barked at them. "Huh?" Dunne grabbed her arm and led her down the street towards the parking lot. She didn't resist, but kept up her patter. "Guess ya gotta sleep with someone, huh? Where are we going?"

"How about I give you a ride home?" Dunne said.

Gillian tried to pull away, but Dunne kept a firm grip on her arm, "I don' wanna go home," she said. "He's there."

"The senator?" Dunne asked, surprised. That Gillian O'Malley was drunk was not that surprising—her penchant for hitting the bottle was well-known and there had been some public incidents over the years. But nothing had ever been said about the health of the relationship between the senator and his wife.

"Nah," she said, "Well, yeah, he's there. But I mean that fucker Gordon," she said. "He's a creepy bastard." Dunne knew she meant O'Malley's chief of staff and longtime aide, Gordon Congdon. He was O'Malley's rainmaker, chief enforcer and problem-solver, and Dunne knew he had a reputation for sharp elbows and a take-no-prisoner style.

They arrived at the parking lot, and Dunne managed to get Gillian into the black Saab. He quickly put the convertible top up, and rolled up the tinted windows, in case some photographer with a zoom lens was snapping away from behind some tree. The last thing Dunne needed was to be publically tied in with the beautiful wife of Senator Malcolm O'Malley. He maneuvered the car deftly through the summer traffic of Winter Cove, past the famous stone Church of St. Margaret, known for its many O'Malley family events: christenings, weddings and funerals, and then took the beach road which led down past the O'Malley compound and the Winter Cove Yacht Club. Glancing over to the passenger seat, Dunne was not surprised to see that Gillian had slumped against the door and fallen fast asleep.

He continued down the sandy causeway that led out to Serpent Point, drove past the granite entrance gate and finally pulled into the circular drive that curved up a slight rise to the elegant front entrance to the O'Malley mansion.

He kept the engine running and reached over to the sleeping passenger, gently shaking her by the shoulder. "Ma'am?" he said, "You're home. Ma'am?" It was no use—she was dead to the world.

Dunne got out of the car and walked around to the other side. Just at the moment, the front door opened and a large burly man with a head of curly gray hair, dressed in khaki pants and a blue button-down oxford shirt, came out onto the wooden porch that ran the width of the house. He stood at the top of the five broad stairs that led down to the drive.

"The fuck you think you're doing?" the man said gruffly. "Do you know where you are?"

Dunne folded his arms across his chest, leaned back against his car and faced the man. "Oh, would you rather I take the senator's wife back downtown where she can make more of a spectacle of herself?" he said. "She's passed out in the front seat."

The man didn't reply, but turned and went back into the mansion. In a few seconds, he came back out accompanied by a broad-chested young man with short red hair and no neck. The younger man came down the steps lightly, opened the car door, reached inside and lifted Gillian O'Malley up and out in a smooth and effortless motion. He gave Dunne a quick nod and carried her into the mansion.

The curly-haired man reached into his front pocket and began rummaging around. "I...I'd like to give you something for your trouble, Mister ..."

Dunne held up a hand. "Don't insult me more than you already have," he said. "Name's Dunne. I ran into her...literally…on a sidewalk downtown. She seemed to be, ah, in some difficulty and was beginning to attract some attention, so I offered to bring her home. Thought it was the neighborly thing to do."

The door to the mansion swung open. Senator Malcolm O'Malley stepped out onto the porch. "Neighborly?" he said, in his distinctive Massachusetts patrician accent. "Don't tell me you're one of Joe Bruno's guinea friends? " O'Malley was dressed in a pair of shorts, a pink shortsleeved shirt and a pair of white boat shoes. His thick, pear-shaped body rested on thin white spindly legs and his familiar swept-back mane of white hair was mussed. His jowly face was frowning, eyebrows creased and his lips pursed on a frown. "I wish to Christ there was some way I could get you goombahs off this island…"

The curly haired man cut him off. "Now, Senator," he said. "I'm sure Mister Dunne here was just trying to help. Listen, sir, my name is Gordon Congdon and I want to thank you for bringing the senator's wife home. If there's anything we can do in return…" He fixed Dunne with a broad smile as if they were suddenly the best of friends.

Dunne stared at the two men for a long moment and then shook his head. "Jesus," he said, "No wonder the country is in such bad shape. You guys have made me sorry that I tried to help the lady."

He looked at the senator. "Name's Jack Dunne," he said. "I'm the partner of Tom Pyle and I'm staying in his boathouse for the summer. Guess that makes us neighbors, huh? I don't like dumb micks and I don't like politicians and I don't particularly like you, but like they say, ya can't always choose your neighbors. Have a nice fucking day."

He turned to go.

It was eight o'clock in the morning when Fat Peter stuck his head inside the garage office and told the two men inside "let's go." Immediately, they dropped what they were doing, leaving the television on, and headed into the garage. Mario got behind the wheel of the black Lincoln town car and backed it into the driveway, while Joey took up his position outside the passenger side. The front door of the ranch house opened and Joe Bruno came striding out quickly, trailed as always by the huge bulk of Fat Peter. They climbed into the back seat, Joey, with a last look around, jumped into the passenger seat in the front and the car roared off.

Once they were cruising down Route 6 heading for the Sagamore Bridge, a tan Chevy sedan fell in behind them, two or three cars back. Fat Peter, who had been heaving his bulk around in the leather seat to peer out behind, saw it. "Got it Scats?" he asked the driver.

"Yeah, boss," Mario said, nodding. "It's the Feds. Right on schedule."

The two-car convoy continued all the way up to Boston, a ninety minute drive. Mario kept the town car at or near the speed limit and the tan Chevy kept its distance, two or three cars behind, but always in sight. Traffic began to pick up as they approached Boston from the south. Joey began to look in his rear-view mirror once they reached Quincy on the Southeast Expressway. Soon, he spotted a red Nissan SUV which pulled in behind the town car and flashed its headlights. He nodded to himself and then turned to the two men in the back seat.   "Robbie's in position, Boss," he said to Fat Peter, who nodded back. "Call the office," Peter said, "Tell them we'll be there in 30 minutes." Joey pulled out his cell phone and dialed.

The traffic slowed to almost a crawl as they approached the Big Dig tunnel entrance near Chinatown. At the last possible moment, cutting over from the center lane to the angry honking of several ticked-off motorists, Mario swung the car onto the exit that took them onto Commercial Drive along the waterfront of Boston harbor. Joey watched in the mirror, and then turned to Mario with a grin. "Robbie cock-blocked the Feds again," he reported. "We're clear."

After a few deft turns, the town car entered the Italian section of Boston's North End. Bruno sat up suddenly, all senses alive. He was home, back in his the familiar space of his own neighborhood. He ordered Mario to take Hanover Street, which halved the neighorbood, on their way to Bruno's storefront office. His eyes took in the street scene, registering everything. He saw two of his associates walking down the sidewalk deep in conversation. He noticed a blue Cadillac parked in front of the Napolean restaurant—it was out of place, shouldn't be there. He noticed that Peter "the Rifleman" Santone was not standing in front of Papa's Pizzeria where he should be. Joe Bruno had managed to keep his business and his power all these years because he had an eye for these telling details.

Bruno noticed a strong-looking young man dressed in sweats and carrying a gym bag over his shoulder walking on the sidewalk. "Ain't that Tony Blue-Eyes' kid?" Bruno asked. Peter squinted out the window for a look. "Yeah, I think so, Boss," he said.

"He still workin' with Langone at the New Gardens Gym?"

Fat Peter nodded. "Yeah. I think he has a fight coming up next month with Vinnie Cozza," Peter said. "He's a nice lookin' kid…good hands, quick feet, cement jaw. Punches like a cannon, Langone says."

"Any hope on the national cards?" Bruno turned to look at the kid as the car passed.

Fat Peter shrugged, but there was the hint of a smile on his lips. Joe Bruno saw it, and knew that Peter thought the kid had something. "Call Vinnie, tell him to go down in the first round," he said. "Put down some bets, let's say 25 grand, do it through the regular channels, on the quiet, got it? We should clear a hundred G's." He sat back. "Oh, yeah, get us some tickets to the fight."

Fat Peter made some notes in his day book.

"What do we got today?" Bruno asked.

"This morning, the usual," Fat Peter said. "After lunch, Sugarman wants you to meet a new recruit he wants to add as a cooker in the meth lab. He likes him, but you said you wanted to approve."

Bruno nodded. "Did you see that blue Caddy back there?" he asked.

"Yeah," Fat Peter nodded. "It's the Feds. We got 'em covered. Car's gotta be a decoy, it's too obvious sitting there on Hanover. Means they're probably somewhere else painting a house, installing a phone, fixing the air conditioning. Playing secret agents again."

"How we gonna talk to this new cooker?" Bruno asked.

"We're meeting Sugarman at Dom's place," Fat Peter said. "He'll close down for an hour and we'll move the kid in from next door. We'll go in through the kitchen. I figured we'd keep it simple and right under their noses…better than tryin' to do cat-and-mouse and get them all excited."

Bruno nodded, satisfied. The town car cut down a side street and pulled up in front of a small bodega, with its ancient hand-painted green sign above the small store window: Angelo's Market. He always felt a twinge of nostalgia coming back here, where his grandfather had first opened the store; where his father had been gunned down in the gang wars of 1958, and now where he, Joe Bruno, ran the mob operations for the city and most of New England.

He waited until both Joey and Scats jumped out of the car and took up positions on either side of the entrance to the market. Once they had carefully scanned the street, searching for anything remotely out of place, they each nodded once, and Joe Bruno climbed out of his car and entered the store.

The narrow aisles were jammed into the small space, and the old heart-of-pine floorboards, darkened with age, were covered with a thin layer of sawdust, just like old times. The white enameled counter down one side of the store was filled with aged cheeses and choice cuts of salamis and other dried meats hung from hooks in the ceiling. Bruno breathed deeply, taking in the smells of the Old World: the cheeses and the meats, the aroma of roasting coffee beans and fresh baked bread. He waved a hand at the ancient storekeeper, someone his father had first hired all those years ago, and strode purposefully to the back of the store, ducking behind a heavy green curtain and entering the back office.

Bruno's two brothers were hard at work in the outer office, working the telephones and their adding machines, compiling the take from the previous day's operations. Bruno nodded at them, but left them alone to finish their work. They would report to him when they were done, letting him know if anything was amiss. He continued on into his inner sanctum, a small but comfortable office where he could use one of several different telephones—all checked daily for bugs and hooked up to the latest technology that could indicate if anyone else was listening in—and where Bruno could meet privately with his associates.

Fat Peter followed Bruno into the inner office. "Okay," Bruno said, sitting down behind his desk, "Let's start the parade." Fat Peter nodded and backed out, closing the door behind. Outside the storefront, in the coffee shop next door and out on the sidewalk, people had begun to gather as the word went out that the Don was receiving visitors today. Some of them had favors to ask, some propositions to make, others forgiveness to beg or excuses to offer. But they all needed a few minutes of Joe Bruno's time. Each of the supplicants was carefully frisked and gruffly instructed not to waste Bruno's valuable time. Soon, each one was sent in, past a series of cold-eyed sentinel—one on the sidewalk, one in the store, yet another standing guard in the back office—finally to be ushered into the inner sanctum for their five minutes with Bruno.

While Bruno often complained about this part of his job, secretly he loved it. He liked being in touch with his people on the street. He liked solving people's problems. He liked the respect his people showed him. To him, these people and their small, seemingly petty problems represented his real life's work. The rest of it, the violence, the vast sums of money that came and went into the organization, the cars and the houses and the women … they were just things, the tools of his trade. But these people who depended on him, Joe Bruno, they were the real reason he got out of bed in the morning. They needed him, and he couldn't live without that need.

After a couple of hours, he motioned to Fat Peter, who always stood just outside the door to the inner sanctum, and the steady flow of people into his office stopped. With a few whispers and quiet words, the people still waiting were told to go away, the Don had finished for the day. Quickly, the street outside emptied as the supplicants left, returned to their lives. They would be back another day. They would always be back.

Fat Peter came back into Bruno's office. Wordlessly, he opened the back door which led into the alley behind the market. The two men walked down the alley and climbed into the back seat of a maroon Chevrolet with dark tinted windows that was idling at the curb. The car sped off and began to follow a labyrinthine path through the narrow streets of the North End, eventually emerging onto Atlantic Avenue. It continued north for three blocks, made a hard U-turn and screeched to a stop in front of a Dunkin Donuts store. The car idled there for fifteen minutes. The black Lincoln town car, driven by Scats, pulled alongside the maroon Chevy and two men, one large and one small, got out of the Chevy and into the Lincoln, which pulled away down Atlantic. If the Feds were watching, and everyone assumed that they were, they would assume that Fat Peter and Joe Bruno had just gotten into the Lincoln.

With the decoy car now driving wildly through the streets of downtown Boston, the maroon Chevy continued slowly back into the North End and eventually pulled up outside the kitchen entrance of Dom's Restaurant. When the watchers had given the signal that the coast was clear, Fat Peter and Joe Bruno climbed quickly out of the car and entered the restaurant.

They exchanged embraces with Dominic Matarazzo, the restaurant owner and one of Bruno's underbosses, and he quickly escorted them into a private function room at the back of the restaurant. There they found pots of fresh coffee, sandwiches, plates of anisette and powdered sugar cookies, and Marshall Sugarman, the organization's chief chemist. The three men hugged and, while Fat Peter made a beeline for the food, Bruno and his chemist sat and discussed business. Methamphetamine was one of the major cash generators for

Bruno's organization. It was relatively cheap to make, and the demand was never ending. Whether taken by male or female, the drug invaded the bloodstream and wiped out all sexual inhibitions. It was far better than Viagra, more potent than any commercial drug and, of course, inherently addictive. Bruno's organization had the reputation of selling the purest meth or crank on the market, and he wanted to keep it that way. Better quality meant he could charge a higher price, and even if his main distribution channel, handled by a motorcycle gang known as 'The Avengers,' cut the stuff two or three times, it was still far better than anything else available in the New England area. Bruno wholesaled the gang one-pound blocks of crystal meth for $8,000 a block, usually 100 pounds at a time. By the time the gang had cut the stuff and repackaged it into tiny glassine envelopes and moved it to customers on the street, the profit margins soared.

There was a knock at the door.

"You check this kid out?" Bruno demanded of Silverman. The chemist, in turn, looked at Fat Peter.

"All the way back to kindergarten, boss," Peter said, powdered sugar dusting his dark sportscoat.

Bruno smiled and nodded. The door was opened and Michael Stern was ushered in. He had been a chemistry major at Boston University, but had to take a year off from his studies to help out when the family business needed him. His uncle had been a bookmaker in the Bruno organization; his father a respected odds maker with whom smaller bookies often laid off their larger bets, knowing the Bruno organization would take the action for a fee. But the uncle had died a year ago and now Stern's father was dying with cancer and it fell to the young man to support his family.

Silverman took over the interview. "Michael, can you give me a good rundown on how you'd make a ten-pound block of methamphetamine?"

The young man looked at the others in the room nervously. Fat Peter took a napkin, filled it with cookies, and left the room. He understood that too many people in the room could clam anyone up, especially in this business.

Once it was just the bosses and the chemist, the young man went through the step-by-step method for taking a solution of phenyl-2-propanone, methylamine and isopropyl alcohol, adding aluminum foil and mercuric chloride to create a chemical reaction and then adding precise amounts of benzene and sodium hydroxide. There would be several more steps: distillations, chemical reactions, fractionating processes and more until, at the end, by dissolving the solution in acetone and adding hydrogen chloride gas, the crystals of methamphetamine would form and be dried and collected.

Marshall Sugarman, himself an MIT-trained chemist, listened. "There are, of course, simpler and cheaper ways to make it," he said.

"But this way yields the best quality," the young man said. "It's a little more time consuming, but the results are spectacular."

"Would it be better?" Bruno wanted to know. He only understood about half of the chemical mumbo-jumbo, but he knew what he wanted at the end.

"Yes, Joe," Sugarman nodded. "About ten percent stronger than what we sell now."

"Then that's the way we'll do it," the boss said. "Work out the details and get the lab set up. I want to raise the prices anyway, and this will be my justification. Get it done."

"You got it, Joe," Sugarman said.

The boss looked at the young man and smiled. "Welcome on board," he said. "Your uncle and your Dad were good men. I expect you will be too."

The young man managed a nervous smile. He had passed the audition. "Thank you," he croaked.

JACK DUNNE AND TOM PYLE ORDERED IN LUNCH and sat eating it in Pyle's office overlooking Boston Harbor. Pyle had spent several days in Washington DC trying to nail down some federal construction contracts. Dunne had been assigned to stay in Boston and make sure the Big Dig problem was under control. This was the first chance the two had had in some time to compare notes and plan strategy.

"So how's the Iraq thing going?" Dunne asked, as a plate of sandwiches and a fresh pot of coffee had been wheeled into Pyle's suite by a pretty girl wearing an apron over her black slacks and white oxford shirt. Pyle Industries had been trying for six months to nail down the job to do some major road and bridge building between Baghdad and Basri. It was a good project for the firm: the Army had helped destroy much of the country's infrastructure in the invasion and now the U.S. government was going to spend several billions rebuilding what they had knocked down. Tom Pyle was spending most of his time pulling all the strings he could to make sure that his company got a nice big chunk of that business.

He shook his head as he helped himself to some lunch. "Everything is pretty much good to go," he said. "With the exception of our beloved senior senator who hasn't signed off on the deal yet."

"What's O'Malley's problem?" Dunne asked.

"The usual," Pyle said. "He wants his share and he's asking for the fucking moon."

"How much?"

"He wants ten million cash and a job for one of his fuckin' nephews," Pyle said. "That family breeds like rabbits and apparently every last one of them has to be taken care of by the taxpayers."

"He chairs the Appropriations committee, right?"

"And sits on Ways and Means and Defense," Pyle said, shrugging. "So he's got us by the short and curlies. I mean, a certain amount is just the cost of doing business, but he's getting greedier every year. Especially now that he's getting ready to run for President. By the way, I put you down to help him raise money."

Dunne exhaled. "I wouldn't give that bastard the back of my hand, which is all he deserves," he said.

Pyle laughed. "Don't worry, I'll take care of it," he said. "I just need to use your name so I can funnel a few more million into his campaign account." Like the head of any big corporation with its fingers in the national pie, Tom Pyle knew how to move campaign donations around, how to construct a list of campaign donors that would withstand any examination, how to make it all legal and aboveboard. He changed the topic. "

"What's going on with your little problem?" he asked.

"It's all pretty much under control," Dunne said with a shrug. "We got the attorney general to back off any criminal prosecution. The governor has appointed an investigation panel that will takes its sweet time looking through thousands of pages of documents and will eventually conclude that the shifting mud under the harbor moved some of the footings and caused the ceiling supports to give way. Blah blah…"

"Will there be any financial penalty?" Pyle asked.

"Oh yeah," Dunne said. "Probably a hundred million or so. But still within our contingency budget. And there's insurance that will kick in for most of it. It won't hurt the profit margin."

Pyle nodded. "Good. What really happened, by the way?"

Dunne chuckled. "It was the quality of the concrete poured in those footings," he said. "The contractor decided to use an inferior grade to try and save a few extra bucks, thinking no one would ever know the difference."

Pyle shook his head. "Typical," he said. "Who was it?"

"Your good buddy Joe Bruno and his pals," Dunne said, fixing the older man with a gaze across the table. "Benito Concrete is owned by one of Bruno's cousins, and they got the job so there wouldn't be any trouble with the Teamsters. The contract was only for fifty-six million, and a good chunk of that went straight to your boy Joe, so I guess Benito had to shave expenses somewhere else. So they poured lousy concrete down the hole and …"

"Joe Bruno is not my boy," Pyle protested.

"Just your neighbor down on the island and the father of your babysitter."

"Well, it doesn't hurt to have him on your side, instead of against you," Pyle pointed out.

Dunne shrugged. Just like the payoffs to politicians like Malcolm O'Malley, payoffs to the mob were part of doing business in today's world. In the end, everyone walked away with something. Except maybe that poor woman whose car got crushed in the tunnel. She was a cost of doing business, too, although one whose entry wouldn't fit neatly onto some spreadsheet or budget line item.

"No chance of any of this going public?" Pyle asked.

Dunne shook his head. "Naw. All the records were falsified to show that the concrete they poured met the specs. And Bruno will make sure that if anyone starts getting close to the real story, they'll disappear."

Pyle nodded in satisfaction. He ate some more of his sandwich and took a sip of the coffee.

"Where are the boys?" he asked next.

Dunne stiffened. This was dangerous ground. "Michael is out in Singapore, watching over a new high rise, and Jason I sent to Dubai. He's got enough work on his plate for the next two years," he said.

Pyle stared across the table at Dunne, his eyes hard. "Keeping them out of the way?"

Dunne shrugged. "It's a big company," he said neutrally. "There's a lot going on. I need good people in a lot of different places."

"Especially out of the country and out of sight," Pyle observed.

Dunne flared with sudden anger. "Well, you could settle that problem once and for all," he said. "Like announce publically and officially that I'm next in line to take over this company. That would end a lot of public speculation and let your boys decide how they wanted to react."

"They'd probably quit the firm," Pyle said.

Dunne shrugged. "That might be best for everyone," he said. "I don't see where leaving them hanging in limbo does anyone any good. We've got the annual meeting coming up in five months. Be a good time to clear the air."

Pyle frowned. He didn't like being crowded, and he didn't like the idea of forcing his own children out of the company that bore their name. Even if it was probably the right thing to do. Blood was thicker than water, he thought. And maybe even thicker than money.

"I'll think about it," he said. He changed the subject again.

"When are you going to bring your wife down to the island? We'd like to meet her."

Dunne sighed. He didn't like getting into his personal life. He understood that Pyle was hoping for a reconciliation; there was a romantic streak hidden deep within the outwardly tough businessman. But still, it was really none of his business.

"I've invited her down for the Fourth of July," he said. "I haven't heard yet if she and Tiger are coming. Soon as I know something, I'll let you and Margaret know."

Pyle nodded, pleased. "Good," he said. "She'll love it. The yacht club has a big fireworks show on the Fourth, and we have a front-row seat. It'll be great."

Maybe, Dunne thought to himself. *And maybe not.*

"Angel has a problem, boss." Fat Peter tried to keep his tone steady, matter of fact, calm. He knew that there was nothing that could set Joe Bruno's anger off more than something involving his younger daughter. Even so, he could feel the man sitting beside him stiffen as they rode back down to Winter Cove in the back seat of the town car.

"Tell me." The voice was low. But the tension in the two words was unmistakeable.

"I was talking to that old fruit who lives next door," Fat Peter explained. "He's been giving her some music lessons from time to time. He likes her. He told me that she wants to sign up for the sailing classes at the yacht club, but they only allow member's kids in."

"Those Yankee fucks don't allow no goombahs like us to join," Bruno rasped. "Even though I could prolly buy and sell any one of 'em six times over, they don't want our kind stinkin' up their joint."

Fat Peter nodded. "I told Angel this," he said. "But she's just a kid. She doesn't understand. She just wants to learn how to sail a goddam boat and be with some of her friends."

"I don't want her hanging out with those stuck-up fucks," Bruno said. "Think their shit don't stink. Most of 'em never worked a day in their life. Like that motherfucker O'Malley. Take away his trust fund, take away his daddy and his uncle and whaddya got?"

"Not much," Fat Peter said.

"Not nuthin!" Bruno exploded. "He's a piece a shit."

They rode in silence for a while.

"Maybe it's time for Angela to realize she can't always get what she wants," Bruno said.

"Maybe," Fat Peter said noncommittally.

More silence.

"What do I gotta do?" Bruno said finally.

Fat Peter smiled to himself. He knew Angel's father would first blow off steam and then begin to address the problem. She was the apple of his eye, after all. "Lemme go talk to them," he said. "Maybe I can work something out."

Bruno's phone rang. He pulled it out of his pocket and flipped it open. Before he spoke, he looked across at his trusted associate. "Was me, I'd work it out with a fuckin' shotgun shoved right up their asshole," he growled. "Yeah," he spoke into the phone. "Waddya want?"

Fat Peter sat back, pleased with himself. And thought, *good thing it isn't you, or Angel would never get those sailing lessons.*

IT WAS A COUPLE OF DAYS LATER that Fat Peter LaGuista was ushered into the office of Jerry Flanagan, manager of the Ocean Cove Yacht Club. The office was on the second floor of the old building, where a small den of offices looked out over the club's parking lot, and the row of whitewashed mansions on the bluff above. The room was barely big enough for Flanagan's desk and chair, a four-drawer file cabinet and the one guest chair in front of the desk. A small air conditioner in the window chugged away softly.

Flanagan was about forty, heavy set, with gray hair beginning to take over the sides of his head. He kept fiddling nervously with his black rimmed glasses and pulling at his neckie, which had a navy blue background filled with gold nautical symbols. When he had received the call asking for an appointment, he had asked around and learned who Peter LaGuista was and, more importantly, who he worked for. Now, he fixed his small eyes on the huge form in front of him as Fat Peter eased his body into the small chair and smiled at him. Flanagan had the impression of a cobra coiled and ready to strike.

"How can I help you?" Flanagan asked.

"My employer has sent me to ask for a favor," Fat Peter began. "Mister Bruno is a longtime resident of Serpent Point and his daughter Angela wishes to enroll in your sailing program for the summer."

"I see," Flanagan said, drumming his fingers on the desk. "And is Mr. Bruno a member? Our programs are reserved for the children of the membership."

Fat Peter smiled. "No," he said, "I don't believe Mr. Bruno has been asked to join the club." He didn't point out that it would be a cold day in Hell before an invitation might be forwarded to Joe Bruno; both of them knew that to be the truth. "But he is, of course, willing and more than able to pay whatever costs might be involved in having his daughter participate in the program. The cost, I can assure you, is of no consequence to my employer."

"I see," Flanagan said. "Well, such an arrangement would be quite unusual. I would, of course, have to submit such a request to the Commodore of the club and it would no doubt be taken up by the board of directors."

"No doubt," Fat Peter said, nodding his enormous head in agreement.

Flanagan flipped open his day calendar. "Unfortunately, the next full meeting of the board is not scheduled until mid-August, by which time the children's sailing program would be almost completed." He shook his head sadly, and closed the book again. "So you see, it would be impossible to accommodate Mr. Bruno's daughter. Perhaps we can make some arrangements for next summer …"

Fat Peter slammed one of his meaty fists onto the top of Flanagan's desk, with a thump that made the man jump. The color quickly drained from his face.

"Now you listen to me, you little shit," Fat Peter growled. The eyes in his huge head had narrowed, and held Flanagan's in a piercing stare that pinned the man to his seat. "Angela Bruno is going to take those sailing lessons, she is going to enjoy herself, she is going to be treated exactly like anyone else's kid and that's the end of that story. Do you understand what I am saying?"

Flanagan found himself suddenly unable to speak. He nodded, eyes wide.

Fat Peter leaned across the top of the small wooden desk and put his face inches away from the blanching Flanagan's. "If I hear the first word from the girl that she has been treated with any disrespect by anyone up to and including the fucking Commodore, if I hear that she has been called 'a guinea' or 'a wop' or 'an eye-tie' or any other name other than her own, if I hear the smallest little complaint about this place from the girl at all, then I will come back here and you and I will have another little conversation. And I can assure you that you will not enjoy it. Do I make myself clear?"

Flanagan nodded again. He tried to swallow, but there was no moisture in his mouth.

Fat Peter reached into his jacket pocket. Flanagan almost lost control of his bowels, but Peter's hand came out holding a stack of bills bound with a rubber band. He tossed it onto the desk. "That's a thousand bucks," he said. "That should cover the lessons, any equipment she needs and any food or drink she wants. You got that?"

Flanagan nodded again.

Fat Peter sat back. "Good," he said. "Angela tells me lessons begin on Tuesday morning. She'll be here. Do we understand each other?"

Flanagan nodded once again. His ability of speech had deserted him. His bowels were in an uproar and he didn't dare unclench his sphincter for fear of soiling himself.

"Excellent," Fat Peter said and rose to leave. "Have a good day."

Flanagan listened to the stairs protest loudly as the huge

man clomped down. His heart slowly began to return to a normal speed. In a minute or two, he was able to rise and make his way to the rest room. He was in there, shaking violently, for quite some time.

DUNNE SAT ON THE NARROW WOODEN DECK of the beachfront boathouse, nursing a tall drink and watching the day slowly ebbing away. The sun had long since disappeared from sight, but the long summer twilight lingered on and on. The darker blues of the ocean seemed to seep up into the night air, mixing with the lighter grays of the dying sky until the two hues merged and the line between them was slowly erased. Only a few wispy clouds high in the sky still reflected the last rays of the sun, remaining defiantly pink. The muscular wind of the afternoon had died down and was just strong enough to keep most flying insects at bay. The only sounds disturbing the peacefulness of the evening were the soft lapping of the surf against the sandy shore and the low thrumming of a fishing boat, heading for the safety of the port at Ocean Cove.

He enjoyed this time of day more than any other. It was as if Nature itself after the rushed madness of the day, the constant striving for survival; was taking a breather, a time to just sit and think quietly about things before finally drawing up the covers of darkness and turning over to sleep. Already, he could see the first stars blink into life high above in the sky.

"Hello, neighbor!" a soft woman's voice startled Dunne out of his reverie. He looked down at the beach, partially hidden behind a hedgerow of wild roses, and saw the pretty blond hair and lithe figure of Gillian O'Malley. She was dressed in a tailored white t-shirt and off-white capri pants, both of which hugged her figure, and was wandering barefoot through the light surf at the waterline.

"Hello yourself," he said back to her with a smile. "Nice night, isn't it?"

"Almost perfect," she said. "If I could only find a few more unbroken sand dollars." She held up the three round sun-bleached specimens she had already found at the water's edge.

She stood there for a moment, and he looked down at her. Her blond hair was pulled back and tied with a red ribbon and in the fading light of the day, she seemed to glow.

"Would you like a drink?" he asked, holding up his own half finished glass. "I'm about to make another gin and tonic."

She glanced once back across the broad green lawn at her own home next door, then looked back at Dunne with a bright smile. "Love to," she said. "Thanks."

She climbed up from the beach and mounted the four wooden stairs to the small deck that had been built at the beach end of the old boathouse. Dunne went inside and mixed her a cocktail and topped up his own. When he came back out to the deck, she was standing, looking out at the darkening ocean, her hair caressed softly by the breeze.

Dunne handed her the glass and they clinked. "You know," she said, not looking at him directly, "I never really got to thank you for getting me home the other day ..."

"It was nothing," he said, knowing that wasn't really true. "Glad I could help."

"So am I," she said. "A lot of other people, men actually, might have tried to take advantage of the situation."

"I'm not a lot of other people," he said.

She smiled, and nodded. She took a small sip of her drink and held it up between them. "This causes me a lot of grief," she said. "I know I shouldn't drink, but sometimes …"

"Well," he said calmly, "We all have our problems, and we all have to find a way to deal with them, some of which are better than others."

"And what are your problems, Jack Dunne?" she challenged him, but with a smile that softened her question.

He smiled. "Believe it or not, I have plenty of them," he said. "And most of them are none of your business."

She laughed. He liked the sound of it. It came from a place deep inside. He thought, she doesn't laugh enough. Neither one spoke for some time, drinking in the peacefulness of the evening.

"I hear you have a little boy," she said finally.

"Yeah," he replied. "Tiger. He's five going on fifty. I think he'll be coming down for the Fourth of July weekend. With his mother." He didn't know why he threw in that last bit of information, but he wasn't sure why he was enjoying the company of Gillian so much either.

"Ah," she said. "Malcolm and I never had children. There just never seemed to be the right time, what with his campaigns and all. I've always regretted it."

"Has he?"

She smiled ruefully and shook her head. "Malcolm is a man without regrets," she said. "That's why he's so successful as a politician. He never looks back and wonders what might have been. He just goes and goes."

"Like the Charge of the Light Brigade," Dunne said. "'Cannon to the right of them, cannon to the left'!"

"Exactly," she said. "And we all know how that worked out! They got their asses blown off!"

He laughed. "Sounds like you're not looking forward to the presidential campaign."

"Just between us?" she said, taking a sip from her glass. "I'd rather strip naked and walk through Times Square. And sometimes being the wife of a candidate like Malcolm O'Malley feels like that, bare for all the world to see ... and judge..." Her voice caught, and she stopped.

"I don't suppose you can just say no."

She laughed again, this time a laugh of sarcasm and bitterness. "No, of course not," she said. "It's my own fault. I knew what I was getting into. You don't marry an O'Malley without marrying all that comes with it, including the public scrutiny, the lack of privacy, the rumors of other women ..."

"The money, the nice houses, the servants ..." Dunne was deliberately cruel. He could not stand self-pity in anyone.

Her head snapped back as if he had slapped her. Her eyes blazed with sudden anger. "Fuck you," she said. "You bastard."

"I might be a bastard, but at least I'm an honest bastard."

She turned away and stared out at the sea. He knew she

wanted to get up and leave, to flee the truth. But she stayed. He gave her credit for that.

"I'm sorry," he said. "That was uncalled for."

She waited a beat and then smiled. "Thank you," she said. "It was also true. My life may not be perfect, but it is what it is."

"Here's to the truth," Dunne said and held up his glass again. They clinked again.

She put her drink down. "I've gotta get back," she said. "Thanks for the drink … and the honesty."

They both stood up, facing each other. She leaned forward and kissed him on the cheek. Then she turned and left, disappearing into the growing darkness and leaving behind only a wisp of her perfume hanging in the air. And three sand dollars, glowing ghostly in the night.

Joe Bruno walked into his kitchen. Fat Peter sat at the table next to the window, a plate of half-eaten pastries and a mug of coffee in front of him. Bruno looked at the huge man and thought, not for the first time, that he couldn't think of a time when he had seen his lieutenant without some kind of food nearby. He shook his head.

"You ever gonna lose some of that weight like the doctor told ya to?" he growled, not without some affection in his tone.

Fat Peter looked at his boss. "Lemme think about it," he said. "Ok, I thought about it. Nope." In illustration, he took a bite of the pastry.

Joe Bruno almost smiled. "Listen, we got a little problem."

Fat Peter put down the food and paid attention.

"Just got a call from Providence," he said. Fat Peter knew that meant the *capo di capi* of the New England mob, Billy di-Grassi. He was the one who called the shots and the only man to whom Joe Bruno paid respect. The next highest step on the rung led back to Sicily, the 'Ndrangheta and the graybeards that still ran the worldwide operations there.

"He's heard that Benito might cave and start talking to the feds," Bruno continued. "He got a call from fuckwad over there—" he nodded in the direction of Senator O'Malley's home across the street – "who's worried that shit might hit the fan if he does."

Fat Peter nodded. He was not surprised. Carlos Benito was a bit player. He had been a small time hood whose legitimate cover business had been asphalt and concrete—resurfacing driveways and parking lots. When the contracts for the Big Dig project had begun to be distributed, Bruno had arranged with O'Malley for his share of the federal windfall, and had used Benito Concrete to get his hands on a good-sized chunk of the money flowing out of Washington. Benito got the contract to pour the footings and passed along most of the money to Bruno, who, in turn, paid the agreed share under the table to O'Malley. It had been a pretty simple deal, one of many that Bruno and the senator had pulled off over the years.

But Carlos Benito had gotten greedy, as small-time hoods usually do. He saw the millions being passed out to Bruno and the senior senator, and compared it with what he saw as the chump change he had been left. So he had cut corners, ordered cheaper concrete to be used on the project, and pocketed the difference. He had been able to move his wife from landlocked West Palm Beach up to Hobe Sound, to a very nice new golf course condo two blocks from the ocean. She had been very happy.

But somebody had to take the fall for the death of Edith Scoggins in the tunnel collapse, and Carlos Benito had finally realized that he was it. The net was closing in, and he was not happy. He had two choices: shut up and take it, or begin to sing. O'Malley's sources in federal law enforcement had apparently told him that Benito, if he wasn't belting out arias, had at least begun to clear his throat. O'Malley, gearing up for his run for the White House, couldn't let that happen, and had called Billy diGrasso in Providence to tell him that. And now, diGrasso had put the problem in Joe Bruno's capable hands.

"He always was a twerp," Fat Peter said now. "Whaddya want me to do?"

"Take care of it." Bruno said.

"Won't there be some questions if he goes bye-bye?" Peter asked, thinking.

"I don't give a fuck how you shut his trap," Bruno snarled. "Just fuckin' take care of it, capisce?"

"Ok, boss, OK," Peter said, holding up his hands as if he were being attacked. "I'm on it."

CARMINE BENITO OPENED THE DOOR of her condo wearing just a short terrycloth robe over her nightie, leaving her long brown legs exposed. When she heard the insistent knocking, she had been having her morning coffee out on the screened-in patio, surrounded by her collection of growing things: the big terra-cotta urns holding the banana palms, the smaller pots filled with ferns and other wispy tropical plants. The little fountain in the corner, with the water shooting playfully out the penis of the little naked marble boy, made a pretty splashing sound. Carmine loved her little patio, its rococo wrought-iron furniture and even the view of the lake and the fairway of the golf course beyond it. She especially loved the warm Florida sunshine, which never went away, and the tangy smell of the nearby Atlantic. And although she wouldn't admit it to anyone, especially her mother, she loved it that her brute of a husband only came down from Boston to join her for the occasional weekend, and perhaps for six weeks in the coldest part of the winter. The rest of the year, she was free, gloriously free of his scowls, his incessant farting, his bad breath and his too-frequent demands for sexual pleasure. Truth be told, he made her skin crawl. But he had provided her with this nearly perfect three-bedroom condo in this nearly perfect part of the world, and he didn't seem to mind that she hadn't been back to Massachusetts in more than three years.

She had glanced out through the leaded-glass windows next to the door, and had caught a glimpse of the white panel truck in her driveway. CableVision, it said. She didn't recall making an appointment for the TV—she rarely watched the thing anyway. Maybe Carlos had ordered some new service. In any case, she opened the door with a smile.

"Miz Benito?" the man had asked with a cheerful grin. He was tall, heavy-set, with jet-black hair and there was something wrong with his nose—it had an odd shape to it, as if it had been broken in one or two different places. He was holding a clip-board in hands with thick, stubby fingers. There was another repairman standing behind the first, but he was facing away from the door, so she couldn't see his face. He was skinnier than the first, his arms and legs long. Both men were dressed in navy blue coveralls and steel-toed work shoes.

"Yeah?" Carmine said. "Don't tell me my husband has ordered another sports channel. We must get a thousand of them already."

The man laughed, revealing an incomplete set of teeth. "Yes, ma'am," he said. "It's the new NFL package. It'll just take us two seconds to get 'er hooked up."

Carmine Benito sighed and swung the door open, letting the men come in. She turned and walked down the hall, flashing those long legs and motioning with one hand to the den off to the right. "It's in there," she said. She heard the door close behind them.

The heavy set man grabbed her by the arms and pinned her against the wall.

"Hey!" she yelled, "What the f---"

"Joe Bruno says hello," said the skinny man, who stepped forward and jabbed a hypodermic needle into the woman's hip. She struggled against the restraint, but it was no use. She looked into the skinny man's face, and saw him grinning. His hair was long and greasy, hanging in dirty strings around his face. His eyes were cold, hard, empty. He waited and watched as the 50ccs of heroin coursed into her veins, carried up to the heart and spread out throughout her bloodstream. It only took a matter of seconds. She stopped struggling. Her face got red, her eyes went out of focus and her head dropped forward onto her chest.

When she awoke several hours later, her head pounding, she was totally naked, her arms were tied to something over and behind her head and she was staring up at a ceiling. She looked around in a daze at the inside of a double-wide trailer. The small windows were covered with darkened blinds, but she could see daylight still as the blinds waved back and forth in the air currents created by an air conditioning fan chugging away noisily. She tried to cry out, but a gag in her mouth prevented all but some whimpering sounds of fear and protest. Her heart began to pound so hard she was sure it was going to burst.

The door to the trailer opened, flooding the darkened interior with bright, harsh light. The heavyset man pulled himself up the steps and into the mobile home.

"Ah," he said, "I thought I heard you say something. About fuckin' time. You been tripping for eight hours now."

Carmine Benito struggled against the restraints that held her arms tightly above her head. Tears of anger and frustration flowed out of her dark eyes. She could see, and thought that she could feel the touch of his eyes as he looked at her nakedness, laughed softly and licked his lips. He was no longer wearing the long blue coveralls of the cable TV company, but wore a simple T-shirt and a pair of shorts. His thick legs were hairy and pasty white, and she could tell that he wasn't a Floridian. But some part of her knew that already. She knew these men were here because of her husband. She wondered what he had done.

The fat man went into the little kitchenette at the front of the trailer home and rummaged around. He came back where she lay on the narrow built-in couch on one side of the trailer, holding a small digital camera in one of his thick heavy hands.

He held the camera up to his face. "Say cheese, baby," he said. "We wanna let that fucker Carlos know that his little putana is still alive down here in the fun and sun capital of the world." He clicked off a half dozen shots, the flash illuminating all the dark corners of the woman's body. Carmine Benito whimpered softly as all of her was exposed.

The fat man held the camera out and pushed the buttons to review the shots he had just taken. "Nice," he said. "You got some cute bod. That shit-for-brains husband of yours is gonna love getting these. I'll bet he sees your cute little snatch, he'll wish he could dive right in."

Carmine was weeping steadily now, tears streaking down her face.

"You better hope he does what he's told," the fat man continued to click through the shots in the camera. "That fuckin' kid out there, he wants a piece of you so bad he's about to burst. You'd think he'd never been laid before. Chrissakes, when I was tying you up, he had his cock out so fast I almost could't stop him in time."

The fat man came over and stood for a moment, looking down on the woman. He reached out a hand between her legs and stroked her pubis with a thick thumb. She shrank, pulling away from his touch. "Yessir," he said softly, his eyes narrowed with desire, "That boy is all pent up. No telling where he'll stick that thing if I give him the OK."

He shook his head, as if to clear away some cobwebs. "But never mind. I been told to keep the putana on ice for now. Until your old man does what he's told. Until then …"

He produced another needle and jabbed her again in the hip. The drug quickly carried her off again. This time, she was glad to go.

"Jason…you there?" The voice came scratchedly through the computer speakers and there was a delay of several seconds before a shaky image of Jason Pyle followed on the screen. He was fiddling with something near the camera and it wasn't until he finished and sat back that Michael could see his brother's face.

"OK," Jason said. "I got ya, loud and clear. How's it going bro?"

"Not too bad," Michael said. "What's shaking out there in Singapore?"

Jason's image moved fitfully as he stood up and again adjusted something on his screen. "The usual," he said. "Spend all day dealing with contracts and specs and all night wining and dining these fucking Japs."

Michael laughed. "They're Singaporean and Chinese," he said, "Not Japs."

Jason flipped his hand. "Whatever," he said. "I'm getting sick of them. How are you doing with the towel heads?"

His brother laughed again. "I'm not sure international is the right place for you, bro," he said. "You don't seem to have the proper grasp of the niceties of diplomacy."

Jason groaned. "Oh, fuck diplomacy and fuck all these little yellow people. I'm ready to come home. How is Plan C coming along?"

Michael paused before he answered. He and his brother had hatched the strategy they called Plan C—for Cabal—several months earlier, right after Jack Dunne had taken over control of Pyle Industries and assigned each of them to far-off lands. Because their father had apparently decided to go along with Dunne's plans for the company and to make him the de facto heir apparent once Pyle retired, the two sons had decided to take matters into their own hands.

The plan was a simple one: find new owners to come in and take over the company, install Jason and Michael as co-presidents, and get rid of both their father and, especially, Jack Dunne. Each brother had sent out feelers. Jason had contacted some of the Chinese industrialists he was working with in the Far East while Michael had had some preliminary discussions with the Arab construction establishment. Specifically, with the Bin Laden Group out of Saudi Arabia. That company was closely allied with the Saudi royal family and had for years been the main infrastructure contractor in the Kingdom.

"Abdullah is in London this week," Michael now reported to his brother. "He said he was going to float the notion that Pyle might be in play and see what reaction he gets. He thinks he can get the Rothschild bank involved, and maybe another player from Germany."

"Can he keep it quiet?" Jason asked. "If any of this goes public, you and I are screwed."

"Not to worry, bro," Michael said. "These Arabs know how to keep things close to the vest. What about the Chinese? Any interest over there?"

Jason nodded, his head moving jerkily on the computer screen. The technology for making video calls via computer was good and getting better all the time, but it wasn't perfect. Sometimes the video would freeze for several seconds while the audio continued.

"Believe it or not, SinoCom, the big national telco, might be willing to throw a couple of billion into the pot," he said. "They want to diversify their base, and they need to build an entire wireless telephone infrastructure throughout the country. I've been telling them they can kill two birds with one stone by owning a piece of Pyle Industries."

"Geezus," Michael said. "That kind of contract would be worth zillions. And take decades."

Jason nodded. "You bet. Keep us in clover for years. And, if you bring in the Saudis at the same time, it'll split the pie three ways—Chinese, Arabs and us. Three-legged stool would be pretty strong, bro."

"Damn right," Michael agreed. "With all our US business, plus the new stuff that you and I bring in, Pyle will be one of the world's biggest companies. And you and I will be sitting in the driver's seat. Instead of that thug Dunne."

"Speaking of him, did you see where he forced Harvey Kay to retire?" Jason said.

Michael nodded into his computer camera. "Yeah," he said. "I mean, Harvey was probably ready to retire anyway, but now

Dunne will install his man as treasurer. Just another reason why we got to stop that bastard, and soon."

"We will, bro, we will," Jason said. "Hey, you gettin' any out there in the desert?"

Michael shook his head. "Not here, Jase," he said. "Man, you make a false move in this country, they'll come along with a sword and whack something off. But I'm going up to Geneva this weekend. Got a nice girl up there, works for the International Red Cross."

"Cool," his brother said. "What's her name?"

"Believe it or not, it's France."

"France? Like the country?"

"You got it," Michael said. "Her name is France, she's from France, and when she makes me come I yell 'Vive le France!'"

Jason Pyle laughed. "That's a good one," he said. "Listen, I gotta call coming in. Let's talk again Sunday."

"OK, bro," Michael said, "Stay cool." He punched a button and the screen went dark.

It was less than two hours later that Jack Dunne viewed the entire conversation between the Pyle brothers, sitting at his own office in Boston. It had been brought to him in person on a DVD by Paul Zec, a small, greasy-haired technician with thick round glasses and a bad case of acne. Dunne watched the entire thing, then clicked off his own computer and sat there for a moment, deep in thought.

"I thought you'd want to see that pretty quick, Mr. Dunne," Zec said.

Dunne glanced at the little man. "They don't have any idea that we've hacked into their networks?" he asked.

Zec shook his head and smiled. "No way," he said. "I personally installed all their machines at home and in their offices. Made sure that everything they do on those machines gets sent directly to our private server downstairs. Cell phones too. Michael likes to have phone sex with that chickie-poo in Geneva. You wanna hear some of that?"

Dunne shook his head. "Naw. I don't care if he's screwing camels," he said. "But I can't believe how fucking stupid those two boys are. Don't they know that as soon as they bring in foreign ownership, they lose every military and government contract in the US and overseas? Jesus, Mary and Joseph."

Zec shrugged. He didn't care about the business end of things. His was a world of wires and bytes, of connections and networks, of listening in and tracking down. He was well paid, could buy any piece of technology he wanted, and nobody ever busted his chops about anything.

Now he saw that Jack Dunne was staring out the window, unseeing, deep in thought. *Oh well*, he thought as he stood to leave, *that's why they pay him the big bucks.*

WILLIE JOHNSON CARRIED THE SILVER TRAY into the music room, and poured out two cups of hot chocolate into the antique Limoges cups, passing one to Timothy Regan and the other to Angela Bruno. There was a plate of freshly baked scones, a small silver dish with butter, another with cherry jam and a third with clotted cream. Angel reached hungrily for the scones, split one in half and heaped on all three condiments. Regan watched her with affection.

"You'd think you hadn't eaten in days, child," he said with a smile.

Angel took a huge bite of her scone and chewed it enthusiastically. "It's been a whole hour since I had breakfast," she said finally. "I'm a growing girl."

Indeed you are, Regan thought, as he noticed the young girl's figure, not for the first time. Regan himself was disinterested, of course, but he knew her expanding hips and swelling breasts would soon attract a great deal of attention from young men her age, if they hadn't already.

"It must be all that outdoor exercise you're getting," he said. "How are the sailing lessons going?"

"Super!" Angel said happily. In between bites of scone and sips of her chocolate, she told him of the classes she had been to so far. There were ten kids all together, six girls and four boys. "Good odds," she joked. The instructor was a college junior at Harvard named Freddie. "He's totally a bae," she sighed. He had paired the class up into twos, and Angel had drawn as her sailing partner a nice young man who attended Phillips Andover named Bob Martin. "He's a little dweeby but has possibilities," she said. Regan was not so sure he knew what either "bae" or "dweeby" meant, but he didn't stop the girl's chattering account to ask. She did mention his long blond hair, icy blue eyes and good tan. "There's another boy my age named Stan," she reported. "He goes to Choate. He wears sunglasses all the time and doesn't say much."

"Sounds perfectly dreadful," Regan said drily. She nodded in agreement.

The first day, she explained, they had just stayed on the docks, while Freddie had explained some of the theories of using the wind to propel a boat through the water. Then they had spent time learning the correct names of all the various lines and parts of the small two-person sailing dinghies they were going to use. But the next class, they had all pushed out into the protected cove of the yacht club, and had tacked back and forth among the large yachts tied to the club's moorings. "It was wicked fun," the girl said. "And Bob and I did the best. Stanley's boat capsized and Freddie had to go help him get it right-side up," she said with a grin.

"And have they treated you well, dear heart?" the old man asked. He remembered the dark look that had crossed Fat Peter's face when he told the man about Angel's wish to participate in the sailing class, and the rebuff he himself had suffered when he tried to plead the girl's case. He remembered thinking that he would not want to be on that man's bad side.

"Oh, sure," the girl said. "Everyone's been super nice. The manager guy, Mister Flanagan or something like that, told me I could order food or Cokes or anything I wanted at the snack bar. Peter was there the first day, sorta hanging out, but I told him he really didn't need to watch over me the whole time. I think he makes people a little nervous. So now he just drops me off in the morning and picks me up later in the afternoon." She paused and ate some more.

"I even met Mister...I mean Senator...O'Malley yesterday," she said. "I was driving us...I mean, I was ..." She paused, thinking.

"At the tiller?" Regan suggested.

"Yeah! That's it! At the tiller," she nodded. "And we managed to pull up right beside the dock without crashing or anything. And Senator O'Malley was standing there getting ready to go out on the launch to his boat and when we were tied up he told me 'Nice job!' And then he said maybe one day I could come out for a sail on his boat. Wouldn't that be super-cool?"

Oh my God, Regan thought to himself, *the spider has met the fly*. "Yes, that would be quite an experience," he said. "As long as some of your other friends go along as well. There's safety in numbers."

The girl laughed and came over to plant a kiss on the top of Regan's wig. "Oh, you funny old bear. You sound just like Peter or my Dad. I'm sure Mister … I mean, Senator,…O'Malley was just being nice."

Regan nodded and managed a weak smile in the girl's direction. *And I'm quite sure he was not*, he thought.

The offices of Benito Concrete and Paving were tucked away in a grimy warehouse district in Saugus on Boston's North Shore, between a metal working shop and an import/export firm. Jets taking off and landing at Boston's Logan airport roared overhead at regular intervals, drowning out most conversation for several seconds.

Carlos Benito was a little worried. He had not been able to reach his wife for the last two days. It was not like her to go off somewhere without telling him. Sure, she sometimes went down to that big outlet mall near Fort Lauderdale with her neighbor Jenny, and they sometimes spent the night in a motel there, but she had always told him about these expeditions beforehand. But this time, there had been no word. And every time he called the condo in Hobe Sound, all he got was the answering machine. He didn't like that.

He was sitting in his dark little office thinking about this when the door opened and Joe Bruno walked in. Carlos rose to greet him, and his heart, which had already started to pound, jumped even more when Bruno was followed through the door by Fat Peter LaGuista and Richie "BugEyes" D'Anjou. Benito's legs began to tremble, and he sank back into his leather office chair.

Bruno stood in front of the desk, the other two men flanking him. "Carlos," Bruno said, looking down at him with cold hard eyes. "How ya doin'?"

"Good, Joe, good," Benito managed to say. "Can I get you any …"

Bruno held up a hand. Benito stopped speaking.

"What's this I hear about you going in to talk to that investigative committee on Thursday?" Bruno said.

Benito's heart sank. The federal agents who had come to interview him had promised that no one would know if he agreed to testify. They said the meeting up on Beacon Hill would be private, closed to the public, that his name would never be released. They said he was looking at 20 years if he didn't tell them what he knew about the contract for the Big Dig concrete. He didn't want to go away, not now, not when things were going so good. He'd just started to get somewhere, what with the money he'd made from that contract, and the extra he'd made by fudging a little on the materials. For the first time, he had a little breathing room. And with his wife safely tucked away down in Florida, never wanting to come back home, he'd been able to enjoy the services of Delores, the girl who right now was sitting in the outer office, painting her nails and deciding where he was gonna take her for dinner that night. No, he couldn't go away now.

"No, Joe, I swear …" he started. Bruno backhanded him across the face, knocking him further back into his chair, which squeaked in protest.

"Don't fucking lie to me," Bruno said, his voice low and cold. "I already know you're going in. What's important to me is what you're gonna say."

Benito shook his head to clear it. He put a hand up to his lips and saw the blood on it when he took it away. He glanced up at Bruno, who stood there glowering at him, and at Fat Peter and Richie, who started at him impassively. He shook his head again.

"I ain't gonna say nothing," he said. "I mean it, Joe. I ain't gonna say a thing."

"You got that right," Bruno said. He motioned to Fat Peter, who reached into his coat and pulled out a handful of photos. He dropped them on the desk in front of Carlos Benito. Benito didn't move. "Look at them," Bruno ordered.

Benito looked at the photos of his wife, naked, bound and gagged. He could see the fear in her eyes, the appeal for help. His heart sank again. He knew what this meant. He was going away, probably for a good long time.

He raised his eyes from the photos and met the glare of Joe Bruno. "I won't say nothing, Joe," he said. "I swear. Please don't hurt her."

Bruno's expression of disgust and hatred didn't waver. He hated weaklings like Carlos Benito. He had come across and dealt with sniveling little shits like this his whole life. They all thought they could get away with something, take something away from him, from Joe Bruno. Time and again, he had proved them wrong. Some of them, he had killed, with his own hands. Others, like this little piece of shit, he had simply forced to do his bidding. He thought nothing of it. They were weak, they were small, they were nothing.

"Here's what you're gonna do, shitwad," Bruno said. "On Thursday, you're gonna tell them you changed your mind, you forgot what happened, tell 'em whatever the fuck you want, but you will not rat on Joe Bruno. And trust me, I will know it if you do, and that little lady of yours will be alligator bait by nightfall. But not until the boys down there have enjoyed fucking her up one side and down the other. You got me?"

Benito nodded.

"They'll likely indict you for perjury or some other goddam thing," Bruno continued. "I will make sure you get a lawyer. He'll drag it out long as he can. But you'll probably do some time. When you come out, you can see your little lady again. You got that?"

Benito nodded again.

"I can't hear you," Bruno growled.

"Yes, Joe," Benito said, his voice hoarse.

Bruno turned on his heel and walked out of the office, followed by his two henchmen. Fat Peter stopped to look down at the man one last time, then turned and walked out, closing the door behind him. The bleached blond girl sitting in the outer office watched the men leave, blowing on her newly painted nails. They were a shade of pink that went nicely with the color of her tight top, which featured a deep V in the front that displayed the twin mounds of her voluptuous breasts to good effect.

Fat Peter stopped briefly as he passed her desk. He reached into his pocket again and pulled out a thin stack of bills, held together with a rubber band. He dropped it on her desk. She moved quickly to swoop it up and dropped it into the depths of her purse tucked underneath her desk. She flashed a quick smile at Fat Peter, who nodded silently at her and followed his boss outside.

"THERE'S THE BEACH, MOMMY!" Tiger's high-pitched voice could not contain his excitement. He had already pointed out the pizza parlor, the grocery store and the "boat place," also known as the Winter Cove Yacht Club. How he was pointing to the strip of sand that lay alongside the causeway which led to Serpent Point.

Kathryn Dunne smiled at her son, but she was unsettled. She was not sure this long weekend was a good idea. She felt that she had allowed herself to be manipulated by the excitement of her son and by the insistence of her husband to come down to the island, even though she still felt she was at an emotional disadvantage. Her reasons for insisting on the separation from Jack Dunne had been real ones, solid ones and nothing, so far, had really changed. They both had begun to live without the other and to deal with how that felt and how it worked. Yes, certainly, it was good for Tiger to see them together again, not fighting, not yelling. But she didn't want to put any false ideas in the child's head. The problems between her and Jack were still there. And she didn't really believe, in her heart, that this weekend would do anything to make them go away.

But here she was, pulling into the sandy ruts that led to the boat house, at her son's directions. It did look pretty, the bluish tint of the weathered shingles set against the deeper blue of the ocean beyond; the whitewashed windows and the hedge of roses waving back and forth in the midday breeze. She thought, *well, you're here. Might as well make the best of it.*

Jack Dunne heard the sound of her motor, and came outside to greet them, wearing some cutoff blue jean shorts and a tattered, old t-shirt. He waved and grinned as Tiger threw open the door of the car and came running into his tanned, strong arms. He picked the boy up and swung him around, carrying him back over to the car, where he gave Kathryn a chaste kiss on the cheek.

"C'mon in," he said. "I've got some sandwiches and iced tea made. I'll bet this young man is hungry."

"Okay!" Tiger yelped. "C'mon Mommy. You gotta see my room. It's got all the seashells I found."

Kathryn allowed herself to be dragged by the hand, while Dunne went back to the car to unload the suitcases. Tiger took her around to the beachside and up the wooden stairs to the deck that overlooked the sea.

"We have dinner outside," he said excitedly. "Isn't that great? That's the barby-cue where Daddy cooks us hangurbers. And sometimes fish!"

He dragged her inside the sliding glass doors and showed her the well appointed den, with its wicker furniture covered in pretty chintz cushions, the small TV in the corner. There was a dinette on one side, and a pass-through counter that led to the small, narrow kitchen, with its four-burner stovetop, small white refrigerator, and one-hole sink.

"The sleepy parts are back here!" Tiger continued the tour down the narrow hallway that led to the three bedrooms in the back of the former boat house, with the one smallish bathroom at the corner. "This is my room. Isn't it great?" He showed off the tiny space with its narrow bed, a small white desk and chair and some shelves, which he had already managed to fill with a variety of shells, sand-dollars, petrified intestinal casings and other beach detritus. Kathryn sat on his little bed and allowed him to put each item into her hands, one at a time, telling her exactly where and when he had found them. It was a good way to create some space, to catch her breath for a moment. She heard Jack thumping down the hall with their suitcases.

"I've got you in here, Kath," he said. She went to see. The room faced to the west and the sun poured into the one window, creating a pool of warmth on the round sisal rug that covered the floor. The bed had a simple wooden headboard and was framed with white tables, each of which had a ceramic brown lamp with a pretty floral shade. A series of watercolors showing beach scenes hung on the wall above the bed. He tossed her bag on the bed, and then carried Tiger's duffel into the boy's room.

"And Daddy's room is just across the hall," Tiger informed his mother solemnly. "You're supposed to knock before you go in."

She laughed and ruffled his blond hair. "I'll try and re-member that," she said. She looked up at Jack, who was standing in the hall, looking in at them. She could read his sadness and his longing in his face. She hoped her own wasn't giving away her feelings. But how could it? There were so many. She smiled at him. "It's lovely, Jack," she said. "Everything you said. A place to get away from it all."

"I'm hungry!" Tiger announced, and his parents both laughed.

"Well, come on," Jack Dunne said. "Everything's ready. Let's eat!"

"Can we eat outside, Daddy?" Tiger asked. "It's much more better when we eat outside."

"Sure kiddo," Dunne said. "But no tossing your bread crusts to the gulls. They're like rats with feathers."

"OK, Daddy," the boy said.

AFTER THEY HAD EATEN, Tiger asked if he could go exploring on the beach. Dunne agreed, as long as he didn't get anything other than his feet wet, and stayed in view. The boy invited his mother to go with him, but she said she'd stay on the deck for a while and talk with his father. He accepted that, and went happily off to the beach, looking for more shells.

Dunne had opened the umbrella that provided shade for the small round table, and he adjusted it now so that Kathryn was sheltered from the harsh afternoon rays. They both swung their chairs around to face outwards so they could keep an eye on the boy and as frolicked along the waterline.

"So, how've ya been?" Jack said. "Everything OK at work?"

Kathryn was grateful for a neutral subject. She brought him up to date on the goings-on at her company, a large mutual fund where she was one of the senior investment advisors. Her background was technical analysis and as she talked about esoteric investing metrics and the application of analytical benchmarks, he found his attention wandering. He was more of a hands-on businessman, who identified, isolated and solved problems. But he liked the sound of her voice, and he loved to watch her as she talked about her work. Her eyes were alive and her hands moved to emphasize her points. He had always admired her intelligence and her dedication, even if he understood very little of what it was she actually did. He tried to pay attention, ask the occasional question and nod in all the right places, but he found himself instead thinking of how much he missed her, missed the sound of her voice and her laughter. He had to bite down hard on the back of his teeth to keep from reaching across to her, to brush the strands of soft brown hair out of her face, to hold her face in his strong hands and to kiss those soft red lips again.

"Are you listening to me?" she smiled at him now. She had seen his eyes go soft and unfocussed.

"Not really," he confessed. "I've missed you Kath," he said.

Her smile faded, and she turned her eyes away from his to search out and find the small boy skipping along at the water's edge, the small waves pushing up in brownish circles on the beach.

"Let's not go there, Jack," she said. "We'll just end up fighting again. Nothing has changed, really. You know that. Let's just try and co-exist for the weekend. For Tiger's sake."

"I don't want to fight," he said. "I just want us to be together again."

She turned and looked at him, searching his eyes. "You know we can't go back," she said. "Neither one of us has changed. You are still who you are, and I am still who I am. That wasn't working, Jack, you know that."

He sighed. He knew what she said was true, even if he wanted more than anything for it not to be true. "I've given a lot of thought to things," he said. "I've tried to see what I can change…"

"No, Jack," she cut him off. "You can't change who you are. I don't want you to change who you are, because then you won't be the Jack Dunne who I once loved."

"But…"

"But nothing," she continued. "The problem is that the Jack Dunne who I once loved is the same Jack Dunne who scares the hell out of me. The same Jack Dunne who is so driven, so determined to get his way, that he will let nothing get in his way. I've seen that Jack Dunne, I've lived with him. He frightens me. I don't know how far he will go to get what he wants. That frightens me. I don't want to be frightened anymore, Jack, I really don't."

"I would never hurt you, Kath," he said. But he knew how hollow and empty that sounded as soon as he said it.

She smiled, a rueful smile. "No," she said. "I don't think you would hurt me. And I know you would never hurt Tiger. But there are ways of hurting someone other than with your fists. Or even with words. It is the way you think and the way you act and deal with things. You are a dangerous man, Jack Dunne, and those close to you either have to live with that danger, or not. I just can't do it anymore. I'm sorry."

She looked at him, her eyes filled now with tears. He looked back at her, and tried to understand. Suddenly she broke away and looked out for Tiger. She couldn't see him. She stood up and scanned the beach. He was nowhere to be seen.

"Where's Tiger?" she said, fighting down a sudden wave of panic.

Dunne also stood up and looked up and down the beach. "He was right over there a second ago," he said, pointing down the beach. "Tiger!" he called out. There was no answer.

Kathryn had already started down the stairs that led from the deck down to the beach. Dunne leapt past her and was at the water's edge in no time. "Tiger!" he called once again. He turned to the west, looking into the sun, and put a hand up to shade his eyes as he peered down the water line. There was nothing but the rocky waterbreak some 500 yards in the distance, beyond the beach in front of Tom Pyle's house.

Dunne began to trot down the beach to the east. "Tiger!" he called out a third time. His eyes swept over the shallow water just offshore, looking for a shadow, something that might be the form of a small boy. He went from a trot into a full run. "Tiger!"

"Jack…Jack…he's here…I've got him!" The voice came from his left. He turned and looked down the broad grassy lawn that cascaded from the side porch of Senator O'Malley's mansion. He saw Gillian O'Malley holding his son's hand as she walked him back towards the beach. Without thinking, he vaulted over the wooden-slat redwood fence that demarked the line between the sandy dunes of the beach and the manicured perfection of the O'Malley's lawn.

"Thank God," Dunne said. He grabbed the boy and gave him a hug. Then held him out at arm's length. "Where the hell did you go?" His voice was harsh and angry, even though he tried to control it. "You were told to stay in sight!"

"There was a kitty," Tiger said, bewildered, not understanding why his father suddenly seemed so angry. "I came over to pet the kitty." His eyes began to water as he sensed he had done wrong.

Dunne folded the boy in another hug, holding him tightly against his chest. "It's OK," he said. "I'm sorry for yelling. Your mother and I were scared when we couldn't see you on the beach, that's all." They stood there for a long moment.

"Hi," Gillian O'Malley said over Jack's shoulder. "You must be Tiger's mother." She walked down to the windbreak where Kathryn stood, watching, her face drained. Gillian reached over the fence. "I'm Gillian O'Malley," she said. "You must have had quite a scare."

"Kathryn Dunne." The two women shook hands. "Yes, we couldn't see him anywhere. Thank you for looking after Tiger."

"Not at all," Gillian said, smiling. "We seem to have a family of cats around here. I hope they're not totally feral. He must have seen one of the new kittens. I was up on the porch and saw him chasing after something, so I thought I'd better some out and see if he was OK."

Dunne and the boy had walked back down to the fence. Dunne lifted the boy over and jumped back across to the far side. He turned to look back.

"Thanks, Gillian," he said. "Really. Thanks."

She smiled. "It's what neighbors are for, Jack. Now we're even. Nice to meet you Kathryn." She smiled down at Tiger, who was sniffling and holding tightly now to both his parents' hands.

"And, young man, anytime you want to come over and chase the kittens, you are most welcome," she said. "You should just make sure you tell your mommy and daddy where you've gone, so they won't worry. OK?"

He smiled up at her. "OK," he said. "Can we go home now, Mommy?"

TWO NIGHTS LATER, THE DUNNES WERE GUESTS for dinner at the Pyle house. Once again, Margaret had booked Angela Bruno as a babysitter to keep Tiger occupied while the adults had dinner. She sent the two upstairs to the den with some DVDs to watch and a large platter filled with hamburgers, hot dogs, chips, pickles and a green salad.

"When it gets dark, come down to the deck and we'll all watch the fireworks," Margaret told Angel.

Pyle was working at the grill, fussing over the marinated chicken breasts and braised short ribs that Margaret had prepared earlier that afternoon. She had told him not to press the younger couple about their problems, and after taking one look at Kathryn Dunne, she hoped he would listen. The younger woman was outwardly charming and gracious, but there was a shadow of sadness that draped over her like the silk wrap she had donned against a possible evening chill.

Pyle had put a goblet of chardonnay in her hands when the Dunne's arrived, and mixed a strong cocktail for her husband. While he puttered at the grill, the two of them talked animatedly about sports and business and politics, while Kathryn sat quietly, enjoying the softness of the evening, saying little. Margaret's heart went out to her and she came and sat next to her.

"Tiger is such a darling little boy," she said, patting Kathryn on the knee. "So well behaved. You should be proud."

Kathryn smiled at the older woman. "Oh, thanks," she said. "He has his moments like any other kid. But he's always been a serious sort. It's scary sometimes, the things you find out that he's thinking about."

"All children are surprising that way," Margaret agreed. "When I first met Tom's boys, they were already teenagers, so I don't really know what they were like when they were small. But even so, I found them to be a constant surprise. Not in a bad way, of course ..."

"No, I know what you mean," Kathryn said. "I guess that's the hardest thing. Not knowing what they're thinking. You might think you know, but you're often totally wrong."

Margaret laughed, reassuringly.

"Are Tom's sons close to him?" Kathryn asked.

Margaret cast a quick look over at Tom and Jack, who were engaged in a deep discussion about the Red Sox pitching staff on the far side of the deck. "Yes," she said. "I would say so. They're both working in the company, which I'm not so sure is the best idea. That by itself can create all kinds of tensions and get in the way of a good relationship." She was suddenly worried that she had said too much. Tom did not like his private life discussed in public. "But they're doing well," she added hurriedly. "Your husband has given each one an important assignment overseas, and from what Tom tells me, they're both doing well. He's proud of that, I think."

"Have either of them married yet?"

Margaret shook her head sadly. "No," she said. "But that's probably for the best. They are both still young and not quite ready, emotionally I mean, for that responsibility. Michael is a bit more settled, but Jason still sees himself as a free spirit. He's already broken more than a few hearts along the way. A shame, really."

Kathryn, sensing that this topic might be a bit touchy, just smiled and nodded.

"How did you and Jack meet?" Margaret asked.

Kathryn looked over at her husband, standing next to Tom, one hand in his pocket, the other gesturing with his half-empty glass in his hand. She remembered the investment conference in Philadelphia. It had only been ten years ago, but it seemed like another lifetime. She had recently joined one of the city's top investment banking firms after graduating near the top of her class at Penn and then Wharton. Her assignment at that meeting was to babysit some of the firm's clients, make sure they were entertained, and introduce them to the rainmakers in the firm. Jack Dunne had been part of a panel discussion on public financing in construction, representing the company he was in the process of taking over. He had been typically brusque that morning, snapping off comments and opinions without worrying if they offended anyone. And there had been some in attendance, including one of Kathryn's assigned clients, who had been put off by Dunne's style.

"He's a wise-ass," one of them had said, leaning over toward Kathryn, more, she felt, to try and peek down the front of her business suit than to whisper wisdom in her ear. "One of these days, he'll get squashed like a bug."

Kathryn had felt differently. She liked his confidence, his outside-the-box way of thinking. She had found a moment, when her Main Line client was engaged with someone else, to approach Dunne, put her card in his hand and look into his eyes. "You've got some interesting ideas, Mr. Dunne," she had said. "I'd like to talk about them with you some time. Call me."

It had been bold and a little forward, but not unusually so. She had kept her approach business-like, and indeed, that was her main interest. He had smiled at her, nodded, and tucked her card away. That was all. She had turned and gone back to her client, back to the babysitting, and forgotten all about it. Except for a slight frisson of disappointment.

"We met at a business conference in Philly," she told Margaret now. "He was a speaker and I was a fledgling at a bank. I gave him my card. He waited about two weeks and then called me."

When he had called, it took her a minute to remember who he was, and she almost ended the call quickly. She was, after all, a hungry and ambitious young executive, and she didn't really have time for romance. But then she remembered his cool gray eyes, and the confidence of his opinions, and she had agreed to meet him for a drink.

"Ah," Margaret said, nodding her head. "Men can be such scaredy-cats sometimes. Tom tells me that he knew Jenny—

that was his late wife—wanted to meet him, but he still took about a month to screw up the courage to call her."

Kathryn smiled. That after-work drink had turned into dinner, and they had sat in the restaurant talking, oblivious, until the manager had come over and asked them to please leave. It was two a.m. and everyone else in the place had long since gone home. The same thing happened the next time they met, a day or two later, and Kathryn had insisted on a few day's pause so she could catch up on her sleep. And she had demanded that they meet someplace during the daytime. That hadn't worked, either—they had met at the museum, spent a restless hour wandering the halls, and she had quickly taken him back to her apartment where they spent the rest of the daylight hours and those of the night in her bed.

"Well, once he did, he was a hard man to say 'no' to," Kathryn said with a rueful smile.

Margaret smiled. "I can see that," she said. "There is something of the wild man in him, isn't there?" Kathryn looked up at the older woman, surprised. "No, no, I don't mean like a cave man, clonking women on the head and dragging them away. I see it more as a sense of something untamed in him. Animalistic? Perhaps unconventional would be a better word, but I'm not sure that goes quite far enough."

"OK, what the hell are you two girls talking about so earnestly over there," Tom Pyle called out from across the deck. "You're making Jack and me nervous over here. Besides, I think I have reduced these bits of animal flesh into something edible. And I'm hungry."

Margaret and Kathryn exchanged a knowing look. "Talk about a cave man," Margaret said under her breath. Kathryn giggled.

THE FIREWORKS BEGAN SOON AFTER THE NIGHT had darkened and the first stars had twinkled into view in the eastern sky. Angel and Tiger had come downstairs, and Tiger had nestled onto Kathryn's protective lap while the rockets soared and exploded into colorful displays, reflected in the restless sea. Hundreds of pleasure boats had gathered off shore to watch the annual display, one of the few activities the Winter Cove Yacht Club shared with the general public ungrudgingly. Jack sat next to his wife and child and watched the lights reflected on their faces, enjoying their sense of wonder and excitement. Tom Pyle stood behind Margaret and rested a hand on her shoulder. Only Angel was alone, hugging her knees to her chest and watching the fireworks exploding overhead.

After everyone had gone home, Margaret had cleaned up in the kitchen while Tom had a small glass of whiskey for a nightcap. He sat in the kitchen and watched as she made things neat.

"What do you think of Dunne's wife," he asked. "You two were over there talking for a long time before dinner."

"I liked her," Margaret said. "She seems very intelligent, very centered."

"Do you think they will get back together?"

She didn't answer at once. She had been pondering that question since she had met Kathryn. "I don't know, of course," she said. "But I don't think so. She's very guarded, as anyone would be in a social situation like tonight. But I get a sense that she's somehow become frightened of Dunne."

"Frightened?" Pyle said. "He doesn't hit her does he?"

"Oh, no," Margaret said quickly. "I don't have any reason to believe that. He seems devoted to her and we know he's devoted to Tiger. But there is an undercurrent of fear in her. I don't know the reasons why. And I think it's that fear that is keeping them apart."

"Humph," Pyle said. "I don't understand. Sure, Jack Dunne is a tough guy. You have to be strong to get as far as he has in this business. But I don't know why anyone would be afraid of him. Or any more afraid of him than anyone else."

"There's nothing about him that concerns you?" Margaret asked.

"Me?" Pyle was surprised. "Hell, I hired the man."

"And you've let him send your boys away."

Pyle stood up. "Goddam it, Margaret," he said hotly. "I've given Jack Dunne the position of president of the company. I've got to allow him to make decisions as he sees fit. The last thing the company needs is any perception that there's a power struggle going on at the top. He's given Jason and Michael important assignments and they're both doing a good job. Why can't everyone just let things be for a while and see how it all works out?"

"Why?" Margaret said. "Who else is concerned? The boys?"

"Well, sure," he said. "They want to know when they can come back, And Dunne is after me to name him the chairman-to-be at this fall's stockholder's meeting."

"Ah," Margaret said. "He wants to be named the heir apparent, officially and publically. And that doesn't concern you?"

"Of course it concerns me," Pyle said. "I just think it's too soon to make any big decisions like that. I've told Dunne that. There's no good reason to be making any public pronouncements about anything. Besides, I'm not planning on retiring any time soon anyway!"

"I wish you would," she said wistfully. "You've worked hard for so many years. Wouldn't it be nice to relax for once? Take some time for you and me?"

"Yes, yes, of course," he said. "I'm trying to slow down. That's one of the main reasons I brought Jack Dunne on board in the first place. He can help keep the company growing. He can make sure there will be a Pyle Industries even after I've stepped down."

"But if you let him take the company over and force your two boys out, will that be worth it? Is that what you've work so hard to achieve?"

He shook his head. "I'm beat," he said. "Can't we go to bed now?"

He did look tired, all of a sudden. And old.

PART
TWO

G ORDON C ONGDON, CHIEF OF STAFF to Senator Malcolm
O'Malley, walked into the little Irish pub on the East Side of
Manhattan and waited for his eyes to adjust to the darkness.
A long mahagony bar, complete with brass railing and old,
rickety stools, ran down the right side of the narrow space,
while the back of the place past the bar opened up to permit a
half-dozen round tables to be squeezed in. Sitting in the last
one of those tables, his back to the wall, was the huge form
of Fat Peter LaGuista. He was eating a huge cornbeef sandwich. Also arrayed on the table in front of him was a platter of
French fries covered in red ketchup and a big bowl of stewed
cabbage.

Congdon made his way through the mostly empty bar
and took the chair opposite the huge man. "Peter," he said in
greeting. "You leave anything to eat for the rest of us?"

Fat Peter didn't bother to reply, but nodded at a leath-
er-covered menu on the table. He continued to eat, silently and
methodically, while Congdon scanned the menu and placed an
order with the white-aproned old man who appeared at his
side.

Peter finally swallowed. "Wassup in DC?" he said.

"The Senator..." Congdon saw the raised eyebrows and silent appeal on the face of the huge man and started over. He was not supposed to allude to his boss in any recognizable way in public in case someone was listening in, whether from the next table or via some kind of electronic eavesdropping. "I mean, Mister Jones was glad to hear that, ummm, the businessman in question had a change of heart, or loss of memory as the case may be."

Fat Peter nodded. Carlos Benito had appeared before the investigative committee at the Boston state house, but had refused to answer any of the questions put to him by the federal agents. He had pleaded the Fifth. He had even refused to acknowledge that his name was, indeed, Carlos Benito. The feds had immediately hauled him before a federal grand jury and charged him with perjury, obstruction of justice, and violations of the RICO Act. An indictment was expected soon.

"The Sen...I mean, Mister Jones is concerned that there may be other, ahh, incidents like this one in the future," Congdon said. "Given that Mister Jones has some rather important future plans, that might not be convenient."

Fat Peter smiled knowingly. "I can imagine that Mister Jones does have such concerns," he said. "But Mister Jones has spent his entire career lying down with dogs, and not just the ones associated with my employer. He shouldn't be surprised at this late date to realize that some of those dogs may have a few fleas."

"That's not my point," Congdon said hotly. "We just want to make sure that this thing is bottled up and bottled up tight."

Fat Peter shrugged. "I can't give you any guarantees," he said. "Like this time. A problem comes up, we take care of it. Can I tell you that no more problems will ever come up? How can I do that? Do I look like a fuckin' fortune teller to you?"

"That wasn't our agreement..." Congdon started. Fat Peter cut him off.

"Our agreement, dickwad, was that Mister Jones would open up the federal money pipe and keep it open," he snapped. "In return for which, some of that flow would go right into his own fat pocket. He did, and it did. End of story. Now he wants to pretend that this was all on the up-and-up? That nobody broke any laws and if they did, that he didn't have anything to do with any of that? "

"The Senator never agreed to break any laws," Congdon, in his anger, forgot the ruse of using the pseudonym.

"Oh no?" Fat Peter smiled again. "Like the law calling for open bids on all public projects? Or the law forbidding kickbacks and payoffs? Or the tax laws about declaring all income? Did the good senator pay his taxes on that six million in cash that went straight into his numbered bank account in the Cayman Islands? Oh yeah, is that bank account legal?" he shook his head. "Don't make me laugh, Congdon. You and your boss are just as bent as me and mine. The only difference is that you pretend he's not. And that you steal in broad daylight and right under everyone's nose. And you pretend what you do isn't stealing at all. At least we're honest about it."

The two men glared at each other across the table in the dimly lit room. Each of them knew that they could destroy the other with a single telephone call. Each of them knew, however, that they, too, would likely be destroyed in the process. It was like détente in the Cold War all over again, the politics of mutual destruction. But they both understood that Congdon and O'Malley had much more to lose. Joe Bruno, after all, was not planning to run for President of the United States. The waiter came with Congdon's lunch and that gave them an excuse to pause, regroup.

"I'm sorry," Congdon said finally, "I didn't mean to imply that the Sen...I mean, Mister Jones isn't appreciative of your services."

Fat Peter nodded and kept his face impassive. *Got you, you bastard*, he thought.

"And if, as we hope and expect, Mister Jones is successful in his bid for higher...ummm....things next fall, then you could probably expect some additional benefits to your business."

"In return for?" Fat Peter said.

"There may be some things you can do for us in the upcoming campaign," Congdon said.

"Such as?"

"Oh, I don't know," Congdon said, although he did. "Perhaps some opposition research. Additional fund raising. Get out the vote drives. Things like that."

Fat Peter nodded thoughtfully. *You mean elimination of potential campaign problems, money laundering and vote buying*, he thought. *This is why Joe hates politics and politicians. He isn't going to like this at all.* "And Mister Jones is prepared to offer what in return?" he asked.

Congdon munched on his sandwich, and waved a hand airily. "Oh, I don't know," he said. "Appoint a new U.S. Attorney for the New England district," he said. "Someone who will concentrate more on some crimes than others. There may even be a chance for the next president to name a new director of the FBI."

"I see," Peter said. "Well, that's all very interesting. I will discuss it with Mister Smith, my employer."

"Do that," Congdon said. "And keep in mind that it could also go the other way."

"The other way?"

Congdon smiled this time. "Sure," he said. "There could be a U.S. Attorney and an FBI that are suddenly very interested in organized crime in New England, or that suddenly get all kinds of new resources and funding to investigate. You never know how it goes."

Fat Peter nodded, acknowledging the implied threat. He also knew it was possible that O'Malley and Congdon could be planning a major double-cross: use the services of Joe Bruno's organization during the campaign and then loose the federal and state dogs against them once they'd won. In fact, Peter suspected that was their plan anyway; Malcolm O'Malley had never been a straight-up guy. That's why Bruno would have to be very careful. Or they'd have to find something about O'Malley that would give them the upper hand, and protection for the organization. "You gotta win, first," he said.

Gordon Congdon's smile widened. "Oh, we will," he said. "You can rest assured of that."

Angel Bruno arrived for her weekly gabfest, disguised as a piano lesson, tanned and happy. Timothy Regan noticed the sparkle in the girl's eyes and her barely contained enthusiasm as she related the events of the last week. She was having the time of her life at the Winter Cove Yacht Club.

"Even though we're supposed to change partners, Freddie lets Bob and me sail together," she said happily. "He said we're totally the best sailors in the class."

"Totally," Regan said, smiling.

"And in August, there's this big race thing…"

"Regatta?" Regan suggested.

"Yeah, that's it," the girl nodded. "Over at Chatham. All the yacht clubs on the Cape get to enter two boats and there are prizes and stuff. Freddie said that Bob and I are definitely going to be one of our two boats. Isn't that awesome?"

"Totally," Regan said. "So I take it you and the young Bob have become close?"

"Oh, he's OK," Angel said. "He can be a little bossy sometimes. Like he tries to tell me what to do when I'm the skipper?

I hate that. When you're at the tiller, you're supposed to be the one in charge, Freddie says. The other person just has to follow orders. But he's a guy and he thinks he knows everything."

"I hope you make him walk the plank, dear heart," Regan said.

Angel giggled, "Oh, you old bear. Our little boats are too small to have a plank. But I have thought about pushing him overboard a couple of times."

"Probably do him some good," Regan agreed. "And how is your family?"

"Oh, everyone is fine," the girl said. "My big sister came down for the Fourth of July. She told Mother that she has a new boyfriend and Daddy went ballistic. Wanted to know who he was and what he did and all that stuff. He can be such a control freak."

"He's probably just trying in his own way to make sure your sister isn't making any rash decisions," Regan said. "A father always wants to protect his daughter."

"I guess," Angel said, looking doubtful. "I overheard Daddy tell Peter to check him out."

"Well, you see? Better to be safe than sorry." Regan imagined the unfortunate young man being confronted with the impressive visage of Fat Peter LaGuista or one of Joe Bruno's other fearful henchmen and being given one of their "or else" ultimatums. Regan imagined that the Bruno girls would be virgins until their wedding days, and maybe forever.

"Well, he'd better not try to check out any of my boyfriends," Angel said, frowning. "I'd be furious."

"How do you know he hasn't done so already, say, with young Mr. Bob the sailor?" Regan asked mischievously.

Angel giggled. "Oh, you old bear," she said. "Bob's not my boyfriend. He's just a friend friend."

"Ah, well that's fine then," Regan said, smiling. "Although it's been my experience over the years that friend friends can easily become boyfriends." Visions of his most recent boytoy evening leapt into his mind, and he forced himself to put them out again.

"But you are the second person who's thought that Bob and I are boyfriend and girlfriend," she said, suddenly turning serious. "Senator O'Malley said the same thing the other day."

"Oh?" Regan felt his heart sink but kept his voice calm.

"Yeah," Angel said. "Bob told me that the Senator talked to him about going sailing on the Senator's yacht. Said he and his girlfriend should come out with him one day next week and he's show us what real sailing was all about. He meant me as the girlfriend," she explained.

"Bob told you all this?" Regan asked.

" Yeah," the girl said. "He thought it was funny, too. But he does want to go out on the Senator's boat. Bob is really into politics and he thinks it would be awesome to spend some time talking about issues and stuff like that. Like I said, he can be a little dweeby sometimes."

"Maybe you should let Bob go by himself," Regan suggested, hoping the girl would agree. Although he feared also for the boy. He had heard rumors about O'Malley, that his sexual tastes ran in all directions and had no gender boundaries.

"But he's supposed to be a really great sailor," Angel frowned. "I could probably learn a lot from him."

Indeed you could, child, the man thought. *But I doubt that the lessons would have anything to do with sailing*. He changed the subject.

"Dear girl," he said. "We have something very important to decide. And that is how we are going to celebrate your birthday, which I believe is soon upon us."

She smiled. "And yours too, don't forget," she said. "It's amazing that you and I have the same birthday. It's like we were fated to become best friends." It was true: they shared the same birth date, separated by nearly sixty-five years.

"So what shall we do to celebrate?" he asked. "We have to do something wild and extravagant."

"A party, of course," she said. "We should throw the biggest party ever. Invite all all our families and friends and the neighbors. Out on the lawn. I mean, you've got the pool, the tennis courts, all that space. We should have everyone over and lots of good stuff to eat and you can play the piano and sing."

A party, he thought, a garden party, just like the old days. Everyone elegantly dressed. Champagne and caviar. He could hire an orchestra. It would be just like Beverly Hills, back in the day. Bogie and Bacall. Fred and Ginger. Spencer and Kate. George and Gracie. When life was simpler and purer.

"Hello?" Angel's voice brought him back to the present. "What do you think? About the party?"

"I think it's a wonderful idea," he said. "Go get Ruby and we'll get the ball rolling right now!"

She ran over and gave him a hug and kissed him on top of his bewigged head. "You are my favorite bear in the whole world!" she said.

A FEW DAYS AFTER THE HOLIDAY, Dunne was working on some contracts in his office in the Pyle Industries headquarters in Boston when his secretary poked her head in.

"Mister P just buzzed," she told him. "He asked if you could come down."

"Now?" Dunne complained, looking at the pile of papers on his desk.

"That's what the man said," she replied.

Dunne pushed back his chair with a sigh and walked down the hall and around the corner to Tom Pyle's office. The older man was sitting behind his impressive desk and waved him in.

"What's up Tom?" Dunne asked. "I've got six different contracts to wade through and I'm trying to get out of here and down to the island before the traffic gets bad."

"The traffic is always bad, Jack," Pyle said with a grin. "We probably ought to invest in a company helicopter. You could wave at all the poor bastards on the Southeast Expressway as you choppered over them."

Dunne, preoccupied, did not laugh. He dropped into one of Pyle's guest chairs. "What's up?"

Pyle looked across the desk at Dunne. Bringing the younger man into the company had been a good idea. With his new energy and the contacts from his own organization, Jack Dunne had breathed new life into Pyle Industries. In just six months, he had brought in a dozen important new jobs and there were deals pending around the world, waiting only for official approval of their proposals. With Dunne assigned to administration, cost control and construction management, Pyle had been freed to do what he did best, which was smoozing and elbow rubbing with prospective clients, government bureaucrats, politicians. He had played a lot of golf, hosted expensive dinners, scheduled future trips taking prospective clients hunting for elk in Wyoming and fly fishing in virgin lakes in the Yukon. As a result, Pyle Industries had become even more of a major player. It looked like the company would have record earnings this year, and the next…well, Tom Pyle had long ago learned never to count the money until it was safely in the fist, but he couldn't see any way that profits would not double over the next twelve months.

Still, he was uncertain about what he was about to say. It would be the first time the two men had gone head to head. But it had to be done.

"I just wanted to give you a heads-up," he said now, looking Dunne in the eye. "I've asked Jason to come back from the Far East to work with me in Washington."

Dunne shook his head from side to side. "I'm not ready for him to come back yet," he said. "I need him out there to keep an eye on the Chinese deal. We're just starting to get our foot in that door, and it's a big fucking door."

"And I need him here," Pyle said firmly. "There are some big contracts about to be let in California, and Jason knows all the players. He lives out there for Chrissakes. If he's leading the charge, we'll have an advantage."

Dunne stood up and began to pace. "For God's sake, Tom," he said. "The China projects are worth six or seven times what anything in California can bring in. And how do you know they'll be able to pay? Haven't you heard? California is broke. The Far East is where the big bucks are. Jason is doing a good job out there. In another six months, twelve tops, maybe I can let him come back stateside. But not now."

Pyle stared at Dunne. "Jack," he said, "I appreciate what you say. But I've made my decision. Jason is on his way back and that's final."

There it was. The words hung in the air. Their eyes locked across Pyle's desk. For a long moment, neither one spoke. They both had known that eventually it would come down to this. They were both strong powerful men used to getting what they wanted. But this time, one would not. Inside, Dunne was furious; he had feared it would come to this, and although he had tried to do everything he could to make sure he had the power to make it happen, he knew, deep down, he did not. In the end, it was still Pyle's company. For now, at least.

"OK, Tom," he said. "I disagree, but it's your company." He turned and stalked out.

Pyle watched him go. He knew, too, that a line had been crossed. There would be no going back now. He had asserted his authority. Dunne had accepted it. But there would be some fallout, some kind of blowback. Something would change. He didn't know yet what that change would be. But he would keep careful watch, because long experience told him that men like Jack Dunne do not like taking orders or being forced to do something they don't want to do. There are always consequences, he thought, always. He would wait and watch and he would be ready.

DUNNE SAT ON THE DECK OF THE BOAT HOUSE later that night, watching the moon rise from the sea out beyond Martha's Vineyard and begin to wash the beach with its ghostly light. He had finished his work earlier that day, slashing his way through the piles of contracts with a cold efficiency, and then making the drive down from Boston to Cape Cod, weaving in and out of the traffic. He had been honked at a dozen times and exchanged upright middle fingers with most of the honkers. He had stopped in Winter Cove to buy a steak, a baking potato and a pre-made salad and picked up several bottles of a delicious Chilean shiraz. He had arrived at Serpent Point around seven, had grilled and eaten his steak by eight and was now sipping on his third glass of wine and watching the moon's reflections in the millions of sparkles on the restless waves.

He was so preoccupied, replaying the events of the day, that he didn't see Gillian O'Malley until she was standing next to him, on his own deck, smiling down at him, her blond hair tossed by the breeze from the sea and streaked in the moonlight.

"Neighbor," she said, "You look like your best friend just died."

He looked at her and managed a smile. "Business," he said.

"Closing time," she sang, patted his shoulder and went inside, returning with a wine glass, which she filled from the half-empty bottle at Dunne's side. "You want to talk about it?" she asked once she sat down and sipped.

"Not really," he said, shaking his head.

"Good," she said. "Business bores the shit out of me."

"How's the senator?" Dunne asked, nodding in the direction of the house next door.

"Politics bores the shit out of me, too," she said. "In fact, my husband bores the shit out of me. He's down in Washington at some fund-raiser or something. At least that's what he says. He's probably banging the latest Bambi."

"Bambi?" Dunne couldn't help from laughing.

Gillian grinned. "Some cute young thing from God knows where," she said. "Comes to Washington, the seat of power, wants to save the world, feed the poor, clothe the naked. Meets Senator Bigshot—either mine or someone else's—at some cocktail party and is thrilled that he's actually paying attention to what she says. Then, before you know it, she's on her back, her panties are off and the Senator is in session. They're always so young and innocent…just like Bambi. Hence the name."

"My, my," Dunne said, chuckling. "You sound almost cynical."

Gillian laughed, cynically. "Just realistic, I'd say," she said. "Washington is crawling with Bambis—always has been, always will. It used to bother me, thinking about it. Used to bother me a lot when some of the Bambis came to cry on my shoulder, thinking that if they confessed their sins to the wife, the bad old Senator would get what was coming to him. I don't let them cry on my shoulder any more. It happens too often. I just tell them to smarten up, grow up, stop believing in some fucking nonexistent Camelot and to go home."

"Ouch," he said. "Puts a little dent in the desire to save the world."

She laughed again, cynically. "Washington is about two things," she said, "Money and pussy. When they're thinking mostly about pussy, the country's usually in pretty good shape. When they start in on the money part, then we all get fucked."

"Can I write that down?" Dunne said. "Might make a good letter to the editor."

She drained her wine and poured herself another. "Just don't quote me," she said. "Wouldn't go with my image as the lovely and long-suffering wife of the soon-to-be-savior of the country."

"Why do you put up with it?" he asked.

She stared off into the moonlight for a moment. "Why do you think I'm a drunk?" she answered.

He was silent for a while. "That could be an excuse," he suggested gently.

"Ya think?" she responded hotly. She continued to look at the sea. He could see tears forming in her eyes. She turned to him, lips quivering. "Why are you making it so goddam hard for me to take you to bed?" she asked.

He responded by leaning forward and searching for and finding her lips. They kissed, and her mouth opened hotly to his. She tasted at first of wine and sadness. He reached up and stroked her face softly and felt her respond. She moved across and into his lap and they kissed, deeply. His hands stole beneath the thin shirt she wore and found her breasts, and her back arched as he stroked their tender tips. She moaned and pressed herself against him in need and desire.

"That's better," she whispered.

He stood and led her inside. There, in the soft moonlight streaming in at the window, he undressed her beside his bed, stopping to kiss her breasts and her stomach and the thin downy covering of her sex. He stripped off his own clothes, and she reached out a hand and caressed his tumid sex, then fell to her knees and took him in her mouth, hot and wet. His breath caught.

"That's much better," she said, smiling up at him.

He lifted her and laid her on the bed, then bent to kiss her stomach. He traced his lips down, down into the warmth below and she opened her legs to his exploring tongue, calling out in wordless ecstasy as he nuzzled and licked, first softly then with hard insistence until she trembled, gasped and then exploded in orgasm. He waited until she stopped her spasms, then he climbed between her legs which opened wider to accept him. He slipped easily into her, and heard her soft cries of joy echo again as he began to move, slowly, oh so slowly. Her legs wrapped around his waist and she reached up to pull his face down to hers. "Don't stop," she whispered, "Don't ever stop."

Joe Bruno was not happy. He was in his office in the back room of the North End bodega and Fat Peter was telling him about his meeting with Congdon. As Peter had feared, Bruno was going ballistic over the idea of helping Malcolm O'Malley campaign for President.

"What I'd like to do is shoot that bloated fuck," Bruno raged. "He thinks we're gonna help him? Why the fuck would we do that?"

"He says because he can get the feds off our back," Fat Peter said.

Bruno laughed, an exhalation that did not have any mirth in it. "And we're supposed to believe him?" he said. "Malcolm O'Malley? You gotta be fucking kidding me. He's a fucking politician. He don't talk out of both sides, he talks out of his mouth, his ears, his asshole and any other fucking hole he's got. He tells us one thing today, another thing tomorrow."

"But if he can deliver, it would be good for business," Fat Peter pointed out.

"When has he ever delivered?" Bruno wanted to know. "It's always 'Do this, Joe' and "If you do that, Joe' with him."

"He did get us that contract on the Big Dig," Peter said. "We cleared about ten million on that deal."

"And now every goddam federal agent, politician and reporter in the state is trying to hang us with the blame for what the fucking little weasel did," Bruno said. "What is Senator O'Malley doing about that? He wants to make sure nothing else happens. I swear to God, Peter, it would be better for us and for the fucking country if we put a couple of caps into that motherfucker's head and that fruitcake Congdon too."

Fat Peter just smiled and let it pass. He knew, and Bruno knew, that eliminating a sitting United States senator wasn't possible. Especially someone like O'Malley, with his family's long history of public service and public tragedy. Peter knew Bruno was just blowing off some steam, and that he would eventually calm down and decide the right thing to do.

"What we gotta do, boss, is figure out a way to get on top of him," Fat Peter said. "Get him by the balls. Then we can do the squeezing, 'stead of the other way around."

"You got any ideas?"

"The wife might be a possibility," Peter said. "She's a lush and she's got hot pants, I hear."

Bruno waved his hand dismissively. "So's every politician's wife in Washington," he said. "This day and age, if they don't fuck around, something's wrong. Naw, we gotta get something else."

"How about Congdon?" Peter suggested. "We know he's a homo. There's rumors that he and the boss get it on when there ain't any bimbos handy."

Bruno shook his head. "O'Malley wouldn't care if that got out," he said. "I'm telling you, Peter, times have changed. We could get pictures of Malcolm O'Malley fucking a German shepherd and the fucking New York Times would probably endorse him for President on account as he's an animal lover."

Peter laughed.

"It's fucking true!" Bruno continued. "The sex things don't work anymore. You gotta catch these bastards with their hand in the cookie jar nowadays. And O'Malley has always been real smart about hiding all that shit from view."

"Maybe we can set him up," Fat Peter said, thinking out loud. "Do a deal, bring him in, drop a dime."

Bruno thought about that, stroking his chin. Eventually he nodded. "Got possibilities," he said. "Lemme think about it. Maybe call Providence, talk to DiGrassi. We try and take down someone like O'Malley, we'd better cover all the bases, *capisce?*"

"OK, boss," Fat Peter said. He was satisfied. He'd turned Bruno away from anger and revenge and onto more productive avenues. That was his job. And he knew how to do it well.

MALCOLM O'MALLEY POURED HIMSELF A DRINK from the crystal decanter on the cherry sideboard filled with Bushmill's Irish whisky. He glanced at Gordon Congdon and motioned at him, but his chief of staff shook his head. Congdon rarely drank, and never this early in the afternoon. He needed to make sure his head was clear. The senator, on the other hand, seemed to function better when he had a slight buzz on.

It was quiet on the fourth floor office of O'Malley's home on Louisberg Square in Boston's expensive Beacon Hill district. The Senator liked this office, with its windows offering a nice view across the rooftops to the Lower Basin of the Charles River. Dozens of white sails dotted the river in the afternoon sun, tacking back and forth in the brisk breezes that swept in from the harbor off to the right.

"So…how'd the meeting with Bruno's people go?" the senator asked, taking a good-size swallow of the golden fire in his glass.

"Good, I think," Congdon said.

"Any more little problems we gotta worry about?"

"Well," Congdon said, "I don't think so. Of course, that fat fuck LaGuista said he couldn't guarantee there'd be no more problems, but they did take care of the Benito situation. He clammed up. Rogers over at the FBI is bullshit, but there's nothing they can do except send him away for a year or two for perjury and obstruction."

"Good, good," the senator said, sitting down behind his Louis XIV desk, its leather inlaid top polished and shining. "By the time he gets out, people will have forgotten the whole thing, moved on. Did you bring up the campaign?"

"I did," Congdon said. "The fat wop was noncommittal. But his eyes lit up when I mentioned the possibility of getting the feds to leave his organization alone for a while."

"I would think so," O'Malley smiled. "Fucking Bruno must spend five million bucks a year on lawyers and payoffs. He'll be hearing cash registers clanging away he thinks we give them an eight-year window of opportunity with the feds held at bay."

"Assuming you get elected and re-elected."   Congdon smiled at his boss. They both knew that the way things were going, Malcolm O'Malley was a shoo-in for the Democratic nomination. And once that happened, they would make sure he got elected. And re-elected. They'd even discussed, privately—just between themselves—whether it might be possible to get the 22th Amendment to the Constitution rescinded. Hell, if Roosevelt could get elected to four terms, why couldn't O'Malley?

"Of course, we'll have to find a way to crack down on him," O'Malley mused. "I can't allow that guinea bastard to think he can operate above the law."

"No," Congdon agreed, "We can't have that."

"Don't be a smart ass." O'Malley frowned at his chief. "I'm serious. Soon as we're in the White House, we're gonna hit the mob and hit them hard, from coast to coast. It's good politics. The people will eat it up when we start arresting all those fucking Italians, the ones importing all those evil nasty drugs and running whores and gambling dens. They'll eat it up, and the media will eat it up."

"You're gonna need a strong Attorney General," Congdon said. "Can't have no civil liberties pussy in that job if you're gonna take on the mob."

O'Malley smiled. "You got someone in mind?"

"Yeah," Congdon said. "Someone who went to Harvard and Harvard Law, good Massachusetts boy, experienced with handling those pukes in the Congress ..."

"You?"

"...someone who'd have the President's back," Congdon said, nodding.

O'Malley chuckled. "I don't know," he said. "When was the last time someone went from campaign director straight to head of Justice?"

"I don't know," Congdon said. "Kennedy? Reagan? Bush? Who cares? You need a strong AG and someone you can trust."

"And that's you, huh?" O'Malley said.

Congdon didn't respond. He knew O'Malley was just toying with him. He knew he could get any job he wanted in the O'Malley administration. He knew too many secrets, both political and personal. He knew where O'Malley's skeletons were buried; hell, he had arranged the internment of most of them. O'Malley owed Gordon Congdon, he owed him big time. And Congdon was going to collect. Once that 270th Electoral College vote had been secured on election night, Gordon Congdon was going to cash in. Big time.

"You think the country's ready for the first fag attorney general?" O'Malley was still joking, even though Congdon didn't think he was so funny anymore.

"Don't ask, don't tell," Congdon shot back. O'Malley laughed and drained his drink. He looked longingly at the decanter, but decided not to pour another. "What do we have tonight?" he asked.

"Meeting with the mayor at seven, then a fund-raiser over at the Copley Plaza," Congdon said. "Gillian is being driven up from the island, should be here about eight."

O'Malley looked at his watch. It was just after five. "That gives me about an hour before I have to get ready," he said. "I wonder what we can do to kill an hour?" He smiled across the desk at Congdon.

His chief of staff saw the look in the senator's eyes. He thought of that 270th vote, foresaw how he would feel the moment that final state went into the D column, put the O'Malley team over the top. He stood up and began taking off his clothes, leaving them in an unkempt line as he walked into the senator's darkened bedroom.

THE TELEPHONE RANG IN THE FOURTH FLOOR APARTMENT on the Quai Wilson in Geneva. Michael Pyle, who had been staring out the tall, narrow window past the green wrought-iron balcony at the blue lake and the mountains of Switzerland rising in the distance, turned away from the view and answered it.

"Bro!" came the greeting from his brother, Jason.

"Hey, Jase," Michael said. "Where are you?"

"Washington," his brother said. "Got in about a week ago and I've been pigging out on Burger King and Budweiser ever since. Funny the things you miss when you live overseas."

"I'd say you're a lucky bastard, but your cholesterol has probably gone through the roof," Michael laughed. "How's Dad?"

"He's good," Jason said. "You know, I'd have predicted he'd be slowing down a bit, you know, losing a yard off his fast ball? But I can't tell any difference. He's still got his A-game."

"Yeah, everyone I talk to back at headquarters says he's still on top of things," Michael said. "So what's up?"

"Good news," Jason said. "I think I've got that bastard Dunne."

Michael sat down on the plush sofa in the elegantly decorated lounge. He could hear France, his girlfriend, bustling about in the kitchen, preparing dinner. "Tell me about it," he said.

Jason told his brother how he had made contact several months ago with someone who worked in the Pyle Industries accounting division. "I had to sorta let her believe that she and I were an item," he explained, somewhat sheepishly. His brother chuckled. Jason's mole, a thirty-something, never-married woman named Marcia, had agreed to keep her eyes open for him. And just before he got the word from his father that he could come back and work in the D.C. office, he had heard from Marcia. There were some discrepancies, she said. Expenditures that were not budgeted. Requests for cash, sometimes in large amounts. Expense reports that showed some unusual charges. Nothing that by itself would raise the eyebrows of an auditor, not even one from the IRS. But Marcia had noticed that all these unusual items had come from one place: the office of Jack Dunne.

"I've got it all down on paper," Jason said excitedly. "Item after item."

"How much does it all add up to?" Michael asked.

"Couple hundred thousand," Jason said.

"That's not a whole lot," Michael said. "Are you sure he's stealing? Maybe there's some explanation for it all."

"Goddam it," Jason exploded, his voice echoing tinnily from the telephone speaker. "Do you want to get rid of that bastard, or don't you? I'm telling you, I've got the goods on the son-of-a-bitch. When I present the evidence to Dad, he'll have to fire the guy."

"I dunno," Michael said. He was always the more cautious of the two brothers. "Maybe you should let me take a look at it before you show it to Dad."

"Don't be a pussy," his brother said.

"I'm not," Michael protested. "It's just being sure. When you go up against someone like Dunne, you gotta be sure. Otherwise, the blowback might rebound on both of us. Why don't you put all the stuff into a FedEx package and send it over? I'll take a look and let you know what I think."

There was a long silence on the other end. Michael knew Jason was frustrated. Jason was always more hotheaded, more willing to leap without looking. Sometimes in this business, that was a good thing. But many times, it could be dangerous. Like now.

"OK," Jason finally said. "I'll send it tonight. But don't dick around. I want Dad to know what kind of bastard he's let into the company as soon as possible."

"Roger," Michael said. France came out of the kitchen with a tray holding two wine goblets, a bottle of Bordeaux, and some cheese twists, freshly made at a bakery two blocks away. They were even better, Michael thought, than a Whopper and fries. "What are you doing this weekend?"

"I'm flying the Citation up to the Cape to say hello to Margaret on Friday, then Friday night I'm going over to the Vineyard. I, uh, promised Marcia a weekend."

"Hope she's worth it," Michael laughed.

"Aw, she's OK," Jason said. "Not the best looking thing in the world, but she's got all the right body parts. And I promised."

Michael laughed again, shaking his head. His brother was a renowned rake and a confirmed bachelor. He smiled fondly as France poured out the wine. "OK, I gotta go," he told Jason. "Fly carefully."

"Roger that," Jason replied cheerfully. "It's great to get back in the cockpit again. I missed flying. Maybe I'll fly over and see you guys. I'd love to cruise over the Alps."

"Yeah, you'd better bring a Boeing with you," Michael said. "I'm not getting in a twin engine plane with you to go over the Alps."

"You are such a pussy," Jason said. "Later."

The weather had turned hot and humid, and the kids in the sailing school were moving slowly on the sunny dock.

"C'mon people," Freddie called out. "Let's get moving. The sooner you get rigged up and away, the cooler you'll be."

Angel carried the blue polyester bag that held the sail for the dinghy, while Bob Martin grabbed the wooden tiller, heavily varnished and glistening in the sunshine. "Man, oh man," Angel moaned as they walked down the length of the floating dock, "I don't know why he's making us do this. It's so hot out today even the wind has stopped moving."

"He hates us," Martin said. "Or else he gets his jollies by making us suffer. If I have a stroke, make sure somebody sues his ass."

Angel giggled, and bent to the task of rigging up the sail. The bottom edge was threaded into the metal channel that ran along the top of the aluminum boom and fastened at both ends, then a halyard was clipped into the top of the sail and she guided it expertly up the mast before she tied if off, nice and tight. The sail waved back and forth listlessly in the brief puffs of hot air that were the only signs of a breeze in the tropical morning air. In the meantime, Bob had clipped the tiller into its clamps on the stern and threaded the sheet line through the pulleys on the boom. Angel climbed into the small boat and Bob, with a final push, jumped in after her and tried to fill the sail with what little wind there was.

Freddie, the college-age sailing instructor, saw the two of them were away and yelled at the other kids to hurry up. "Angela and Roberto are already gone," he yelled. "Get a move on!"

"We haven't gone far," Bob muttered under his breath. The dinghy had traveled all of twenty feet out into the harbor, and whatever headway they were making would have lost a race with a snail. Bob glanced at his crew. Angel sat in the bottom of the dinghy, wearing a pale blue bikini top and a pair of cut-off jeans. He noticed the swelling of her breasts, just filling out the bra cups of her suit, with just a hint of her nipples poking through. Her skin was dark, in part because of all the time in the sun they had spent in recent weeks, and in part because she was naturally olive skinned. He made himself stop staring. She already inhabited most of his erotic dreams, and he didn't want her to catch him staring.

But Angel's attention was elsewhere. She was watching a long white yacht gliding silently across the quiet harbor on its way dockside. She recognized the boat as the *Filibuster*, Senator O'Malley's 60-foot ketch. The boat was not under sail, but motoring in to the dock, and she could see the curly grey hair of the senator as he sat behind the great wheel aft of the mizzen mast.

"Watch out for the senator," she called out to Bob, pointing at the approaching vessel.

"Hey," Bob said. "I'm under sail and he's motoring. He's gotta watch out for us. Rules of the road."

"Yeah," Angel said, "But he's a bigshot senator and we're just a couple of kids, so we'd better get out of his way."

"We'll just see about that," Bob said with a grin. He kept the tiller steady and a little puff of wind came up and filled his sail, moving the dinghy forward with a bit more speed.

"Bob, I wouldn't do that," the girl said, watching as the two boats, one huge and the other tiny, converged. "He's bigger than we are."

The boy laughed now, enjoying himself, and he kept his hand steady. It was Freddie, watching from the dock, who suddenly called out. "Bob! Bear off…bear off, goddam it!"

The shout caught the senator's attention. He spun the great wheel to starboard, pulling his bow away from the tiny boat. Bob finally pulled his tiller over and the dinghy responded sluggishly. The two boats passed each other, port to port, missing a collision by a matter of inches.

"Goddam it," the senator yelled, jumping to his feet and peering down at the two kids in the smaller boat that passed by his stern, "What the hell do you think you're doing?"

"I'm under sail, sir," Bob said. "I believe I have right of way."

"You little peckerhead," the senator was furious. "If you put a scratch on my hull, I'll fucking have your ass."

"Martin!" Freddie yelled from the dock. "Get your ass back here. NOW!"

"Uh-oh," Angel said. "We're in for it now. I told you not to mess with him."

"Aw, fuck him," Bob said. But he said it softly so that only Angel could hear it. His heart was pounding. He swung the tiller over the other way and pointed the little boat back towards the dock, where the other kids were watching with wide eyes and grins.

About forty minutes later, Angel and a crestfallen Bob Martin were sitting on one of the patios of the yacht club, watching as their classmates were skimming back and forth across the harbor in a freshening breeze that pushed against the hot humid air. They had been dragged into the office of the harbormaster, along with Freddie, and been subjected to a loud harangue about irresponsible helmsmanship, suspended from class for the day, and told to go sit and watch until the class was dismissed for the day. Bob had been angry at first—"They can't put us in Time Out like this is kindergarten," he had muttered—but he gradually calmed down. Angel had been silent through the whole thing, not wanting to seem disloyal to her friend, even though she had tried to warn him. Finally, he had blown out a breath and caught her eye.

"Did you see how mad O'Malley was?" he said with a sly smile. "I thought he was gonna pop a gasket."

She giggled. "I guess that means he won't invite us to sail on his yacht again," she said.

The two of them sat there and watched while the dock attendant dragged the gasoline hose over to O'Malley's yacht and pumped in fuel for what seemed like ten minutes. It was a bit later that one of the waiters from the yacht club restaurant came down the dock with a big wicker picnic basket and took it aboard the *Filibuster*, followed a minute later by another one pulling a large cooler on a two-wheeled dolly. The second waiter passed the cooler over to the first, who took it below. The teens heard the sound of bottles clinking as they were stored.

Two men dressed in khaki shorts, polo shirts and docksiders came out of the main building of the club, walked down the dock and climbed aboard the big yacht. "One of those guys is Gordon Congdon," Bob whispered to Angel. "He's O'Malley's chief of staff. I've seen his picture in the newspaper."

The door opened again, and this time the senator himself came out, holding the door open for two young women. He motioned gallantly towards his yacht, and they made their way down the wooden dock. One woman was dressed in a blue-and-white striped top and a pair of form-hugging white shorts, while the other wore a bathing suit and a terry cloth wrap. They giggled something to each other and climbed aboard, helped by one of the men already on board.

"Looks like the senator's got a party boat going out today," Bob muttered softly.

The dock attendant came out and untied the stern ropes while O'Malley fired up the engines. When he was ready, he nodded, and the attendant tossed the line aboard and O'Malley guided his yacht slowly away from the dock and pointed it out into the sound.

"She's pretty, isn't she?" Angel said, watching the boat move slowly away and out into the channel.

"The sailboat or the blonde bimbo?" Bob said.

"You are such a guy," Angel said. "Why do you think either one of those women is a bimbo? Maybe they just like sailing."

Bob Martin rolled his eyes. "You can't be that naïve," he said.

KATHRYN DUNNE HAD MADE A POT OF TEA when her husband brought Tiger home from a weekend spent in Winter Cove. She had declined an invitation from Jack to spend another weekend on the beach, without giving a reason. But she did want to have a conversation with her husband, on her ground and on her terms, when they came back that night.

She hugged and kissed her son and listened to his enthusiastic and rushed report of all the fun things he and his Dad had done that weekend. They had gone fishing on a friend's boat and Tiger had managed to catch a small bluefish. Tiger had described the fish as being huge, while Jack, smiling, had held his fingers perhaps a foot apart.

Kathryn had sent Tiger off for a bath, and once he was splashing happily in the warm sudsy water in the tub, she had poured the tea for Jack in the breakfast room.

"Sounds like you two are really enjoying the Cape," she said as she put down a plate of cookies.

"Be better if you'd come with us," Jack said.

She shook her head. "I don't think so," she said. "Might be a little crowded."

He looked at her sharply. "What does that mean?" he asked.

"Tiger has told me about your neighbor," she said, looking at him directly. "The lovely Mrs. O'Malley who comes over at night. Has dinner. Stays late."

"He's just a kid," Dunne said quickly, trying to keep from looking guilty. "He's making stuff up."

"Children are not stupid, Jack," she said. "They know if something is going on."

"Listen, Kath…" he started. She held up a hand.

"You don't have to explain, Jack," she said. "You're free to make your own decisions. Just don't insult me by trying to lie about it."

They were silent, uncomfortable in the breakfast room that was suddenly claustrophobic.

"I think it's time we moved on, Jack," Kathryn said finally. "We both need to begin to start new lives. It doesn't have to be mean or ugly. You're still a good man and a good father to Tiger, and you always will be. We just shouldn't be together anymore. We can't go back, so we might as well face it and go forward."

"I don't want to lose you," he said.

"You lost me a long time ago," she said. "When you stopped caring what I thought about anything you did. When you decided you had to be the top dog in everything you did, and with everyone in your life. You never cared what I wanted. You never even asked."

"You can't complain about anything I've given you," he said, waving his hands at the house. "You've never wanted for anything."

"Except to be let in on Jack's life," she said. "Your real life."

He shook his head. "I don't understand," he said.

"I know you don't," she said. "That's part of the problem. You're so caught up in Jack's world, in trying to be the guy running everything, the top dog, you can't see what it's been like for me, and for Tiger. We don't get a choice, we just get told what to do, what to be. There's no room in your life for anyone else, anyone else's input. Turns out to be a lonely place to live."

"Listen," he said, "If this is about Gillian, I'll stop … get rid of her. I don't really know what that's all about anyway."

"You don't?" Kathryn said. "That's easy. You're in a pissing contest with every man you meet, and the way to defeat Senator O'Malley is to fuck his wife. Not that I'm sure he cares all that much about her. You do this with everyone in your life, find a way to beat them down, defeat them. That's why you so enjoyed being a mercenary soldier during the war…you got paid to prove you were better, stronger, more powerful than the enemy. You haven't stopped doing that ever since. It's just that now you do it in different ways."

He said nothing.

"With O'Malley, you fuck his wife. With Ted Pyle, you take over his company and send his own boys away. With me?" She stopped, thinking. "With me, you put me in a box I don't want to be in. Dutiful wife. Does what she's told. Shows up, shuts up, says 'yes, dear,' raises child." She laughed, ruefully. "I don't know yet what you're going to do with Tiger," she said. "But I'm afraid you'll find a way to try and control him, make him conform to your image of the perfect son. I pray to God he'll have inherited enough of your strength to fight back. I don't."

"You make me sound pretty goddam awful," Dunne said.

"I know, and I'm sorry," she said. "I don't mean to. I will always admire and respect you. I just can't love you any more. I don't love you any more."

There. She had said it, that which she had wanted to say for a long time, but couldn't. Her words hung in the little room. There was nothing he could say.

"Momma," came Tiger's cry from the bathroom upstairs. "I wanna get out now."

She stood up. "When do you want to take him again?" she asked. "Next weekend?"

He stood up too. "Naw," he said, rubbing his jaw. "I've got some business stuff I need to take care off for the next couple of weeks. It might be August. I'll call and let you know."

"Are you OK?" she asked.

"No," he said. "I'm not. But I'll deal with it."

IT WAS A FRACTIOUS NIGHT in the Bruno household on Serpent Island. Angela had announced at dinner that she wanted to invite Bob Martin, along with most of the rest of her sailing class, to the party at Timothy Regan's scheduled for the following weekend.

"No," her father said flatly. "You're too young for dating."

"Da-ad," she said, rolling her eyes. "It's not a date, it's a party. And I'm turning sixteen already."

"It's a boy, it's a party," Bruno said. "It's a date. The answer is no."

Rosa Bruno looked at her husband. "*Cara mia*," she said. "It's just a cookout. We will all be there. How can there be any problem? And all of her friends will be there, too, isn't that right, Angela?"

"Of course," she said. "And Freddie the instructor will be too. He doesn't let any funny business happen when he's around."

"There, you see?" Rosa turned to her husband. "It's all very innocent."

"I'm telling you that she's too young," Bruno snapped, slapping his hand down on the table.

Tears of frustration welled up in Angel's eyes, and she fought to keep them from spilling down her cheeks. She looked imploringly at her mother, who shook her head slightly. Her father's head was down, and he was shoveling food into his mouth with fury. He had made his mind up, and he was not going to be argued with.

Angel looked at Fat Peter, who was sitting across the table from her. She could see the understanding and sympathy across his face—he always understood—but he also shook his head in warning. Don't go there, his look said.

She sighed. Poked at her plate.

"*Manga*…eat!" Bruno snapped at her. "Your mother spent all day preparing your food."

"I'm not hungry," Angel said. She pushed back her chair, ran upstairs to her room and slammed her door.

Bruno threw back his head and drained his glass of wine. He replaced it on the table and glared at his wife. "Don't you start with me," he said. "She is too young for boys. Too young." He looked over at his consigliere. "And you," he snapped. "You are a man. Have you forgotten what it was like to be a boy? All you could think about was getting into a girl's pants…any girl!"

Rosa made a noise of disapproval and got up, taking some dishes away into the kitchen.

"It's true!" Bruno continued, talking to the back of her retreating form. "I don't care if this boy is from the yacht club or the street. He is a boy and boys are thinking of nothing but sex…morning, noon and night."

Fat Peter was silent. He was taking his own advice not to argue with his boss. He would pick the right time to try and reason with Joe. But this was not it.

"Bah!" Bruno said. "A man cannot find peace in his own house, even at his own dinner table. *Basta!*"

He stalked out of the dining room and thumped down the stairs into the basement of the home. He fumbled in his pocket and pulled out a key on a chain. He fitted it into the lock of a heavy oak door. The tumblers clicked and the door swung open noiselessly. Inside was another door, this one made of steel. Bruno punched in the numbers on a security pad and this door, too, clicked open. He went inside, reached up to the left and flicked a switch.

The lights came on, a row of recessed cans that had been installed in the ceiling. They illuminated a long, rectangular room that had been carved out of the sandy soil beneath the house. In the center of the room was one leather recliner, and next to it a small wooden table. There was nothing else. Bruno smiled and closed the steel door behind him. It clicked shut.

This was his sanctum. He had spent several hundred thousand having it built, secretly and carefully. All of the workmen who had been hand-picked for the project had been well paid…very well paid. They had worked mostly at night, and special care had been taken to disguise all signs of construction. Debris had been secreted out, and materials hidden as they were brought in. Bruno wanted no one to know about this secret and special underground chamber. Once the work had been completed, and all the workmen had received their cash, Bruno had spoken to Fat Peter. And then, over the next three months, one by one the workmen had been quietly eliminated. One at a time. Their deaths had been made to look like accidents. Or random crimes. But they had all died, and with them died the knowledge that Joe Bruno had a special, secret, climate-controlled underground room buried beneath his house at Serpent Point.

And then he had begun to decorate his room. On those long rectangular walls, he had hung magnificent works of art from the Renaissance and the Romantic Ages. He had marble friezes that had once decorated the Parthenon and tapestries that once hung in the finest castles of Germany. He had priceless icons that had inspired centuries of believers in hidden monasteries of Russia and illustrated manuscripts painstakingly colored by Irish monks in their cold seaside cells. He had the Rembrandt and the Vermeer that had been brazenly stolen from the Isabelle Gardiner Museum in Boston twenty years earlier. Bruno had not been behind that heist, but he found out who was, and he had taken those works he most wanted.

Now, he poured himself a glass of wine, and went to sit in the leather chair in the center of the room. He picked up a remote control and the music of Enrico Caruso singing the arias of Guiseppe Verdi filled the room. He punched another series of buttons and his specially designed lighting system began to illuminate each of his works, one at a time, giving him a minute or two to concentrate on each work, each painting.

He could admire the genius of the artist, see each individual brush-stoke, look into the faces of the subjects and feel what they felt, even though they were just pigment smeared on canvas hundreds of years ago.

This was the only place where Joe Bruno could relax, sitting here in this hidden room, admiring his collection, listening to the ethereal sounds of the great Italian tenor, and enjoying the taste of a great wine. This was why Bruno did the things he did. These were his spoils, his reward. Sitting here, looking at his collection, he could forget the outside world, and all its problems, and be transported to a place that was, he felt, as close to heaven as a man would probably ever get. In this world, or in whatever came in the next.

He didn't come down into this room as often as he'd like, but at the same time he didn't want the effects of coming here to ever wear off. The Catholic priests had beaten into his head the idea that too much of a good thing could be bad, especially for one's soul. His special room was supposed to be a reward, not a reminder that he was destined to reside forever in hell. He wanted to appreciate the beauty he had collected in this room, not think of the lives that he had ended or destroyed to make such a thing happen.

He emptied his mind of all other thoughts. He sipped his wine, listened to the music and admired, again, the brilliance and the beauty that surrounded him. This was his reward, this was his escape, this was his penance.

TIMOTHY REGAN WOKE EARLY ON THE MORNING of the party. The bright August sun poured in his windows and he hurried through his morning routine, even as Willie kept trying to slow him down. "Important that you look good this mornin'" Willie said. "All the folks comin' to see you today."

It was true. Everyone else who lived at Serpent Point had said they would stop by this afternoon, from the Bruno family next door to the Senator and his wife across the street and Tom Pyle and his "housekeeper." Regan smiled at that. How delightfully old fashioned, he thought, in this day and age. But what do you call your live-in lover? Especially when you are over 60 years old and have children in their 30s?

In addition, Regan was expecting most of Angela's friends from her sailing class to attend. The girl had said her father, under pressure from her mother, had finally agreed that the classmates could attend. In return, Fat Peter was also coming to keep a close eye on the girl and make sure she was chaperoned at all times. Regan didn't mind; he actually liked Peter LaGuista and found him to be a reasonable, if somewhat scary, man.

The last two weeks had been filled with preparations. Regan had hired the "orchestra," actually just a small combo he had known and worked with for years; gone over the details with the caterer, ordered the flowers, arranged with the gardeners to have the pool cleaned and the grounds manicured. Ruby had brought in a half dozen cleaners who went over the house inch by inch until every corner sparkled with wax and polish. Willie had hired some young men to supervise the parking of cars.

After his breakfast, Regan had gone over all the details one more time, to make sure nothing had fallen through the cracks. He wanted this party to be perfect, not only for the sake of the girl, but for his own. He told himself that he didn't really care what his neighbors thought of him or his lifestyle, but of course he did. He understood that Serpent Point had attracted a most unusual collection of the rich and powerful. A gangster, a senator, a business magnate and… himself. All of whom were both fabulously wealthy and yet somehow inherently flawed.

But he didn't have time to dwell on that now. The caterer's truck pulled up and the first thing to be unloaded was the huge, triple-tiered birthday cake. Regan hovered nervously while the men carefully carried it into the dining room and installed it in the place of honor at the center of his large mahogany table. He fiddled with the lighting to make sure the floods perfectly illuminated the cake, glistening white with blue and yellow florets and the lettering with each of their names.

There were dozens of details, things to check. Finally, late in the morning, Willie dragged him upstairs to dress. Fine linen trousers, alligator loafers, starched white collarless shirt and a paisley smoking jacket in the finest silk. "My oh my," Willie said when he was finished, looking at himself in the full-length mirror in his dressing closet. "You ain't looked this good in fifty years."

It was true, Regan thought, admiring the wavy brown wig, which covered his few remaining tufts of white hair, and the flawlessly applied make-up, which hid his wrinkles and spotted face…he looked at most to be forty, forty-five. Back when Timmy Regan, the Irish Nightingale, had been able to sell out the concert halls and arenas and have them standing in line for tickets our in Vegas. Back before the lyrics were all about sex and filthy things. When the songs were about romance and love.

His reverie was broken by the sound of a downstairs door slamming and a shout. "Bear! Old bear! Where is the birthday bear?"

He came down the stairs and hugged Angela. She was dressed in a pretty pink summer flared dress that danced around her tanned legs, and was tucked in at her waist, with thin straps over her shoulders. Her hair was the color of peat and tied in the back with a lacy pink ribbon. She looked happy. And radiant.

"I can't believe it's finally here," she said. "You look fabulous! Is that our cake?"

The words, the questions, tumbled from the girl's mouth in a rush of excitement and joy. His heart filled with joy. If nothing else happened today, this feeling of happiness would have made all the work worthwhile.

"Where is the rest of your family?" he asked. "Are they coming?"

"Yes, bear," she said. "They'll be along in an hour or so. Daddy is still grumbling and muttering, but Mama will make him get dressed. Isabelle is down from Boston with her new boyfriend, and he looks scared to death!"

Ruby came out from the kitchen, her black face glistening with a sweaty sheen. "Child, you look pretty enough to eat," she said, giving Angel a big hug. "I can't believe you're sixteen years old. Why, it seems like just yesterday you was born!"

Regan took the girl out onto the expansive deck that wrapped around the back of his home and showed her the croquet lawn he had set up, and the dance floor that had been laid down near where the band was going to play. "Of course," he told her, "When the band is taking a break, there will be a DJ who will make sure the music is a bit more modern for your liking."

Angel laughed. "You've thought of everything, haven't you?" she asked.

"I tried, child, I tried," he said.

Joe Bruno, in the next house over, was not a happy camper. "Tell me again why I gotta go to this fruitcake's party?" he asked his wife.

"Because she is your daughter, it's her sixteenth birthday, and because she wants you there," Rosa Bruno said, the tone of her voice telling him that he'd better start getting ready. "You don't have to stay long, but you have to make an appearance."

Bruno glanced at Fat Peter, who had already changed into a clean shirt, which hung down loosely over his waist to hide the gun that was always clipped to his belt. Peter shrugged. He gave his boss a look that said you gotta do what you gotta do. Bruno frowned. "Okay," he said, "I'll go, for Angela's sake. But I ain't staying more than 30 minutes. I got stuff to do, for Chrissakes."

"Like what?" Rosa said, "Park yourself in front of the television and watch a ballgame? God forbid you should have a good time, maybe ask your wife to dance."

"Dance?" Bruno exploded. "Now I gotta dance?"

"No, you don't have to dance," his wife said patiently. "I was just saying, it wouldn't kill you …"

"Dance!" he muttered as he headed upstairs to dress.

Senator Malcolm O'Malley was going ballistic. "What the hell do you mean, Joe Bruno is going to be there?" he shouted at his chief of staff. "Do you realize what the press will do if they see the two of us together? The fucking future President of the fucking United States? Together with the top crime boss of New England? Are you out of your fucking mind?"

Gordon Congdon endured the senator's fury patiently. "Relax, Senator," he said when he could finally get a word in. "There will be no press. I put some guards on this morning at the entrance to the Point. No one gets in without my approval. It's a private neighborhood party. You show up, say hello to the faggot, kiss the little girl on the cheek, say something nice and you're back here in twenty minutes, tops."

"I'm staying," Gillian O'Malley said. "I like these people. I like Angela and I like Tim Regan…he's a dear old thing. It's their goddam birthday party. Loosen up, you old fart."

"Well, you stay then." O'Malley said hotly. "And try not to get falling down drunk for once. I'm running for President and I don't need to be seen socializing with the fucking wops and the fucking fags. It's bad enough I can't keep them out of my own neighborhood."

"I wonder how many people would vote for you if they could hear the way you talk about people," Gillian said. "Fags, wops. Don't forget the niggers the Irish fag has working for him."

"I am *not* a racist," O'Malley said. "How dare you insinuate that I'm a racist."

She just laughed.

JACK DUNNE GOT TIGER DRESSED IN A CLEAN PAIR OF SHORTS and a T-shirt, and tried to get him to leave his Boston Red Sox hat behind. But Tiger would have none of that.

"My hat," he said, pouting at the idea that he couldn't wear it. "Papi wears one. Dusty wears one. Youk wears one."

"You look better without it," his father tried to reason. "People can see your hair."

"Want my hat," the boy said, frowning, and in the end, his father relented.

They walked out onto the beach, heading for the Pyle house, where they were to meet Tom and Margaret. But looking back, Dunne saw Gillian O'Malley waving from her lawn. He sent Tiger on ahead and waited for her to catch up.

"Hey, gorgeous," he said. "Going to the party?"

"Of course," she said, giving him a chaste little kiss on the cheek. "Even Senator Grumpy said he'd stop in. He's pretending to be talking to someone on the Ways and Means committee, so I said I'd meet him over at Regan's."

"Great," Dunne said, smiling. "Can't wait to have another brilliant conversation with that turd."

"Be nice," Gillian said, giggling.

Tom Pyle and Margaret were on their back deck, listening to Tiger rambling on about something. Margaret was holding a wrapped package in her hands.

"Damn," Dunne said, slapping his forehead, "I forgot. We got something for Angel for her birthday. Why don't you guys go ahead, and I'll meet you over there in a minute."

Dunne returned to the boathouse and retrieved the gift, a CD of a group that he had been told Angel liked. He slipped it into his jacket pocket and cut through the hedges between his and Pyle's houses, crossed the narrow lane that ran down the spine of the island and entered the curving driveway that led to Regan's house. There was a black SUV parked cross-wise, blocking the drive, about halfway between the street and the house. The driver's side window was down, and they could see two men sitting in the front seat.

Dunne walked up to the driver, who peered out at him.

"Help you?" the driver said.

"I doubt it," Dunne said. "Your car's in the way."

"What's the name, wise guy?" the driver said, indicating a clipboard he held on his lap.

"Who wants to know?" Dunne replied.

"Listen, dickbreath," the driver said, "Nobody gets in unless the name is on the list. So stop being a pain in my balls. The fuck's the name?"

"John J. Kiss My Ass," Dunne said. "Get this heap out of my way."

The driver sighed. The man in the passenger seat got out of his door on the far side of the car and started to walk around the front. He was thick around the middle and his hands were the size of hams. But he moved quickly, with a kind of feline grace. The driver opened his door and started to push it open, but Dunne leaned against it and slammed it shut.

"Sir," said the passenger, approaching Dunne, "You gotta give us your name, so why'n't you stop dicking around so you don't get hurt?"

He reached out and tried to push one of his meaty hands into Dunne's chest. Dunne reached out and grabbed the four fingers of that hand and bent them back sharply. The man cried out and sank to his knees. "Ow," he said, "Fuck." The driver yelled out "hey!" and tried to push the door open again. But Dunne had his hip against the car door and kept his weight on it, even as he continued to bend the passenger's fingers backward. There was an audible click as two of the fingers broke. The passenger gasped once, but didn't say anything else, his eyes locked with Dunne's.

"Mr. Dunne!" Jack looked up as his name was called. Standing in front of the car was Fat Peter LaGuista. He was holding his hand out. "Please, sir, let him go. They didn't know it was you. I apologize for the trouble."

Dunne let go of the fat man's fingers. The man looked at the fingers now bent awkwardly and, with his other hand, reached over and snapped them back into place. He kept his gaze on Dunne the entire time, silent, not even flinching.

"My apologies," Fat Peter continued. "Please, come in. Enjoy the party. I'll take care of this."

Dunne continued to stare at the man whose fingers he had snapped. They were both breathing hard.

"Vinnie, take Joey to the hospital," Fat Peter ordered. "And for Chrissakes, next time try to be a little more polite." He turned to Dunne. "Mr. Dunne, I'm very sorry. The boys just got a little carried away. They were just trying to go with what they were told. I'm sure you can understand …"

Dunne didn't say a thing. He finally nodded at Fat Peter, and with a final glare at the passenger, he stalked off toward the house.

Fat Peter turned back to his men, shaking his head, a frown on his face. "Jeezus," he said. "What the hell are you doing, breaking balls with the neighbors? And how'd you let that fucking animal get the drop on you? Christ Almighty, I gotta do everything myself."

From Timothy Regan's point of view, it was a glorious affair. The house, the deck, the lawn were filled with mobs of people, his friends, his neighbors. The shouts of laughter from the children, Angela's sailing class friends mostly, rang out across the lawn as they conducted a spirited croquet competition. The band, set up near the pool, sounded sublime, and Regan himself, at the urging of many, sang a few of his old standards which seemed to be well received.

Regan tried to circulate throughout the afternoon, keeping a close eye on all his guests to make sure they had everything they wanted or needed to have a good time. The caterers kept bringing out more food and the bartenders kept glasses full throughout the afternoon.

Regan noted the activities of his odd group of neighbors, too. Senator O'Malley had made a brief appearance before begging off with a claim of the press of official business. And, like a well-choreographed routine, no sooner had the senator left than Joseph Bruno arrived, with his beaming wife on his arm. Lurking in the background, if a three-hundred-pound, six-six man could be said to be lurking, was Fat Peter. If there had been any paparazzis lurking in the shrubbery, hoping to snap a photo of the gangster and the senator together, they would have gone home disappointed. But Regan knew there were none—Fat Peter and Bruno's men would have seen to that. Regan had also learned that the Senator's chief, Gordon Congdon, had arranged for a private security roadblock at the entrance to Serpent Point. In fact, Regan had been told that another of his neighbors, Jack Dunne, the associate of Tom Pyle, had confronted one of Bruno's apes on the driveway. That would have been interesting to watch, he thought.

Regan had personally greeted the Brunos. He rarely got the chance to interact with anyone other than Angela or Fat Peter, and he was quite curious about them. Regan had always been interested in that sort—he had met many men in the world of organized crime when he used to play Las Vegas. He had found most of them to be quite boring, interested only in money, specifically, how much he, Timothy Regan, could make for them. But there was always that undercurrent of danger about them, that emptiness in the eyes, which gave him a little frisson of excitement. It was what made them different from other people, and Regan was always interested in differences. It was what made life interesting.

Joe had said nothing, and because he was wearing wraparound dark glasses, Regan couldn't observe the man's eyes. His wife, however, was gracious and thanked Regan profusely for giving Angela such a nice party. When Regan looked around again a few minutes later, Joe Bruno was nowhere to be seen. He is like a ghost, Regan thought. A dangerous ghost.

The old man did notice that the senator's wife, Gillian, stayed for quite a while after her husband had left, chatting gaily with Jack Dunne. When the senator had arrived, Regan noted that Dunne had disappeared, and Gillian stayed dutifully by her husband's side as he had made his quick rounds, meeting and greeting the guests. But once the senator had left, Dunne reappeared and Gillian stayed, never leaving his side. Interesting, Regan thought. He watched the way Gillian looked at Dunne, hung on his every word, reached out and touched his arm from time to time and decided, yes, the two of them were involved. He knew these things. Regan had always been able to read people, like tea leaves, and discern from their comportment what was really going on. It was a like a gift that he had. Or sometimes a curse.

Regan was happiest that Angela had enjoyed her party to the utmost. He had sung Happy Birthday to her, with the backing of the orchestra, and to the applause of all the guests, they had jointly cut the birthday cake, and fed pieces to each other almost as if they were bride and groom. She had been the center of attention throughout the afternoon, surrounded by a gaggle of young girls who could barely hide their excitement and even jealousy. The boys in attendance had at first huddled together, as boys tend to do, but soon they all joined together, playing games and dancing on the wooden floor that had been laid down. In the end, her eyes alight and her face flushed, Angela had confessed that it had been the best day of her life.

Late in the afternoon, as the guests began to leave, Regan had nodded at Fat Peter and, in a corner, out of sight of anyone else, had slipped him some folded bills, hundreds. Peter had taken them without comment and put them away. Regan felt a momentary pang of guilt, but quickly pushed it away. It was his birthday, too, after all. He deserved a gift, something special to mark the fact that he had defeated death for another year. And later that night, he knew, his gift would arrive. His young, delectable, sweet-smelling and oh, so innocent gift.

JASON PYLE BROUGHT MARCIA RUDEN to his father's house on Serpent Point to meet Margaret. He had left his father in Washington, and flown up to the executive airport in Bedford just north of Boston where Marcia was waiting. Then he had made the short hop down to the busy municipal airport at Winter Cove on the Cape. The field at Winter Cove catered not only to the private aircraft of wealthy property owners up and down the length of Cape Cod, but also hosted the prop-jet service to the nearby islands of Nantucket and Martha's Vineyard.

Marcia had been quite overwhelmed by the whole experience. Until a few months ago, she had been a quiet, single, Jewish girl from the Boston suburbs, who lived at home with her parents, an only child, with a social life limited to Hadassah meetings at her synagogue and the occasional movie and coffee with friends. Her job at Pyle Industries as an auditor was interesting, if not intellectually challenging, and between work, home and worship, the days and weeks seemed to fly by in a comforting pattern that she found reassuring.

And then Jason Pyle, the blond, grinning *goyim* filled with such confidence and brio, had singled her out and began paying attention to her. There was a part of her, deep down, which mistrusted this man and his sudden interest in her. But there was another part, one that she didn't even know she had, which welcomed his attention and convinced her that it was real and that she deserved this chance at love and adventure.

He had given her some important work assignments to do for his Asian negotiations. That had led to an invitation for coffee. Then dinner. Then a movie. All very innocent and very above board. There had been an afternoon walk through the Public Gardens when the trees were coming into bud and the feel of spring was in the air. He had kissed her by the Duck Pond, and she had felt her heart lurch for the very first time.

He had been overseas almost constantly since then. But he had continued to stay in touch, and she had continued to do special jobs for him in addition to her usual work. And now he was back, and flying her in the company plane down to Cape Cod, first to meet what he called his "assistant mother" and then to take her away for a romantic weekend on Martha's Vineyard. She was not sure her chest could contain the beating of her heart.

She had never been in a private plane before, and although she was petrified, she forced herself to stay outwardly calm. And she watched as this handsome young man, someone who probably was five or six years younger than herself, although they hadn't had that conversation yet, expertly worked the controls of the twin-engine airplane, made those engines growl with a low-pitched anger that she felt in the pit of her stomach, and sent it hurtling down the concrete runway before it lifted magically into the air and soared into the achingly blue sky.

They skirted the city of Boston, and Jason pointed out the landmarks she had never seen from this angle before—Fenway Park, Symphony Hall, the rings of the two major highways that encircled Boston, even her own neighborhood. She was mesmerized by it all.

Far too soon, for her liking, they had swung out over Nantucket Sound before they landed in Winter Cove. Jason helped her down from the plane's tiny cockpit and led her to a battered old Jeep, which Pyle Industries kept at the airport. He stopped in briefly at the private air terminal and ordered the plane to be refueled for the trip over to the island. He drove them slowly through the town, now crawling with the summer tourist trade, and eventually out the long causeway that led to Serpent Point.

Margaret was waiting with a pitcher of iced tea and sandwiches, which they took out to the back deck and enjoyed along with the views of the sparkling blue ocean. Marcia Rudin could not remember a day when she had felt so happy, so gloriously alive. She had listened while Jason regaled Margaret with his stories of the Far East, some of which she had heard, some new. They had lingered as the sun began to drift slowly out to the west, laughing and chatting.

At one point, Jason had gone inside to call the airport to make sure the plane was ready. Margaret had smiled at Marcia as they watched him go.

"He is such a dear boy," she said. "Always so full of life."

Marcia said nothing. Her heart was too full for mere words.

"But he has always been a hard one to pin down, dear," Margaret said next. Marcia looked at the older woman with surprise. "He seems fond of you, but you mustn't get ahead of things. He has broken many a heart. Just a word of warning."

Marcia felt a surge of fear, just for a moment. The fear that this woman's words were prophetic. That she didn't really deserve Jason and all his attention and love. That something was horribly wrong. But she forced that fear away, tamped it back down deep inside. No, she told herself, this was real, these feelings were not made up or false. She was not some teen-aged girl, she was a mature woman. She could tell reality from make-believe. She would not let this woman's comments unleash her buried fears and undermine her happiness.

Jason came bounding back out of the house.

"OK," he said, "Flight control says we're good to go in about forty minutes. Air is clear, weather is good for now. There's a little mist drifting in out on the Vineyard, but not for a couple hours yet. Let's get cracking!"

There was the usual bustle of departure, the hugs and kisses and expressions of thanks and invitations to come back soon. Marcia and Jason bundled into the little Jeep and re-traced their steps to the airport. She watched as Jason did his preflight check, walking all around the little plane, twisting the flaps, kicking the tires, opening the gas cap and sticking a finger inside to make sure the fuel was topped up. They climbed inside, Jason revved up the engines and they taxied down the tarmac. Jason got his clearance from the tower, the engines growled angrily again and they were airborne.

Marcia stared out the little window at the ocean far below. In the golden light of sunset, the water was a dark blue-green, the color of the spines of the books on the Talmud in her father's library. She watched the pleasure craft making little wakes like waterbugs, and saw the churning path of the huge ferry returning from Nantucket. It was all so beautiful, so magical. She might have drifted off to sleep for a moment.

Then, suddenly, the engines coughed, and coughed again. Then they went silent. All they could hear was the rushing of the air. She glanced over at Jason, and, despite his reassuring grin, she saw the concern in his eyes. He reached down and punched the ignition button. Silence. "What the fuck?" he said to no one in particular. He punched again. Nothing.

Marcia turned to look out the window again, at the perfect scenery in the perfect world on the ocean below. She heard Jason key the radio, and heard his voice, calm but edgy, saying "Mayday, mayday …"

DUNNE PARKED HIS CAR NEXT TO THE BOATHOUSE, but walked around to the front of Pyle's house and entered through the main door. There were already a half dozen cars parked in the circular drive. Inside, he was greeted by a woman he didn't know, who showed him into the living room. Tom Pyle stood looking out the tall windows at the sea, a glass of whiskey in his hand. The day was overcast, the dirty white clouds covering the ocean like a pall. Other people Dunne didn't know gathered in small knots around the room, speaking in hushed tones.

"I came as soon as I heard," Dunne said, as he and Tom shook hands. "Any word yet?"

Pyle shook his head. "No," he said. "The Coast Guard is still doing a search of the area where they think he went down. They had him on radar until he was about two miles off Oak Bluffs. A fishing boat reported hearing something, but the mist had set in and they couldn't see anything."

"Jesus," Dunne said. "Is there anything I can do?"

Pyle shook his head sadly. "I don't think so," he said. "Jason was a good pilot, always did things by the book. But when your time is up, it's up."

"Have you called Michael?"

"He's on his way back from Geneva," Pyle said. "Should be in later tonight. He was pretty broken up."

Pyle's eyes welled up. He couldn't speak. Dunne reached over and squeezed his shoulder. "Tom, if there's anything at all that we can do, just say the word" he said. "The whole company is at your disposal." Pyle silently nodded his thanks.

Dunne turned and made his way around the room, speaking to the others, offering his condolences. He looked for Margaret, and was told she was in the kitchen. He steeled himself and went there.

There were two other women in the kitchen with Margaret, watching with sad eyes as she wiped down the already sparkling countertops with a wet rag. She was trying to stay busy, trying not to think, trying not to lose it. Dunne came in and she stopped fidgeting.

"I…" he said and stopped. "I'm so sorry, Margaret," he finally managed.

She said nothing, but just looked at him. Her eyes were angry and accusatory. The silence grew and became uncomfortable.

"Well," she said finally, her voice thin and quivering with anger. "That's one of them out of your way."

He kept his gaze even. One of the other women turned and left, feeling the hot wave of Margaret's emotion filling the small space of the kitchen. The other came over and stood next to Margaret in silent support.

"I'm not sure I understand," he said.

"I'm quite sure that you do," she said.

Dunne hesitated. He knew that Margaret wanted to provoke an accusatory scene. He remembered his Special Forces training, and maintained a steely, noncommittal visage. Show nothing, he had been instructed all those years ago. Admit nothing. Stay calm while the others rage. Maintain your emotions. The true warrior stays calm while the fire rages all around. He looked into her eyes which stared back at him, accusing, angry, unforgiving, and then he nodded at her and left.

He went out the back door onto the deck, and then down to the beach to his own house. He looked out at the sea from his deck, calm and gray. Somewhere out there, in a hundred feet of water, Jason Pyle's plane rested on the bottom, broken and bent.

The end comes for all of us, he thought. He had long ago stopped worrying about death. It had been a daily companion back in the deserts of Iraq and Kuwait, something that happened as often as the sunrise and with the same regular monotony as the sunset. Back then, he had learned not to worry about it, not to welcome it, fear it, not even to think about it. It could not be controlled, the time or the circumstances of one's own death. All that could be controlled were one's own actions, from minute to minute, hour to hour, day to day. So he had gotten his orders, made his plans, executed the operations as best he could. He had lived, while many others had not. There was no reasonable or rational explanation for all that… it just was. One day, he would die and someone else would live.

That's the way the merry-go-round worked. You got on at the beginning and got off when the thing stopped turning. You had no control over either point, so why worry about it?

Gillian O'Malley was sitting on his deck, a drink in her hand. He looked into her eyes and saw immediately that she had been drinking. Heavily.

"Isn't it awful?" she said, her voice catching. "I was just over there. Margaret is devastated, like she lost one of her own. In a way, I guess she did."

"Yeah," he said, sitting down next to her. "It's a tough one, to lose a kid."

"I called Malcolm down in Washington," Gillian continued. "He's talked to the Coast Guard commandant over at Woods Hole. It's supposedly pretty deep where he went down. They don't know if they'll be able to spot the wreckage."

Dunne shook his head. "Do they know if anything was wrong with the plane?" he asked.

"No, not that anyone knows," she said. "He refueled here at Winter Cove before taking off, so he didn't run out of gas. Air traffic says he called in a mayday, said his engines had just quit and he couldn't get them started again. He was trying to make it to the Trade Wind field on the Vineyard. But they lost him on the radar when he was still several miles offshore. If they can't find the plane, it's going to be hard to know what really happened."

"Most private airplanes aren't required to have flight data recorders," Dunne said. "So even if they find the plane and can get it off the ocean floor, they may never find out what happened."

"Really? How do you know that?" she asked. "I thought all planes had those little black boxes."

He shrugged. "You learn things. We've got three private planes in the company fleet. I ask the pilots how things work."

"Then poor Tom and Margaret might never know," Gillian said. "That is so sad." She rattled the ice cubes in her drink. "Do you think you could make me another?" she asked.

"Are you sure you need one?"

"Don't you start in on me," she snapped. "I don't need it. Between my husband, his boytoy chief of staff and about six other babysitters I know, I don't need drink counters. I need a goddam drink!"

"OK, OK," Dunne said, getting up and heading inside to the kitchen. "Maybe we're all just worried about you, not trying to control you."

"I'll worry about myself, thank you," she said to his retreating back. "Gin and tonic, and make it a strong one."

He brought her a new drink, and one for himself. "My wife knows about us," he said, sitting down.

She reached for her bag and, rooting around, took out a cigarette and lit one. "So what?" she said. "You're separated, right? What, did she make you feel guilty?"

He was silent.

Gillian laughed. "She did. My God. That's rich. Big Jack Dunne, hard-nosed businessman, trying to take over Tom Pyle's company under the noses of his sons. But little wifey sheds a few tears and turns him into a jellyfish."

His eyes narrowed, but he held his tongue. She was drunk. Raving, sloppy drunk.

"Man up, for Chrissakes," she continued. "Make a goddam decision. Go on, go back to her. That's the right thing to do. Me? I'm just your little piece on the side, the next-door whore."

Her self loathing was spilling out now. "There are two kinds of men, you know that?" she said. "One kind thinks sex is their God-given right, to have as many women as they can convince to drop their drawers." She stopped and took a long slurp of her drink. "My husband is one of those. Of course, he inherited his beliefs. Did I ever tell you about the time his old man tried to rape me? "

"No," Dunne said, "I don't think you ever mentioned that."

"'S true." Gillian said, her words slightly slurred. Dunne wondered if she would remember this conversation the next day. "It was after he'd had one stroke, but before the big one that left him a vegetable. He came thumping into my room early one morning."

"Thumping?"

"He had a cane," she explained. "You could hear him coming down the hall. Well, I heard him thumping and then he was in my room, trying to cop a feel. I'll never forget that look on his face. His lips were smiling with pleasure, but his eyes were empty."

"What did you do?" Dunne asked.

"I slapped him upside the head and told him to get the hell out," she said, laughing at the memory. "He took off like a horse for the barn. I heard later from all my sisters-in-law that he did the same thing with them. It was like an initiation to the O'Malley family or something."

She stopped and drank some more, and then smiled, almost to herself. "I got him back, though," she said. "Years later, after his strokes. He couldn't move, couldn't speak. Except for one word. 'Goddam.' That's the only thing he could say. One day, I was the only one in the house, except for his nurse, and I knew she was in the can. So I went into his room. He was sitting in that chair of his, in his hot little bedroom. I went right over to him, looked him in the eye, and then I reached into his pajamas and grabbed him by his shriveled little winkie and I squeezed that sucker as hard as I could."

"Ouch," Dunne said, wincing. "What happened?"

She laughed. "He said, and I quote, 'Goddam. Goddam. Goddam.'"

"You said there were two kinds of men. What's the other kind?" Dunne said.

"Ah," she said. "The other kind still try to fuck as many women as they can, they just pretend to have a conscience about it. At least until the next hottie comes along. Funny thing how the sight of a new pussy can erase every bit of a man's sense of morality. "

"And how many kinds of women are there?" Dunne said. "While we're analyzing the human race."

"Basically one," she said. "We believe in every man we meet. Until they disappoint us, betray us, leave us in the lurch. Which they do, every last single goddam one of them."

She was bleary eyed now. "I'd better get you home," he said, standing up and holding out a hand. "Before you pass out."

She slapped his hand away. "I can get my own self home," she said. She stood up, stumbled, and carefully made her way down onto the beach and headed toward her own empty mansion.

IT WAS A CLOUDLESS AND BREEZY LATE SUMMER DAY when the kids from Winter Cove arrived at the Chatham Yacht Club on Pleasant Bay for the annual regatta. Teams from several other Cape Cod clubs—Wianno, West Dennis, Bass River and Stone Horse—had also sent teams to compete. Sunlight sparkled on the round basin of Crow Pond, filled with sailboats bobbing on their moorings, and beyond on the expanse of the Bay, hemmed in from the open Atlantic by the long finger of the barrier island known as North Beach.

Angela, Bob and the other kids from the Winter Cove club had driven down the Cape in a van driven by Freddie, who had given them last minute instructions. "First thing, check all the fittings and clamps," he had said. "Look for any frayed wires or bent masts. These rich fuckers take sailing seriously and I've heard stories about them providing inferior boats for the visiting teams. Or sabotaging them."

The kids in the van rolled their eyes at each other. Some people took this stuff wayyyy too seriously, they thought. Once they arrived, they were led out to the docks, where the dinghies to be used for the regatta were all resting, hulls up, at the end of one wooden dock. The masts, booms and sail bags were laid out nearby. Once everyone had arrived, the re-gatta chairman called all the competitors together to go over the race rules and instructions. The course was fairly simple: once past the starting line, just outside Crow Pond, the sailors would follow a counter-clockwise route around three bright yellow inflatable markers before heading back to the starting line. Capsized boats could be righted, unless the crew needed assistance from the regatta fleet boat which would be follow-ing the fleet. Life jackets had to be worn at all times, on pain of disqualification.

Once the prerace was finished, Freddie took his group off to one side for last-minute instructions. "OK," he said, keeping his voice low. "The wind is out of the southwest, so you should be able to tack back and forth parallel to the starting line and then swing over to a starboard tack for the first leg. It's import-ant to communicate…that means the crewman should let the skipper know what's going on and where the other boats are at. Got it?"

They nodded.

"Go get 'em!"

Angel and Bob quickly rigged their boat and pushed off from the dock. Freddie had assigned Angel to be the skipper, because Bob, being heavier, would be better suited to counter-acting the heeling action in the brisk wind. She was nervous, but confident that she could steer the boat where it needed to go.

Once all the boats had been launched, the race boat sounded the five-minute warning with a blast from its ship's horn. Angel was busy trying to avoid all the other sailing dinghies which were fighting for position on their side of the start line, not to mention the other boats at anchor in the little harbor. Bob kept glancing at his wrist watch and calling out the time left before the start.

"Two minutes," he said. "Don't get too far past the last marker!"

"I won't," the girl said. Her heart was beating rapidly. She planned to come about with one minute left and run parallel to the line, then peel off at the horn and head for the first race marker, about a half-mile down the bay. "One minute!" Bob yelled.

"Ready about!" Angela called out. She swung the boat around, and the two switched sides. Another boat cut right in front of them, and she had to fall off quickly to avoid a collision. Bob cursed. But Angel swung the nose back again quickly and held it right on line. The breeze picked up and the little boat sped up, heeling over gracefully on its side.

"Yeah!" Bob yelled, leaning back over the water on the high side. "Keep her there, Angel!" He counted down the remaining seconds, and just as Angel turned the nose back to the left, the horn sounded again…one long blast. "Perfect!" Bob said. "You hit the line right on the button!"

There were four other boats that seemed to have timed the start correctly, and they all leapt through the light chop of the bay and beat into the wind on the first upwind leg. Two of the other boats were a bit upwind of Angel, and she looked over at them with concern. "They could steal our wind if they get ahead of us," she said.

"Point her as high as you can," Bob said. "I'll keep her trimmed tight. Let's squeeze out as much speed as we can."

Despite their best efforts, the three leading boats arrived at the first marker at roughly the same time. Because Angel was almost side-by-side with the other two boats, she had to take the widest turn around the mark. That gave the other two boats a slight advantage, and they forged ahead by a length or two as the three made the first turn. The next leg was downwind, parallel to the thick vegetation of the barrier island, with the wind coming over their shoulders. Bob let the sail out to catch more of the wind and the two of them crouched in the center of the keel, as they had been taught, to center their weight and increase their speed to the maximum.

The three boats in the lead flew downwind towards the second marker, their hulls surging forward with every gust. Angel was able to get her nose almost up to the sterns of the two boats in front of her, but no further. When they were about a hundred yards from the next marker, she began to formulate an idea.

"We've gotta cut this one tight," she said. "Get ready for a sharp jibe."

Bob saw immediately what she planned to do, and nodded his head. "OK, Angel," he said. "You gotta cut it hard or we'll go on the wrong side of the marker and have to make a circle."

"I know," she said. "But once we come around, you've gotta get that sail trimmed fast or we'll never get past them."

"Right," he said. He coiled the rope in preparation. Angel kept an eye on the marker and the other two boats and when she thought they could make it, she yelled "Now!" and pulled the tiller over. Normally, a sailboat turns into the wind nose first, and the sail flops over to the other side in a controlled movement. In a jibe, the boat turns stern first and, especially when coming off a reach, with the sail out wide to catch the trailing wind, the sail shoots across in a jarring motion. And that's what happened as Angel and Bob ducked under the swinging boom and Bob quickly trimmed the sail in tight. The little boat shuddered and then shot forward on its new tack, heeling over again and slicing through the water.

Angel bravely kept the nose steady even as their boat approached the side of the boat closest to them. She and Bob could see the eyes of the sailors in the other boat go wide as they saw them approaching. It looked like she was aiming to ram them amidships. The boy who was at the tiller of the other boat even yelled "Hey!" at them as if to ward them away. But she kept on, grinning maniacally, aiming at the yellow inflated marker beyond.

It was close. But the bow of Angel's boat slipped past the stern of the other by a matter of just a few feet. She felt like she could have reached out and touched the other skipper on the back of his neck. But they passed, one sailing away from the mark, and Angel headed right for it. The other two boats now tried to make the same maneuver, but they were slower and less prepared, and they flopped about losing precious seconds while Angel and Bob continued slicing towards the marker.

Bob pulled the sheet in even tighter as Angel gripped the tiller with white knuckles. The wind was trying to push the boat to the wrong side of the marker, and she was trying to keep that from happening. "C'mon, c'mon," she muttered as they drew closer and closer. Finally, a gust came up and the little boat leaped forward, and Angel was able to guide the nose past the marker. She heaved a sigh of relief as she swung the tiller over and pointed the nose of the boat toward the finish line. Bob adjusted the sail and then gave out a huge yell. "Awesome! We got three lengths on 'em now! They'll never catch us."

It was true. The other two boats had rounded the last marker clumsily and now sailing hopelessly in Angel's wake. The last leg of the race took another fifteen minutes, but there was nothing anyone behind them could do. Angel's boat crossed the line first to the sound of the horn, and many of those watching from other yachts in the little harbor sounded their own horns to congratulate the winner.

Angel and Bob were grinning from ear to ear as they sailed back to the dock, and dropped the sails. Freddie grabbed Angel in a huge hug that lifted her feet off the dock and then slapped Bob on the back. Others came forward to shake their hands.

There was a cookout after the race. Angel was still so excited she couldn't eat anything more than a handful of potato chips. Bob wolfed down several burgers. He told anyone willing to listen about their last-second maneuver and how they almost rammed the other boat before crossing just behind.

After the lunch, the commodore of the yacht club, speaking through a squeaky microphone on the public address system, announced the prizes. "And to present the winning cup to this year's champions, we're honored to have with us Senator Malcolm O'Malley."

The senator, dressed in casual sailing clothes, his famous shock of graying hair blowing over his tanned foreheard, beamed as he waved at the applause. He announced the names of Angela Bruno and Bob Martin and draped a ribboned medal over each of their necks, and then posed with them while pictures were taken of the winners with a large silver chalice.

When the ceremonies were over, the senator leaned down at the two happy sailors. "That was quite a race you ran," he said. "Gutsy. Bold."

"Thank you, sir," Bob said. "It was Angel's idea. She saw the angle and decided to take it."

"Nicely done, young lady," the senator said. "I tell you what. Why don't the two of you ride back to Winter Cove with me? On the *Filibuster*?"

"That'd be great!" Bob said, his eyes lighting up.

"I don't know," Angel said. "We're supposed to go back with Freddie and the others."

Senator O'Malley waved away her objections. "I'll speak to him," he said. "It will be OK. I mean, we're all going to the same place, right? But you kids deserve a treat, the way you sailed today. It'll be an honor to have the winning sailors aboard."

He went off to speak to Freddie. Bob punched Angel in the arm playfully. "Not bad, eh?" he said. "Won the race and we get to sail with a U.S. senator! Wait'll my Dad hears about this!"

Yeah, Angel thought to herself. *My Dad better not hear about this, or else.*

It was a week after Jason Pyle's flight had disappeared. There was still no sign of the missing plane. After three days of sweeps in the cold water off Martha's Vineyard, the Coast Guard had reluctantly called off the search. It was as if the ocean had opened up, swallowed the plane whole, and closed over it again.

Tom Pyle sat in his upstairs study in his home on Serpent Point, looking out at the gray ocean. Michael had just left for the airport in Boston, on his way back to Geneva and the contracts he was trying to close in the Middle East. There had been no further point to his staying and waiting for the word which would likely never come.

But Tom and his son had spent a lot of time talking, and Margaret had joined them from time to time. They had talked about a lot of things in the last week. Painful things. Memories of Jason. They had laughed and cried. And they talked of business things. Pyle had asked Jack Dunne to fly out to Singapore and see if he could help step into the breach left by Jason's death. Dunne had gone at once.

Michael had shared with his father the doubts that he and Jason had about Dunne and his plans for Pyle Industries. The folder of material that Jason had sent to Michael in Geneva lay open between them. The two men had agreed that the dossier was troubling, but …

"It could mean what Jason thought it meant, but it also could be read another way," Michael summarized. "It could all be explained away. It's not a smoking gun."

Tom Pyle agreed. Some of the things that Jason accused Dunne of doing he had known about, and even approved. But there were other things that troubled him. Secret things. Things he should have known about, but didn't.

In the end, they agreed that they should do nothing, for now. But they also agreed that they would keep a closer eye on Jack Dunne. And Tom Pyle promised his son that he would make no public pronouncements about the company and its future executive team any time soon. Not until they could determine just where Jack Dunne's loyalties really lay.

Michael had returned to Europe satisfied, at least, that his father would look at his new CEO with a more jaundiced eye. He had been able to plant a seed of doubt in his father's mind, even if he hadn't been able to convince him to fire Dunne outright. Jason would have been angry and upset. But that was Jason, hot-headed and impetuous. And Jason was…gone.

After Michael had left, and Margaret had gone to her room to take a nap, Tom Pyle sat in his study, looking out at the sea and thinking. As with any problem, business or personal, he tried to take himself out of the process. Remove the emotions, remove the ego. Look at the problem dispassionately. Peer at it from the outside in. What is the right thing to do? It was hard, very hard, to do that in this case. His son was dead.

But as he played with the problem, he began to see what was needed. And, finally, he flipped open his personal directory, found the listing for the name he was thinking of, and dialed it.

"Thank you for calling the Federal Bureau of Investigation," said the female voice. "How may I direct your call?"

Pyle asked for the name he wanted, and was connected.

"Agent Harris."

"Jerry? It's Tom Pyle."

"Yes, sir, how are you doing? Sorry to hear about about your boy."

"Thanks, Jerry. I appreciate it."

"How can I help?"

"Do you remember when you told me about someone, former Bureau guy, who does freelance?"

"Yes."

"I think I can use him," Pyle said. "Or someone like him."

"Not someone," Harris said. "Him. Name's Greg Greenfield. GeeGee to his friends. He's the best. I'll have him call you."

"Thanks, Jerry," Pyle said. "Appreciate it."

"No problem," Harris said. "Good luck."

O'Malley motored the *Filibuster* out of Chatham harbor and then, with the push of a couple of buttons, automatically raised the mainsail. With the wind coming out of the southeast, from the general direction of New York City, he pointed her nose at Nantucket. Then he had Bob haul a line that unfurled the large jib sheet and the yacht heeled over smartly in the brisk breeze.

When he turned off the throbbing diesel engine, the silence was glorious as the boat stretched against her lines and splashed against the waves slapping at her bow. "Wow," Bob said as the boat cut through the ocean, "She's really moving!"

"I had her built for speed," the senator said happily, standing at the wheel at the rear of the cockpit. "And comfort, of course. Speaking of which, there's a cooler underneath that cushion if you want anything to drink. How about a beer, Bob?"

The teen laughed at the idea of a United States senator offering him an alcoholic beverage. "Sure," he said, "Don't mind if I do. Angel? Want one?"

"No thanks," the girl said. She sat on the long bench seat in the cockpit, hugging her knees to her chest. She felt shy and strangely uncertain, riding on this beautiful yacht, the biggest boat she had ever been on, with these two suntanned, self-assured men. She didn't know why she felt that way. There was really nothing to fear. It was all just new and different and somehow strange.

Bob passed a can of beer from the cooler to the senator and popped the tab on his. He looked suddenly handsome to Angel, standing there with his long blond curls blowing in the wind, the sun full on his face, looking relaxed and happy and somehow in his element. She felt happy for him.

O'Malley noticed her reticence. "C'mere, skipper," he said, smiling. "Take the helm."

"Oh, I don't know," she said, but he insisted, smiling, and she stood up and grabbed hold of the wooden spokes of the huge wheel. She felt like Captain Ahab, standing on the heaving deck of the *Pequot* sailing the seven seas in search of the great white whale. The thought made her giggle.

"Great, isn't it?" the senator said. "Now, with a boat like this, out in the open sea, you gotta keep an eye on the compass to steer." He pointed to the post in front of the wheel where a domed glass bowl contained a floating compass that fought against the heaving motion of the ocean. A red pointer showed the direction the boat was heading, and the senator told her to try and keep the nose on 260°. It wasn't as easy as it looked, as the churning waves and the wind kept pushing her nose one way or another, causing her to have to make constant adjustments with the wheel.

"If it gets too tiring, I can just put her on auto-pilot," the senator said. "But that's cheating, really. You gotta feel a boat with your feet to know what she's doing. Otherwise, you're just riding, and you can do that in a car, for Chrissakes."

Angel understood what he meant. She could feel the boat through her bare feet, feel it surging and slowing, feel it when it hit a wave and was stopped momentarily in its forward movement, feel it leap forward again as the constant pressure from the wind pushed against the sails and strained against the taut ropes that held the sails. She lost herself in the battle to keep the boat headed where she wanted it to go, and forgot everything else: Bob, the senator, where she was.

She was dimly aware of the senator's hand on her shoulder as he pointed to the tell-tales on the jib sail. These were little lengths of twine affixed to the sail that rode in the wind spilling over its surface. When the boat was pointed in the optimal direction so the wind split over the sail like over the wings of an airplane, the little piece of string pointed straight back to the stern. When the bow went slightly offline, the whirling pattern of the wind made the rope dance, flop or rotate madly. "It can drive you mad, trying to keep her straight," he told the girl, "But that's part of the fun of it."

She bit her lip in concentration as she focused on that little string, while also keeping an eye on the compass, and spun the wheel to adjust for the constant heaving of the sea. It was hard, no, it was impossible to keep the boat on a steady heading for long, but she managed to keep the bow traveling in the general right direction as it sliced through the waves, heeled over to one side so the rushing sea swept over the edge of the gunnel, and the spray from the beating of the bow into a swell was sent flying back into their faces.

And then she was aware that the senator's hand had slipped, down to her waist and was beginning to drop even lower onto her buttock. And she stood back, her hands falling from the wheel. The senator reached out and took the wheel in both of his hands, as the bow began to swing quickly into the wind. Angel went back and sat down on the bench. "It's Bob's turn," she muttered.

The senator grinned and motioned for the boy to come over and take the wheel. He repeated all the instructions and watched as Bob learned how to guide the boat. Angel hugged her knees again and watched. But the fun of the day had gone. She wanted to get off this boat. She looked at the senator, and at those hands that had been on her body, and she shuddered.

32

Tom Pyle and Jack Dunne met in Pyle's office when Dunne got back from Singapore. Dunne reported on the situation in the Far East, and said the Chinese contracts were still pending, but things looked good.

"They have more goddam central committees out there," Dunne groused. "And each one of them need greasing before anything gets done. It's like Beacon Hill on steroids. But then, the contracts they have to pass out are worth more, too."

"Speaking of Beacon Hill, we've got problems," Pyle said, leading back in his chair. "Attorney General Finnegan called me last week. Said he may have to release the information about the Bruno contract in the tunnel. Said some nosy Nellie from the Globe has the story and is planning to run with it."

Dunne waved his hand dismissively. "Did you mention the words 'governor' and 'girlfriend' to him?" he said.

"He was whining," Pyle said. "Said there was nothing he could do about it, if the newspapers had it."

"Hell there isn't," Dunne said. "He could shut it down if he really wanted to."

Pyle shrugged. "Well, it doesn't sound like he's going to," he said. "You'd better go higher up the food chain."

"I'll take care of it," Dunne said. He looked across the desk at the older man. Pyle seemed somehow smaller, older. He seemed reduced from the Tom Pyle he had known just a few weeks ago. "How are you holding up?"

Pyle looked back at Dunne. "I'm fine," he said. He wasn't going to show any weakness. Not now. Not to Dunne.

Dunne pressed. "You don't look fine," he said. "Why don't you take some time off? You've been through a lot. Take Margaret and go somewhere. Europe, maybe, or the Caribbean. I can take care of things for a while."

Pyle shook his head. "I appreciate your concern," he said, "But I'm OK. It's better for me to keep busy. I'd rather be working than sitting around the house. I'd go batshit doing that. Besides, we've got a lot going on…Asia, Europe and now this crap right here in Boston. I'll be fine. You take care of Finnegan."

Dunne called Gordon Congdon and they met for lunch at Locke-Ober, the quintessential Boston businessman's restaurant just off Winter Street. The place had seen its ups and downs over the decades, but was still a good place for a private and quiet discussion in the dark rooms with their heavy Victorian décor. Dunne had the lobster stew and Congdon ordered the baked scrod with crab.

"What's up with Tom's kid?" Congdon asked, as his vodka martini arrived, soundlessly delivered by the aproned waiter.

"Don't know," Dunne said. He was sipping iced tea. He didn't like to drink during the day. "They haven't found the plane. Probably never will. Pyle seems OK, but I'm a little worried about him. He's not so young anymore, and this was a pretty big shock to the system."

Congdon looked at Dunne while he sipped his drink and broke off a piece of bread to dip in the flavored olive oil that had been poured in a small dish. Was Dunne telling him this to signal a changing in the guard? Was he being told the old man was on the verge of being shoved aside? He wondered.

"It'd be hard on anyone," he said. "Losing a kid."

Dunne nodded. He asked about the campaign. Listened while Congdon talked about the senator's fund raising position, the endorsements he had rolled up, the plans to launch the campaign later in the fall. He nodded in the right places, listening with only half an ear.

"There's something we could use some help with," Dunne said after their lunches had arrived and they'd stopped talking to eat. *Here it comes*, Congdon thought. "Charlie Finnegan has been trying to keep a lid on the tunnel investigation," Dunne said. "He's been walking a fine line between finding someone to blame for that woman's death, and letting a whole lot of cats out of the bag. Cats that neither one of us wants or needs to be let loose right now."

Congdon asked the waiter to bring him a glass of water. He had already drained most of his martini, and he could feel it burning a hole in his gut. Jeezus, he thought, am I already so old that I can't drink at lunch anymore? Or maybe it was a sign that something serious was going on here.

"Cats, huh?," he said, smiling. "Meow."

"Go ahead and laugh," Dunne said, "But I've heard some reporter from the Globe is asking some questions. If she finds out who owns Benito, then Joe Bruno 's name is involved. If the Bruno connection gets out, it's gonna splash just as much crapola on the senator as it will on us."

"Is that a threat?" Congdon said, his eyes narrowing.

"That's a statement of fact," Dunne said. "It would not be good for our business if it became public knowledge that we occasionally throw some of our contracts to the Mob, in the interests of peace and quiet on the labor front. It would not be good for your business if it also became public knowledge that such contracts were helpfully arranged by the senior senator from Massachusetts, in return for some fairly healthy campaign contributions, among other things, from both parties."

Congdon sighed. He didn't like little pissants like Jack Dunne, men who thought that because they made lots of money in the world of business they were entitled to move the levers of power. Real power. The kind that Gordon Congdon could move in Washington. He could move levers and make billions of dollars appear or disappear. He could move levers and make people disappear. Dunne and men like him were concerned about their contracts worth a few million here, a few million there. Child's play! Congdon had the kind of power that could send armies into battle, replace prime ministers and kings, and provide access to the secret vaults of the wealthy and connected anywhere in the world. That kind of power made Jack Dunne's problems insignificant by comparison. *And yet…and yet.* It was true what Dunne said. The senator's image would be hurt by disclosures of some of these local political dealings, especially if the Mob were involved. It would not be fatal. Voters didn't care that much anymore about organized crime. After the Godfather movies, and *Goodfellas*, most people looked at the Mob like they were a mostly loveable group of cut-ups, with their pretend codes of loyalty and *muerta* and all that macho Italian bullshit. There was nothing Congdon could conceive that would prevent Malcolm O'Malley from becoming the next president of the United States, and prevent Congdon from gaining access to even greater levers of power. But now was not the right time to let anything happen that might derail the momentum.

"I'll have the senator give Charlie Finnegan a call," he said. "See what we can do."

Dunne motioned for the check. "Appreciate it," he said. "You be sure and let us know what you need for the campaign."

"Oh," Congdon said, "We will. You can count on that."

Charlie Finnegan, the attorney general of the Commonwealth of Massachusetts, was holding a late afternoon staff
meeting in his large corner office in the State House in Boston. His six assistant AGs were sprawled around the comfortable leather chairs and matching love seat that were arranged
around the marble fireplace, while Charlie himself sat behind
the massive rosewood desk. The fireplace had not worked for
more than a hundred years, and even if it did, Finnegan would
have had to arrest himself for violating one of the state's many
anti-pollution statutes had there been a fire burning in it.

Finnegan liked these staff meetings, in which he got to
fire questions at the staff and watch them squirm uncomfort-
ably as they tried to answer. Finnegan was a big man, beefy
around the middle. His bristle-like hair, close-cropped, stood
at attention atop his lined forehead. He had always wanted
to be a law professor, like the ones he imaged who walked
the musty hallways at Harvard, learned and erudite, firing off
questions about The Law, questions that were themselves brilliant and multi-faceted and that illuminated for the intimidat-

ed students the necessity for reason, the importance of precedent, the respect for impartiality.

Of course, Charlie Finnegan himself had never been to Harvard. He had, in fact, attended Suffolk University, the commuter's school, on a scholarship, and barely made it through. It had taken him three tries to pass the Massachusetts bar exam, a fact that had long ago been excised from his official campaign biography. His legal career had been anything but brilliant. His first five years had been spent processing contracts as a junior lawyer for Massport, a job he had been given as a reward for a thousand-dollar campaign contribution placed with a state senator from his home district of Somerville, a grimy little town on the outskirts of Boston. He had finally managed to work his way out of that dead-end job and hooked on as an assistant district attorney for Middlesex County, prosecuting drunk drivers, wife beaters and bad-check writers.

But he had been smart, kept his nose clean and had done his homework. He found out which of those drunk drivers, wife beaters and check kiters had had good connections among their family and friends; and they had been shown official mercy. After years of piling up favors in this way, he had begun to move inexorably upward through the political ranks, eventually to D.A. for Middlesex County, and then to Attorney General for the state. Now, he wanted the other corner office at the State House, the one reserved for the governor, and thanks to his continued use of judicious prosecutions, he had amassed enough favors and passed out enough goodies, he thought, to get there.

So a lot of the questions he was firing at his assistants had to do with whose toes were getting squashed in the various cases under consideration. Most of the lawyers on his staff were young and idealistic. Finnegan liked to have prosecutors like that, the ones who actually believed in using the office to fight injustice and bring the guilty to the bar, and to do the people's work to do what was right. At the same time, he depended on his chief assistant, Elena Halloran, to keep track of the political ramifications of the office's work. She was a bit older than the others, in her forties, and was married to a powerful senate committee chairman, so her idealism had long since been leavened by a sense of what was real. Charlie depended on Elena to tell him if a certain case might have political implications, and exactly whose ox was getting gored in the cases that came across his desk. And he especially liked the fact that she would tell him about it after an enjoyable and energetic session in bed, at the hotel suite that her husband's senate committee kept on reserve just a few blocks from the State House.

Finnegan was firing questions at the staff when his secretary buzzed in to tell him that Senator Malcolm O'Malley was on the line from Washington. He sighed and asked her to find out if he could call O'Malley back, but she told him the senator said it was important. He sighed again and waved his staff out of the office. Elena looked at him questioningly, but he waved her away too. "I'll handle it," he said, nodding back at her.

"Charlie!" the senator's voice boomed in his ear. "I'm not interrupting anything am I? How's Martha and the kids?"

"Senator," Finnegan said into the receiver. "Everyone's fine, thanks. What's up?"

"Coupla things," the senator said. "I've got a fund raiser down here in the District in three weeks. I want you to come down. Gordon says he's got about twenty victims lined up, about half from Wall Street and half from Hollywood. We think if you're here, talking up your campaign, you can score some major bucks from among the pigeons."

"Great," Finnegan said. "Sounds good. Thanks for the heads-up. I'll run it past Fletcher at the campaign office. What do you want us to cover?" Finnegan knew that there would be a price to pay for entry into O'Malley's fund-raiser. He'd have to pay for the booze, or the catering, or the hall rental, or something. That was the way things worked. Sure, he might be able to raise a few hundred thousand in donations, or promises of donations, but he'd have to lay something out, too. Tit for tat. But he'd do whatever O'Malley wanted, pay whatever he was told. Finnegan could read the political winds as well as anyone else, and they told him that Malcolm O'Malley was going to ride his famous name, his famous family and his famously deep pockets all the way to the top next year, and Charlie Finnegan intended to be holding tightly to his coattails in order to move up one floor to the Governor's office.

"Not a thing, Charlie, not a thing," the senator said, surprising Finnegan. "I want to have a network of support when I'm in the Oval Office, people I can depend on all across the country. That's what I'm going to tell the pigeons. That I'm going to need people like Charlie Finnegan in the state houses and in the Congress so we can get things done for America."

Finnegan stifled the urge to laugh out loud. He wondered why O'Malley was laying it on so thick. O'Malley knew that Finnegan was a good soldier. They were both Massachusetts Democrats. They both knew how things worked. They both knew that Finnegan would do anything O'Malley wanted, up to and possibly including murdering his own mother.

"Well, thanks, Senator," he said into the phone. "You know you can count on my support."

"Great, Charlie, great," the senator said. "Listen, there is one thing you can do for me."

Thunk, Finnegan thought. The sound of the other shoe dropping. "What's that, senator?" he said, keeping his voice even, neutral.

"It's that commission looking into the tunnel collapse," the senator said. "Is there any way you can get that buttoned up before the first week of November? I want to make my official announcement exactly one year before Election Day next year. Our theme is 'One Year to Change America.' Like it?"

"Catchy," Finnegan said, thinking *stupidest slogan ever*. "Why do you need the commission report issued before your announcement?" He thought he knew, but he wanted O'Malley to say it out loud.

"Just to tie up all the loose ends," the senator said. "Loose ends can often come back and whip you in the ass. The commission is going to rule that the foundations were not poured properly, right? Contractor tried to cut corners? That Benito fellow. Nothing else, right?"

"Far as I know, that's correct," Finnegan said. "But I have heard that Maxine Wiebe from the Globe is nosing around. She's trying to find out who owns Benito."

"And does anyone own Benito?"

For the second time, Finnegan had to resist the urge to laugh out loud. Everyone knew that Benito Concrete and Paving was a wholly owned subsidiary of Joe Bruno's organization. Just like everyone knew that Pyle Industries had been told to hire Benito to pour the concrete footings and had likely hired several other subcontractors that were Bruno fronts so that a significant cut of the billions in federal largesse would flow into the gangster's bank accounts. And everyone also knew that this little game of spread-the-money-around was done so the work would not be held up by union discord. And that everyone knew that Senator Malcolm O'Malley himself had laid down the word that this was the way the deal was going to be done. But of course, even though everyone *knew* all these things, no one would ever admit them, out loud and in public. Least of all the attorney general of the Commonwealth, who wanted to be the next Governor.

"Not to the best of my knowledge," Finnegan said, lapsing into his best ass-covering lawyer-speak.

"Well then," the senator said. "There shouldn't be any problem."

"No," Finnegan agreed. "But Maxine is a good reporter. You know her?"

"Maxine Wiebe," the senator said. "I think I may have talked with her before. Jewish girl? Dark hair? A little tubby? Bad complexion?"

"Yeah, that's her," the attorney general laughed. "But she can be a bitch when she gets her teeth into something."

"Well then, Charlie," the senator said. "Don't let her."

"Senator?" Finnegan was confused.

"Don't let her get her teeth into this," he said.

"I can't tell the press how to run their business," Finnegan said.

"Of course not, Charlie," the senator was trying to be patient. "She can ask all the questions she wants. It's the answers, Charlie, the answers."

"I'm not sure I'm following you," Finnegan said.

"Make sure the records of the Benito company are clean," O'Malley said with a sigh. "Benito bid for and got the contract on its own. Nobody else was involved. Before or since. Got it, Charlie?"

Finnegan got it. He didn't like it, but he understood. "OK," he said.

"Excellent, Charlie," the senator was back to his effusive self. "I'll have Gordon contact your man Fletcher and they can work out all the details on the shindig. You just plan to come down, make a nice speech, do a little hobnobbing. I'll have Gordon get you a nice suite at the Ritz. Bring Martha down. It's good to let the pigeons see the wife."

They rang off. As soon as he replaced the receiver in its cradle, the door to his office opened and Elena Halloran entered, looking worried.

"What did Senator Slimeball want?" she asked.

"He's booked me into one of his cash-o-thons," Finnegan

said. "Down in DC in a few weeks. Wall Street and Hollywood. Big bucks."

"How much?" she asked. She was asking how much they would have to lay out, not how much they would be taking in. She knew how the game was played.

"Nothing," he said, and enjoyed the surprised look on her face. "Well, almost nothing."

He laughed as she shook her head knowingly. "We've got to sanitize the records of Benito Concrete."

She was surprised. "The company that poured the rotten footings?" she said.

Finnegan nodded. "That's the one," he said. "They and they alone were responsible. Nobody else. That is now the Gospel according to O'Malley. Do a sweep through the corporate records and make sure. Maxine Wiebe from the Globe is asking questions. Make sure she doesn't find out anything."

Elena nodded. "I get it," she said. "No Bruno connection." She thought a minute, chewing her lip. "I know someone over at the Secretary of State's office," she said. "I'll call her."

Finnegan nodded approvingly. That's why he liked Elena so much. She understood these things. Plus, she knew how to put her tongue to good use.

Maxine Wiebe had one of those feelings. It was nothing she could print, not even anything she could mention to her editor. It was just a feeling. But she had had feelings like this before, and they almost always turned out to be something that was real, was printable, was a story.

She had been assigned six months ago to report on the special Legislative Commission on the Construction and Oversight of the Thomas P. "Tip" O'Neill Tunnel Project, as per Senate Resolution 272 duly enacted and passed, blah blah blah. Neither Maxine nor her editor nor anyone in the entire state expected this commission was going to seriously investigate the construction contracts involved in the massive, $15 billion tunnel project. There was, almost literally, not a single member of the Great and General Court of the Commonwealth, also known as the state legislature, who did not have a hand, if not a sucking pipeline, into a part of that $15 billion stream of revenue that had poured into the hole that had been dug out of the ancient mud below the streets of Boston. Then there were the august Councilors of the city of Boston, the aldermen and selectmen of the surrounding cities and towns, the union chiefs, the mobsters, the bureaucrats and the lawyers... by the time one finally got to the end of the gravy train, it was no wonder that what had first been estimated as a $3 billion public works project had metastasized into the most expensive construction project in the history of the world. Maxine had always been surprised that someone remembered to actually build the damn tunnel, amid the decades-long feeding frenzy of graft that had taken place.

But the commission had been set up because of the public hue and cry over the death of poor old Edith Scoggins, killed when a poorly poured concrete abutment failed, and a heavy steel ceiling beam fell onto her car. The public had been outraged that after all that money had been spent, the tunnel was not entirely safe. The occasional spouting leaks that had plagued the first few months of operation, leaks which any engineer knew were not unusual for an underwater project like the Big Dig Tunnel, had also raised the public ire, and the calls for Something To Be Done had multiplied.

Maxine Wiebe was not naïve. She knew the politicians who had stolen the money in the first place were never going to admit that money had been stolen. She knew that they didn't want to conduct a major investigation into where the money went, because such an investigation, if conducted honestly, would lead right into their own pockets. She knew they would take the path of least resistance, find the easy scapegoat, toss him under the bus, call the case closed and move on to the next thing.

So she had been patient through the long months when the commission held its interminable public hearings. Witnesses by the dozen had been called, duly sworn, and testified for ass-numbing hours about concrete, stress tests, points of failure, standards of construction, deviations from norms, inspection procedures and on and on, week after week. She knew this was all part of the obfuscation process, and so she waited. Once a month or so, she would dutifully file another piece on the story. She'd explain the physics of tunnel construction and the chemistry of concrete and the mathematical calculations of materials under stress. She waited, biding her time, knowing the story was in there somewhere, buried underneath the reams of reports and stacks of files. And eventually, the scapegoat had been identified and brought forward. The hapless Carlos Benito had made his appearance in the bright lights of the television cameras, had refused to answer the commission's questions, and had been sent off to the federal prison at Devens to meditate upon his manifold sins and wickedness. The commission had adjourned pending publication of its final report. The final report, Maxine knew, would blame Benito Concrete for deliberately using a bad load of concrete, knowingly cutting corners, cheating the taxpayers, fraudulent record-keeping and otherwise being the one and only bad actor among the cast of thousands in the long-running drama that was the Big Dig. Benito would spend time in jail, the attention of the public would move on, and the politicians and others would spend their ill-gotten gains, even as they looked for the next opportunity to belly up to the public trough. And Maxine knew that the public, sadly, would believe that to be the truth. Because everyone could understand there being one bad apple in the bunch. That only stands to reason. But the idea that the entire political establishment was corrupt and bent was too much for the voting public to swallow.

But there was something about Benito Concrete that gave Maxine Wiebe that funny feeling. She had made a few calls to her usual list of contacts at the State House. Everyone she talked to said they knew nothing about the company or about Carlos Benito. That set off a few bells in her head. Boston, although a big city, is not that big; certainly it figured that if someone like Carlos Benito had the wherewithal to get himself into the cafeteria line of corruption at the Big Dig, he would be big enough that someone would know something about him. There would be gossip to share. Stories to tell. Especially now that Carlos Benito had been fingered as the main culprit in the story, Maxine expected that people would be standing in line to tell her something. Things like "I coulda predicted he'd get caught, because back in '92, there was this deal ..."

But instead, there was nothing but silence. Her sources hemmed and hawed and said they didn't know a thing about him. Total stranger. No dirt. No gossip, other than someone said his wife lived pretty much full time down in Florida. Hardly front-page news. This uniform wall of blankness made Maxine's antennae vibrate.

What's up with that? She wondered. Why are people still protecting the guy? Why are they afraid to dish? It must mean, she decided, that rather than the money-grubbing little businessman caught with his hand in a big cookie jar, Carlos Benito must be connected, and connected to someone very, very big. And scary. And powerful.

"The mob?" her editor helpfully suggested.

"That's my guess," she had said. But she had nothing to corroborate. No proof. No witnesses. No sources. Nothing, nada, niente.

"Keep digging," her editor said and turned back to something else. What else could he say? He couldn't run a story based on his reporter's Spidey sense. He needed facts: cold, hard, implacable, irrefutable pieces of information. Verified by at least two sources.

Maxine had run Benito Concrete and Paving through Dun & Bradstreet, the Better Business Bureau, Lexis-Nexis, City Hall. Nothing. She had called in a favor and had the Globe's crime-beat reporter ask his sources at the local office of the FBI if they had anything on Benito. Nope, came the reply. Nothing. Clean as a whistle. Of course, Maxine knew that the local FBI office itself was about hip-deep in Mob informants, but still… She put in a request for the firm's state tax records, which was denied, and then filed a Freedom of Information Act request for the documents. But that would take weeks to wind its way through the bureaucracy. And many times, when FOIA requests had been made for sensitive documents, those documents managed to get themselves disappeared. Permanently.

So she still had nothing. Except that funny feeling.

And then, finally, she got the break she had been waiting for. The one she knew had been out there waiting for her.

The phone rang late one afternoon in her cubby in the Globe newsroom on Morrissey Boulevard.

"Yeah?" she said. "Wiebe here."

"Is this Maxine Wiebe?" said a male voice.

"Yeah," she said. "Whaddya want?" She glanced at her telephone to see who it listed as the caller, but the caller ID screen was blank, probably blocked on the caller's end.

"I got some information on Benito Concrete," the caller said, his voice low, almost a whisper. "You interested?"

"Yeah, maybe," she said, trying to keep any excitement out of her voice. Play this cool, she told herself. Don't blow it. Play it cool. "What about them?"

"I know who bankrolls 'em," the voice said.

"Oh yeah?" she said, "Who?"

The caller laughed, low and throaty. "Hold on, sister," he said. "Ain't gonna be that easy. First, I gotta have your word that my name never, ever appears in this story. Ever. Or else I'm a dead man. You got that?"

"Yeah," Maxine said, her heart racing with excitement. "I got that, loud and clear. I can promise anonymity. But I gotta see proof that what you're telling me is on the level. I'm not in the business of printing rumors or innuendo. Or bullshit."

The caller laughed again. "Oh, sister, what I got ain't bullshit, you can count on that. I got the proof all right," he said. "Don't you worry your pretty little head about that."

"Listen," she said, "Why don't we get together? You show me yours and I'll show you mine."

"You're a pistol, ain'tcha?" he said, chuckling. "OK. You know a bar called Killebrew's?"

She wrote down the name. "Uh, I don't think so," she said. "Where is it?"

"Southie," he said. "Take the T to the Andrews station. Cross over Dorchester Street. It's on the corner of Preble. Can't miss it."

"Got it," Maxine said, scribbling down the directions. "What time?"

"Let's say six. Can you get here in an hour?"

"Fine," she said. "How do I find you?"

"As you come in the door, there's a row of booths to the right. I'll be in the last one, against the wall. I'm about sixty, got grey hair and I got on a Red Sox sweatshirt."

She laughed. "So does everyone else in South Boston," she said. "OK, I'll find you. What's your name?"

He laughed again. "We'll discuss that when we meet. Just call me Mister X for now."

He hung up. Maxine replaced the receiver and pumped her fist. Yes! This was what she had been waiting for. She had shaken enough trees and finally the coconut had come tumbling down. She stood up and looked over the top of her cubicle to see if her editor was in his glassed-in office at the end of the newsroom. But it was empty and his light was off. He must be out this afternoon, she thought. Well, she'd fill him in tomorrow on what she learned tonight.

MAXINE LEFT THE GLOBE BUILDING and walked over to the Red Line subway station. She waited on the mostly empty inbound platform and was one of perhaps a dozen passengers when she boarded a car on the next train heading north towards downtown. It was rush hour, but everyone was rushing to get out of the city, not in.

The Andrews station was just one stop down the line, serving the blue-collar, very Irish South Boston area. She climbed the concrete stairs, pushed through the turnstile and walked out onto the sidewalk. The station entrance was on Dorchester Avenue. She turned south, where the divided highway of Dorchester Street intersected with Preble Avenue. Standing at the corner, she saw the gold-leaf sign on the window across the intersection: Killebrew's Bar & Grill.

She started across the crosswalk in the southbound lanes of Dorchester Street. From behind her, coming out of Dorchester Avenue, a blue sedan accelerated, swerved into her path and slammed into her back. Maxine Wiebe went flying up into the air, feet above her head, and then crashed down hard on the pavement. A woman across the intersection screamed. The blue sedan kept moving, tires squealing, turned right on Southampton and disappeared in a cloud of blue smoke.

The whole thing took maybe five seconds. And Maxine Wiebe lay there on the street, a wreath of red spreading out slowly around her head.

35

The Winter Cove Yacht Club held a little party at the end of the summer for the kids who had participated in its summer sailing programs. Angela Bruno decided not to even mention it to her father, after the hassle she had gone through a few weeks earlier about the birthday party at Regan's house. She did tell her mother, who agreed that the best thing was just to plan to attend the dinner. Besides, she told her daughter with a smile, Joe Bruno was going to be up in Boston that night on business.

So Angela dressed in a summer print skirt and a white tee, tied her hair back with a silk ribbon, threw on a light sweater and joined her classmates at the yacht club on a Wednesday night. Bob, Freddie and the other boys all wore dress shirts, neckties and sport coats, along with long slacks; and the other girls had, like Angela, dressed nicely. The main function room at the Yacht Club had been gaily decorated with balloons and streamers.

Even though the head chef had complained, Freddie, the chief sailing instructor, had asked that the club order in some pizzas from the popular pizza joint in downtown Winter Cove, and there were several coolers with soft drinks. Someone, probably one of the mothers, had taken digital photos of the sailing class all summer long, and those images were being projected onto a white screen from someone's laptop.

It was a relaxed and fun evening for everyone. They had all become quite close during the summer, and the teens all enjoyed looking at the photos, making jokes and laughing. Angela found herself feeling sad that the summer was over, and decided that she would miss Bob Martin after all. She wasn't interested in him romantically, but he had turned out to be a nice guy, and she knew would miss his joking, his laughter and his company. They exchanged e-mail and Skype addresses and promised to keep in touch when he went back to prep school.

After they had eaten all the pizza, and helped themselves to a nice sheet cake the chef had made and decorated with sailboats and seagulls in red and blue icing, Freddie had presided over a hilarious prize-giving session. Everyone won something, but Angel was pleased to be given a tiny faux-silver cup for Most Improved Skipper. Bob won Navigator of the Year, despite, or maybe because, he had almost rammed Senator O'Malley's yacht that morning some weeks ago.

It was about eight-thirty when the party broke up. The sun had set, and a slight chilliness in the air presaged the coming of autumn. While it felt good against her skin after the long days of August's humidity and heat, the chilly breeze made Angela a little sad. She realized that summer was over, school waited just around the corner, and she felt that life was passing by at a dizzying pace. She didn't want it to stop, of course, and she was anxious to become an adult and experience all that awaited her, but she just wished she could pause for a while and savor this time and this place and not let it go. Not quite yet.

Angel had told her mother she would walk home. It was perhaps a mile from the yacht club down the sandy causeway and through the gates of Serpent Point. She wanted to be independent, at least for one night. And her mother didn't like to drive at night anyway. Fat Peter was coming down later from Boston, but Angel didn't want to bother him. She told Rosa that she'd be home around nine.

So, with some time to kill, she walked out to the end of one of the docks to enjoy the cool night air and just be by herself for a while. She was glad she had taken part in the sailing program that summer. She had learned a lot and made some good friends. She wondered if she'd ever see Bob Martin again. What would he be like next summer? What would she be like next summer? These were things she had to think about.

"Well, hello there," said a deep male voice behind her, startling her out of her reverie. "It's my favorite little sailor girl."

Angel turned and saw Malcolm O'Malley. He was dressed in a blue-and-white striped dress shirt, a rumpled pair of khaki shorts and a pair of tan, ratty topsiders. The sleeves of his shirt were rolled up to his elbows and his hair was uncombed and wind-tossed. He was smiling.

"Hi," Angela said shyly and smiled back.

"Hey, I just talked to your friend Bob back there," he said, nodding back at the clubhouse at the far end of the dock.

"We're gonna go out on the boat and star gaze a little. Wanna come?"

"I don't think so, but thanks" Angel said. "I told my mother I'd be home soon."

"Oh, we won't be long," the senator said. He reached down and grabbed a line that was tied to a fiberglass rowboat, drifting on the tide. He climbed down into the boat and then looked back, holding his hand out. "Come on, don't be a party pooper. I've got this great telescope on board. And the moon is bright tonight." He nodded up into the sky where the nearly full moon was shining brightly. "I'll get you home in time."

"OK," Angel said, deciding she didn't want the evening to end quite yet anyway. Besides, if Bob was coming, it would be all right. She climbed down into the dinghy. The senator untied the boat, pushed off and pulled on the little outboard engine, which sputtered into life.

"What about Bob?" Angel asked as the boat puttered away from the dock.

"He said he had to hit the head," O'Malley said. "I'll drop you off and then go back and get him."

He maneuvered the little craft past the yachts bobbing on their moorings and pulled up next to the *Filibuster*. He helped the girl on board, then cut the engine and followed her into the cockpit.

"What can I get you to drink?" he asked, ducking down into the galley below and flipping on the interior lights. "Coke? Pepsi? Cup of tea?"

"Uh, I guess some tea would be nice," the girl said. It was even chillier out here on the boat. Even the light of the moon seemed cold, bathing the deck and the side rails and the hal-yards in a ghostly blue-white light. Angel looked back at the dock, hoping to see Bob waving for his ride. But there was no one.

She heard O'Malley whistling to himself as he bustled about below.

"Where do you go to school?" he called up while he worked. "And when do you start back?"

"I'll be a junior at St. Mary's" she called back. "We start a week after Labor Day."

"Ahh," O'Malley said, poking his head up through the hatch and grinning at her. "The nuns of St. Mary's. You know what? I went there for a few years myself, until they sent me off to prep school. I think I still have the scars on my knuckles to prove it!" He laughed and ducked back inside. The water was boiling and the kettle whistled insistently.

Angela looked back again for Bob. The dock was empty in the bright moonlight.

"Here ya go," he said, holding a mug of tea up through the hatch. It was steaming, tendrils of vapor rising up and swirling around the rim. She took it with thanks, and held the mug in both hands, absorbing the heat. O'Malley ducked away again and in a minute, he reappeared holding a long padded case. He handed up a second cup of tea for himself and then came up himself into the cockpit.

He unzipped the case and extracted a long black tele-scope. Angela sipped some of her tea. It was peppermint, hot and sweet and delicious. She sipped some more and felt its warmth spread through her.

"Like that?" O'Malley asked, watching her. "Peppermint is a nice calming tea at night."

He busied himself with the telescope, peering into its eyepiece and adjusting the focus as he gazed up at the moon. "Awesome," he said, "You can practically see where they landed up there!" He looked over at the girl. "But you probably don't remember when we first landed on the moon, do you?"

Angela laughed. "I don't think I was born yet," she said. And laughed again. Her fingers were tingling.

He laughed too. "No, I guess not. That was in 1969. You probably weren't even a gleam in your parents' eyes back then."

For some reason, she thought that was very funny and began to giggle. O'Malley laughed too. She drank some more tea. The warmth oozed into her, coursed through her veins.

He held out the telescope. "Here," he said. "Have a look. It's a great night for star gazing."

"Silly," she said. "The moon isn't a star. It's a moon." That made her laugh again, so hard her side began to ache a little. She took the telescope in her hands, putting the half-drunk cup of tea down. The telescope felt heavy, heavier than she thought and she almost dropped it.

"Whoops," O'Malley said, and helped her catch it. "Nice and easy."

She tried again and this time was able to hoist the heavy thing up to her eye. She bent her head back to direct the piece up at the moon, but that made her feel dizzy and she lurched a little, shaking her head to try and clear it.

"Here," he said, "Let me help." He scooted around behind the girl and, reaching around, helped her aim the telescope up at the moon. She tried to line her eye up with the viewer, but couldn't seem to manage it. Her head felt light and loose, as if it might fall completely off her shoulders at any minute, bounce on the deck and fall with a splash into the sea. The image of that happening made her giggle again. She felt his long arms stretched around her and could feel the warmth of his chest behind her as he stood close.

"Maybe you should just look at the moon without the telescope," he said softly from behind her. So she did. It was beautiful, that bright white disc in the sky. Wisps of passing clouds drifted past but the air was so clear she could see the black and grey striations of the moon's valleys and mountains.

"I think I can see the space ship too," she said, her voice dreamy. She giggled again.

Then he put down the telescope and his arms closed around her. He pulled her gently back toward him, towards the heat of his body. His hands closed over her breasts and she felt his hardness pressing against her buttocks. It was all too, too funny. She laughed as he touched her, laughed as he reached under her pretty dress, laughed as his fingers reached between her legs, laughed as they touched her, invaded her. She laughed and laughed and laughed.

ANGELA DID NOT KNOW WHERE SHE WAS WHEN SHE AWOKE. She was aware only of a dull throbbing pain in her head and another between her legs. Someone was shaking her roughly by the shoulder.

"C'mon, c'mon," a voice was rasping in her ear. "Wake up already. Fun time's over."

She slowly came back to consciousness. She was lying on the padded bench in the cockpit of a sailboat. She shook her head and saw that it was Senator O'Malley shaking her shoulder. It must be Senator O'Malley's sailboat. Her head hurt. Her sex hurt too, and it felt damp down there. Was she having her period?

"Here," O'Malley said and held something out to her. It was a pair of panties, white cotton panties. She realized in horror that they were her panties. How had he gotten those? She grabbed them quickly, embarrassed beyond thinking, and crumpled them up in her hand. "Get in the boat," he ordered her harshly. She didn't want to move, but she obeyed.

She found it hard to concentrate, to think. Her eyes kept closing and her head lolling over to one side. But she was dimly aware as he steered the little boat back to the dock, yanked her out and almost carried her down the dock, around the clubhouse and into the parking lot. He opened the side door of his black sedan and pushed her in. He came around, got in behind the wheel, turned the ignition and wheeled quickly out of the yacht club lot. She could feel in her head and in her loins the bumps in the pavement as they rumbled down the sandy road of the causeway and she was thankful when they finally reached the smooth pavement at the entrance to Serpent Island. Her head was still spinning when he pulled to a stop.

He reached over the top of her, opened her door and said "Get out. Go home."

She looked at him with dazed eyes, confused, uncertain. He repeated. "Go on. Go. Your house is right over there. Go sleep it off. You'll feel better in the morning."

She looked where he was pointing. There was her house. The light over the side door from the kitchen was on, and a pool of golden light spread out down the driveway. She looked at it.

"Get the fuck out of my car, you little wop slut." he hissed, and pushed on her shoulder.

Angela got out of the car. O'Malley reached over and closed the side door behind her, then squealed away down the road and up into his circular drive. She watched him go, watched the red lights on the back of his car disappear into the night. She looked back at her own house, at that spreading pool of golden light. She felt something in her hand and looked down. It was her panties, crumpled and wrinkled. And bloodstained.

That's when she knew what had happened.

RUBY JOHNSON WAS SITTING IN TIMOTHY REGAN'S KITCHEN at the old oak table with its sturdy turned legs, working on a crossword puzzle and sipping some tea. The house was quiet. Regan was in his den, watching something ridiculous on television and she really didn't know where Willie was; probably upstairs getting Regan's bed ready or something. She really didn't care, either—she was trying to figure out a seven-letter word for "Draws a conclusion."

She heard a scratching and then a tentative knock at the kitchen door. She put down the newspaper with a sigh and got up. She opened the heavy inner door and saw Angela standing outside on the back stoop. Ruby opened the screen door with a welcoming smile. Then she saw the girl's face, its look of anguish and pain, eyes unfocused yet troubled. Angela wavered and began to collapse, but Ruby was quick, and caught the girl in her large strong arms, picked her up as if the girl had been made of feathers and carried her inside.

Angela began to weep, a sound that came from the very marrow of her, and Ruby just held the girl, held her tight to keep her from breaking apart. They stood and swayed together in the warm kitchen, the girl sobbing and the older woman holding on.

Willie came in from upstairs, his arms full of something, and saw the two together. At first, he smiled, thinking this was a nice thing, Ruby and the girl. Then he heard the cries of anguish from the girl and he saw his wife's eyes, closed tightly as if in prayer, and he knew something was wrong, very, very wrong.

"What ...?" he started to say, but Ruby's eyes flew open and the look she had in those black eyes stopped Willie cold. They were the eyes of all injured and abused women, eyes of pain and anger, eyes of the whipped and the raped and the beaten and the scorned. The look in those eyes hit Willie in his very gut, and he could only stand there and do nothing but wait.

"Bath," Ruby finally said. "Run us a bath." Willie nodded and went into the Johnson's private suite of rooms behind the kitchen, what in the old days they called the servant's quarters. He set the drain plug and turned on the water, adjusting it to be hot but not scalding. He made sure there were clean towels and washcloths handy. He went back into the kitchen and nodded at Ruby and she carried the girl, effortlessly, through the door.

Willie went into the den. Timothy Regan was asleep in his big leather chair, the television droning on in the background, sending its blue glow into the room. He turned off the set, and Regan woke with a start.

"There's trouble, sah," Willie said. "Trouble with Miss Angel. She in the bath with Miss Ruby right now. I don' like the look of this."

Regan was instantly awake and wanted to go to the child at once, but Willie stopped him. "No," he said, "Miss Ruby with her now. Leave them be."

The two men sat silently, each lost in his own worried thoughts. Time seemed to have crawled to a halt, but it was only a half hour later than Ruby came into the den, shaking her head.

"That pore girl," she said. "Best I can tell, she been raped. By that no-good mother-fucker Senator 'cross the way." Willie was shocked; Ruby never, ever swore, never said anything worse than 'durn.' "What she says, how she actin', I 'spect he drugged her up somehow. She not making lotta sense and still is groggy. I put her in my bed for now."

"Son of a bitch," Regan said, mostly to himself. "That goddam son of a bitch."

Willie turned and walked quickly into the billiards room. There was a glass case on one wall which held half a dozen shotguns, beautiful weapons with burled walnut handles and polished barrels. Willie took out the key, unlocked the case, and took one of the guns down.

"What do you think you're doing?" Regan had followed him and now stood at the doorway to the room, watching.

"I'm gonna go blow the mother-fucking head off that mother-fucking bastard," Willie said.

"You'll do nothing of the kind," Regan snapped. "I will not have you spending the rest of your life in jail leaving Ruby and I to fend for ourselves. Your life is worth far more than that monster across the street. Put the gun back, Willie. I'll deal with this."

Reluctantly, Willie returned the gun to its pegs and closed and locked the glass case.

"What you gonna do?" Willie said, turning to look at his employer. "*You* gonna shoot his ass?" He laughed sarcastically at the thought. "You cain't swat a fly without crying your fool eyes out." He shook his head, looking at the frail old man, dressed in his ridiculous wig and outlandish clothes. "You gonna call the police? They in the pocket o' the man over there. They ain't gonna do nuthin' and you know it. Specially since that girl is the daughter of you know who." He jerked his head in the general direction of the Bruno house.

Regan held up his hand. "Let me think," he said. He turned and went to the telephone in his den and dialed a number.

"Hello? Mrs. Bruno? Good evening to you. This is Timothy Regan, next door? Yes, yes, it was a delightful party and I'm so glad you and Mr. Bruno could stop by. We'll have to make it an annual affair! Yes, lovely. Listen, I wanted to call to let you know that Miss Angela has stopped by over here. Yes, that's right. I didn't want you to worry about her. Ruby is making her some cocoa and we're having a delightful little chat. Yes, of course. Is Mister LaGuista at home this evening? Perhaps you could send him over for her? In about an hour? Lovely. Thank you, Mrs. Bruno. Nice chatting with you, too. Bye-bye."

He replaced the receiver. Willie had followed him into the den and stood there listening.

"What you gonna do?" he said. "You gonna tell her Daddy that his little girl got rogered by the sumbitch? You don't think *that* bad ass gonna blow his fuckin' head off? He'll rape his wife, burn his house down and kill his fuckin' dog!"

Regan shook his head. "Now, Willie, calm yourself," he said. "I agree with you. Joe Bruno must never find out about this. I intend to have a little discussion with Mr. Peter. He will understand. He will know what has to be done."

"I dunno," Willie was still upset. "I still think you should just let me go shoot the motherfucker. Be a lot simpler that way."

But Timothy Regan wasn't listening. He was deep in thought.

Fat Peter arrived at ten. Regan met him at the door and led him into his den. They sat. Willie brought in a decanter of brandy and two snifters, and poured each man an inch of the reddish brown drink. Regan quickly explained what had happened, and told Fat Peter that the girl was sleeping in Rosa's bed. Fat Peter's face never changed; he barely even blinked. When Regan was finished, Peter took a quick sip of his brandy.

"The question now," Regan said, "Is what do we do? My man Willie's first instinct was to take one of my shotguns, walk across the street and eliminate the senator post haste. While I understood the impulse—indeed, agreed with it—I thought it best not to act precipitously."

Fat Peter watched the old man with his small dark eyes. He kept his face blank, even though his mind was racing. He nodded once in agreement.

"It goes without saying that Malcolm O'Malley deserves to enter the lowest circle of hell." Regan continued, holding his own brandy glass and swirling it around to release the wonderful aroma. "But I think that merely eliminating him from the earth would be too easy, too simple a reaction. Before you arrived here tonight, I have been thinking. What, I asked myself, would cause that man the most pain?"

"That's easy," Fat Peter said. "I break both his legs, the big bones, the femur. Each leg. With a baseball bat. And then, I rip his nuts off and shove them down his throat and watch him choke to death on them."

"No, no, my dear Peter," Regan shook his head disapprovingly. "You are still bound by the thoughts of inflicting physical pain. Again, I understand the impulse, I really do. I, too, would want to hurt the man if he was standing here before me. But think. What does Malcolm O'Malley want more than anything else?"

"He wants to be President," Fat Peter said. His eyes widened slightly as he said it. He was beginning to understand where this strange little man was going.

"Precisely," Regan said, leaning forward and patting Fat Peter on the knee, as if he were a schoolboy who had given the correct answer. "He wants that so bad, he is willing to do anything, to say anything to get it. Given the rest of his family history, he feels it is his birthright, his destiny."

"So when I shoot him, he won't get to be president," Fat Peter said. "So what?"

"If you *can* shoot him," Regan said. He saw the smile playing at the corner of Fat Peter's lips. "I know, I know," he continued, quickly. "I am not in doubt of your considerable talents along those lines. But the man is a sitting senator and soon, when he announces for President, he will be protected by the Secret Service. He may be harder to kill than you think."

He let that sink in for a moment. "What if, before you shoot him, he is humiliated?" Regan asked. "What if that which he seeks more than any other thing is snatched away from him? As cruelly as the innocence he has taken away tonight? What if he suffers disgrace, embarrassment, perhaps even exile? Will that not hurt him as deeply as a broken femur, and result in a worse punishment?"

"That's not our style," Fat Peter said. "Man who did what he did, needs to die. After feeling a great deal of pain."

"And then what?" Regan asked. "He will become a martyr. He will become another O'Malley tragedy, the latest in a long line. People will feel sorry for him, pity him, remember him with fondness. I would rather have him remembered as the horrendous human being that he is, than be recalled as a beloved political leader whose life was tragically cut short. No, Peter, dying is too good for a man like Malcolm O'Malley. There is not enough physical pain that will atone for the crimes he has committed. He must be destroyed while still living. It is the only way."

"You know when Joe finds out about this, the man is dead," Fat Peter said. "No matter what plan you got, Joe finds out, the man is as gone as yesterday."

"I know that, Peter," Regan said. "That's why I wanted to talk to you first. I want you to listen to what I have to say. Think about it. If you decide that you must tell your boss the truth, then so be it. You, and he, will do what you must do and, I can assure you, I will shed no tears for the senator. I hope you will think I have a better way."

Fat Peter shook his head. "What about the girl?" he said. "What about Angela? How you gonna stop her from telling her momma, much less her daddy, what the man did to her?"

Timothy Regan nodded. "I think she will listen to me," he said. "I will tell her that if she tells her father, her father will have O'Malley killed, if he doesn't kill the man himself. And then her father will be sent to prison for the rest of his life. She will not want that to happen. I will tell her that if she lets me launch my plan instead, that will hurt O'Malley more than anything else."

"OK," Fat Peter said, sitting back in his chair. "Let's hear this plan. Better be fuckin' good. Because you gotta remember one thing, one very important thing. If Joe finds out and knows you or I didn't tell him, we're as dead as O'Malley."

Regan sat back and swirled his brandy thoughtfully.

"Back in the days of Imperial China, they had a special method for executing the worst criminals," he started. "The really bad men like Senator O'Malley. Like me, they believed that a simple and quick execution was not penalty enough.

One swipe of the executioner's blade and the life was ended. That did not provide enough retribution for a truly bad man's horrible crime. So they instead would inflict the *lingchi*, what they called the 'death by a thousand cuts.' The prisoner would be brought into the public square and tied to a post. Then, his body would be cut in many places, shallow cuts, and he would slowly, painfully, bleed to death. It was humiliation, it was pain, and, the Chinese believed, it would affect the man in the after-life. That is what I want to do to O'Malley," he said. "I want to cut him in a thousand places and watch him bleed to death in public."

"Coupla caps to the head is quicker and cheaper," Fat Peter said.

"Money is no object, dear boy," Regan said with a wan smile. "I have millions and millions of dollars and no family to leave it to. To use my money to avenge what has been done to Angela would be an honor. To watch that man squirm would be worth every last dime."

"How?"

"A thousand small cuts," Regan said. "We know there are other girls out there that he has raped. Boys too. I know some of them. They have come here." He looked at Fat Peter who nodded. He knew this. He had helped arrange it. "They will talk, for money. One will speak, and be accused of telling his story just for the money. Then two will speak, then four, and soon their voices will become a din in his ears."

Fat Peter was nodding, a smile playing at his lips.

"Then the women will begin confessing, in public," Regan continued. "The same process will occur. O'Malley will be humiliated. The depths of his depravity will be revealed, slowly, over time, like each of the thousand cuts. His political supporters will begin to back away. Then, we will tell of some of his business dealings, his political shenanigans. Maybe even his relationships with certain, er, criminal elements?"

Peter shook his head. "I can't let Joe or the organization get hurt," he said.

"Of course not," Regan said quickly. "But I am sure that O'Malley has done shady deals with other organizations of a similar nature. Perhaps there are some you would wish to injure, for your own gain?"

Fat Peter nodded now. He thought of some of the New York families that often got in the way of the Providence organization, and by extension Joe Bruno. And Miami. And Las Vegas. And Chicago. He knew that O'Malley had been cozy with all of them in the past.

"And we might begin to have questions asked about O'Malley's taxes," Regan continued. "How it is that one of the richest men in America, from one of the richest families in history, pays so little in income taxes? And has so much money stowed overseas in numbered accounts. And so on and so on…"

"If any of that sticks, he's in a world of hurt," Peter said.

"Oh, I think enough will stick, each little cut will draw some blood," Regan said. "He will grow desperate as he sees that his dream is dying, just as the victim of *lingchi* could feel his lifeblood draining away, one drop at a time."

"He'll ask us to eliminate the threat," Fat Peter said. He quickly related the meeting he had with Gordon Congdon a few weeks ago, when the senator's chief had asked for the Mob's services in the upcoming campaign in return for lenience from the FBI in an O'Malley administration.

"You know he would double-cross you, don't you?" Regan asked. "You can instead double-cross him. Seal his fate. You can destroy Malcolm O'Malley without firing a shot. He will still be alive, but you will have killed him, killed his hopes and dreams."

"And then I can shoot the motherfucker," Fat Peter said.

"As you wish," Regan said. And he smiled.

FAT PETER DUCKED BACK THROUGH THE HEDGES and returned to the Bruno house. He was still not sure what to do, even after listening to the strange little man describe his plan for revenge. As a man of action, it went against his grain. And yet … There was a chance the old fag was right. Quick, brutal action against O'Malley might not be the best move. There would be repercussions—even Fat Peter knew that you can't kill a sitting U.S. senator without repercussions. Bruno had always said that you had to make sure you were stronger before you hit an opponent; had to make sure the blowback wasn't worse than the gain. He'd have to think about it, roll the whole thing over in his mind.

But he agreed to go along, for now. He had looked in on the sleeping Angela, curled up in Ruby and Willie's big bed, hugging a pillow to her chest, looking in sleep like a girl of six. Her face had been flushed, her hair damp. He had decided to let her sleep, and when he went back, he told Rosa Bruno that her daughter wanted to spend the night at Regan's, was having fun and didn't want to leave, and that he saw no harm in it.

Rosa had frowned, but she trusted Peter's judgment and so she had relented and gone to bed herself.

Regan had said he would talk to the girl in the morning. He would explain to her his plan of revenge, and tell her that if her parents found out what had happened to her that forces beyond her control, anybody's control, would take over. Things would happen that she might not like and certainly her life would be changed, probably not for the better.

Fat Peter did know one thing for sure. He knew that he, too, would speak to Angel. He would let her know that he knew what had happened. In fact, he had insisted to Regan that the old man tell Angela that Peter had been informed. He wanted to look into the girl's eyes himself. He wanted to see what was there, in the depths of her soul. Because he knew that if she asked him, if she even hinted that she wanted Malcolm O'Malley to die, that he would do it. Immediately, brutally and without concern for the repercussions That was not a vow, not a resolution, it was a fact of life.

It was around midnight when Gillian stirred, lifted her head and glanced at the numbers on the clock beside Jack Dunne's bed. "I've got to go," she said softly. "Malcolm will throw a double gasket if I'm not home soon."

Dunne refused to release her from the warm and humid embrace of his arms. "Stay," he said. "Fuck him."

She giggled and nestled in tighter against his chest. "I'd rather fuck you, darling," she said. "Again and again. But there's no sense antagonizing him. He doesn't really care what I do, any more than I care what he does. But we've agreed to keep up appearances for propriety's sake if nothing else. For the campaign."

"And you're going to keep pretending even when he's in the White House?" Dunne asked. "For four, eight more years?"

"It's our little bargain, darling,' Gillian said. "It's all been decided. After his presidency, we'll separate. He doesn't want a divorce. That's against the teachings of his church. It's funny how a man who is so immoral in so many ways is scared stiff of those men in dresses in the Vatican. He thinks he can lie, cheat and steal and fuck anything that walks, but if he gets a divorce he's going to spend the rest of eternity burning in Hell." She giggled. "I don't care. I will get a nice house anywhere I want and a comfortable income for life. And then we can spend the night together. Many, many delightful nights…"

She stretched her head up and kissed him, feeling the rough sandpapery texture of his face. He was frowning. She rose from the warmth of the bed and began to dress quickly in the dark.

"When is your little man coming down again?" she asked. She wanted to change the subject. She could feel the anger pulsing from Dunne. She knew it was a male impulse, this need to control and possess the female. That was why Malcolm allowed her to dally with anyone she wanted, as long as she came back to him at the end of the day. That way, he was claiming her, controlling her, telling all other males that she was, in the end, his. And this was what made Dunne furious. He possessed her body, but he couldn't have her. Not as long as she belonged to Malcolm O'Malley. But she didn't care anymore. She was getting what she wanted: access to O'Malley's wealth and success, and the enjoyment of Dunne's athletic and responsive body.

He answered, after a pause. "Next weekend," he said. "Labor Day."

"Is Kathryn coming too?" she asked, brushing her hair out so she didn't look as though she had spent the last two hours engaged in Dunne's bed, a wonderful two hours in which she had taken and given pleasure several times over.

"No," he said. "She's pushing ahead with a divorce. She'd rather spend eternity burning in Hell than spend another month being married to me."

"Don't be maudlin, darling," Gillian said. "Life goes on. You've still got your job, your beautiful little boy, and you've got me." She bent over the bed and kissed him again. "Not a bad deal."

Closing the door softly behind her, Gillian O'Malley disappeared into the night. The scent of her perfume swirled in the air behind her and then it, too, disappeared.

Dunne lay in his darkened room for a long time after she had gone. Yes, he thought, I still have my job. But Pyle has been noticeably cool since Jason died, and Michael had been almost combative. The Big Dig problem had not yet been put away, but Dunne had done all he could on that front. Still, there were the big Asian and Middle East contracts looming. If those came through, Pyle Industries would be millions of dollars richer and Dunne would once again be in a good position to make his move for the top. He had to get those contracts signed. Then he could decide what to do about Michael, about getting him out of the way. Pyle would have no choice but to name Dunne as the heir apparent.

But he knew that the job, his work life, was just a way to keep from thinking about the other problems in his life. As long as he could bury himself in the problems of making and keeping money, he didn't have to think about himself, or anyone else in his life.

He didn't want to think about Gillian. Yes, she was beautiful. Yes, she was sexy. In bed, she alternated between coquette and slut, one minute soft and pliable, the next hard and demanding. The sex was not the problem. She was erratic, seemed always on the edge of madness. She had lately been drinking less, but Dunne knew she could lapse into the bottle at any moment. He sympathized with her domestic situation, but he also hated it. He felt she was being held as O'Malley's slave, almost. He wanted to free her from him, but he knew it was really none of his business. He didn't like it, but he didn't see how there was anything he could do about it.

And then there was Tiger. He worried about the effect the divorce would have on the boy. He had always been so happy-go-lucky, so bold, so outgoing towards people. But he had seen the looks of painful disbelief on his son's face when he had looked at his mother and father together, a look that said why? He had seen his son's sadness, feelings he knew the boy had never had before. Dunne winced, thinking about it. He didn't want his son to feel like that, ever. He knew it was impossible to go through life without sadness, but he felt responsible for bringing this particular sadness onto the boy, instead of protecting him against it. He hoped Tiger would not forever blame him for it. He hoped the boy would one day understand that this thing, this impasse, between Kathryn and himself was not about the boy at all. "Forgive me," he whispered aloud.

DUNNE AND HIS SON ARRIVED AT SERPENT POINT just as they had several months ago: on a bright, sunny and slightly cool day, riding in the black Saab convertible with the top down and the wind rushing through their hair. Tiger had been worried about his favorite baseball cap being blown away, so he had carefully tucked it underneath the seat for the ride. The traffic had been heavy as all of New England, it seemed, was heading for the Cape, for one last glorious weekend at the beach in the summer sun.

Tiger had not slept this time, but jabbered excitedly all the way down to Winter Cove. He was excited about heading off to the first grade, talking about how he had already met his teacher and some of the other kids in his grade. How his mother had purchased a nice new backpack for him, and a box of pencils, a ruler, and lots of paper. Dunne had listened with a smile on his face, enjoying the boy's excitement.

They stopped for burgers, fries and milkshakes at a take-out place outside the village and then drove out to Serpent Point to have their lunch on the deck at the front of the boathouse. The waves lapped gently on the sandy beach and the gulls skirled noisily overhead, especially after Tiger began throwing the odd French fry over the railing to watch them dive and fight for each morsel.

"What do you want to do this weekend, Tiger?" his father asked.

The boy shrugged, watching the birds. "I dunno," he said. "Something will come up."

Dunne laughed. Tiger was right: something would come up.

Dunne had noticed a girl walking slowly along the water's edge, nudging at things with her toes, bending over occasionally to look at something close up. As she drew near, he saw that it was Angela Bruno. He called out a greeting and she looked up, smiled and came up the beach and onto the deck.

"Hi Mr. Dunne," she said with a brief smile. She looked at Tiger and her smile widened. "And how's my favorite Tiger cub?" It was her pet name for the boy, and although he didn't like cuteness, he seemed to enjoy that. He went over and gave her a hug. She tugged on his cap playfully and they laughed together.

Angel sat with them on the sunny deck and they talked. Dunne thought she seemed a bit subdued, less the bubbly child, more reserved. She must be growing up, he thought. The ugly duckling turning into the beautiful swan, molting the feathers of youth for the coat of adulthood. Outwardly, she seemed the same, but there was something different about her. Something he couldn't quite put a finger on.

After a bit, Tiger began to yawn and Dunne said it might be time for a little nap. Angela hugged the boy again, said goodbye and continued her walk down the beach. Dunne put the boy in his bed and hung his ball cap on the bedpost over his head. Tiger was asleep in minutes.

Dunne went back out onto the deck with a cold beer from the refrigerator, glad to be able to sit down and read the morning newspaper. The headlines on the front page were still all about the hit-and-run accident that had killed one of the paper's star reporters several days ago. The state police had taken over the investigation and were said be looking into several possible leads in the case. The woman's editor had been quoted as saying that Marcia Weibe had been looking into a possible connection between the Big Dig project and organized crime, but that he had no further details.

Well, well, Dunne thought as he read the reports. A possible connection to organized crime? That was a sign that pointed right at Joe Bruno's organization. And the way the woman had been killed—hit-and-run with a nondescript blue sedan that had still not yet been found—sounded exactly like a Mob hit. Dunne knew that Bruno would stonewall, could stonewall, until the end of time. But if the cops ever found that car, the earth would shift and shake and who knew what might happen then?

It was another problem. He sat there in the warm sun, thinking about it, until he fell asleep, the newspaper slipping from his hand.

Dunne awoke an hour or so later. He started, looking around to see where he was. A slight cover of cloud had obscured the sun in haze and turned the ocean from sparkling blue to gunmetal gray. He stood up and stretched. He looked at his watch, and walked inside to check on Tiger.

The boy's bed was empty. His ball cap was missing from the bedpost.

"Tiger?" Dunne called out. There was no answer. He checked the bathroom and looked in his own bedroom. Both were empty. He went quickly back out onto the deck and scanned the beach in both directions. Just an older man and his wife, far down to the east. The rest of the beach was empty. He cupped his hands. "Tiger!" he yelled.

Dunne fought against the panic that was beginning to rise in his chest. Keep calm, he told himself. Breathe. He fell back automatically on his Special Forces training: assess the situation, organize a response, execute. He quickly circled the boathouse, checking to see if Tiger was hiding, sitting in the car or playing somewhere nearby. He then went back to the beach and, after looking up and down both ways, turned and headed toward the O'Malley mansion. Tiger had once wandered there attracted by some kittens. He walked hurriedly, keeping himself from sprinting, until he reached the fence that surrounded the vast green lawn. It was empty. He called out again: "Tiger? Where are you?" He jogged now down the beach to the long stretch of sand that ran beside the causeway entrance to the island, checking behind some of the large boulders that lay next to the beach. He caught up with the elderly couple walking hand-in-hand and asked if they had seen a young boy wearing a Red Sox cap. They hadn't.

He turned and sprinted back to the west, past the boathouse, heading now towards Tom Pyle's house. He scanned the water, looking for any sign of the boy and hoping he wouldn't see one. He kept calling, again and again. The Pyle's backyard and deck were empty and the house seemed empty. Dunne kept on running down the beach until he reached a marshy area thick with reeds. He called again and again, but there was only silence.

Shit, he thought, Shit, shit. He ran back to the boathouse and again did a quick search inside and out. When he came back onto the deck, he saw Gillian O'Malley running down the beach toward him. He went to meet her at the water.

"What's happened?" she asked, seeing the panic in his face.

"Tiger is missing," he said. "We were both napping and when I woke up, he was gone."

"OK," she said, "Don't panic. He's probably just hiding somewhere. You've checked the beach?"

He nodded.

"Right. Let's go look on the drive and at the neighbors," she said. "Maybe he went to visit Angel."

Together, they quickly walked to the narrow lane that wound through the center of the island. They started at the cul-de-sac in front of Pyle's house and headed back towards the entrance gates. They both kept calling for Tiger and waiting for the answer which never came.

Gillian ran up Timothy Regan's drive while Dunne continued on down the lane. He came to the fork which led in to Joe Bruno's house and garage and turned down it. As he neared the house, Fat Peter came strolling out of the garage, trailed by another dark-haired man wearing a blue blazer and a pair of well-pressed jeans.

"Mr. Dunne," Fat Peter said in greeting, "What's up?"

"It's my son, Tiger," Dunne said. "He's gone missing on me. Have you seen him in the last half hour?"

Fat Peter shook his head.

"Is Angela here? We thought he might have come over to see her?"

"Naw," Peter said. "She went out with her mother, half hour ago. They were going into town, do some shopping."

There was a rustling in the hedge and Gillian came bursting through from the Regan place next door. "Any luck?" she asked. Both men shook their heads.

"You checked the beach?" Peter asked. Dunne nodded. "Well, he can't get too far. Angelo…" He turned to the dark-haired man. "Get Benji and take a walk around. See if you can find the little boy." He turned back to Dunne. "What's his name?"

"Tiger," Dunne said. "He's six. Wearing blue jeans, a blue sweatshirt and a Red Sox cap." Angelo turned and went back inside the garage.

Gillian put her hand on his arm. "Jack?" she said. He looked at her. "I think you ought to call the police. They know how to do this kind of thing."

"Lady's right," Fat Peter said. "He gets into the marshes back there…" He nodded at the mainland side of the island, where the serpentine tidal creeks snaked through the muddy flats. He didn't finish the sentence, but the warning was clear.

Without a word, Jack Dunne pulled out his phone and dialed 9-1-1.

WITHIN HALF AN HOUR, SERPENT POINT WAS CROWDED with official vehicles. Three police cars were parked outside the boathouse and a rescue truck from the Winter Cove fire department blocked the lane that wound through the center of the island, its staccato red-and-white emergency lights flashing soundlessly. But the driver had flipped the switch that broadcast the traffic on the truck's radio through some outside speakers, and the raspy static of the call and response from the dispatcher echoed through the air.

Three orange-suited men from the rescue squad had begun to search along the edge of the marshes on the mainland side of the island. Two others had begun to walk along the beach again, and one had called in a request for a marine unit to cruise the offshore waters, looking for a little body.

Two of the police officers had begun the process of visiting the residents of the island, looking through the yards and asking questions. An unmarked car pulled into Dunne's drive and a deputy chief got out. He asked if he could speak with Dunne. Gillian went along.

Inside the house, the policeman flipped open his notebook and began the routine, taking down name, age, identification. To Dunne, it was painfully slow. Every second that ticked away was one that could have been spent looking for his son. A uniformed officer stood impassively by the door, listening. Suddenly, his radio, attached to his left shoulder, burped. He bent his head to listen, then unclipped his microphone and spoke a few words into it. He looked at the chief. "They found something," he said. "Over at Round Pond."

Dunne was the first one out the door, brushing past the officer. He leapt off the deck and sprinted out onto the lane and down towards the entrance gates to the island. Round Pond was a perfect circle of tidal creek, free of reeds and other growth, which lay a dozen yards from the roadway. Dunne and Tiger had gone there several times to toss crackers and bread crusts to the ducks that liked to swim in the protected water, and the noisy gulls which liked to preen and bathe.

He was there in no time. The orange-suited rescue crew was standing near the far edge of the pond, where a grassy sward gave way to the rough tumble of reeds and briars. They were looking at something. It was a baseball cap. A small one, a child's cap. It was dark blue with a big red B embroidered on the front.

Dunne looked at it for a long moment, then he turned and started towards the pond. One of the rescue men put out a hand and stopped him. "We've called for a diver," he said. "If you go in there it will just disturb the mud, make it harder to see anything. I'm sorry."

Dunne's reaction was instantaneous and unbidden. His hands went around the man's throat and he began to squeeze. "That's my son, goddam you," he said through gritted teeth. "My son."

The other crew members quickly leapt to their comrade's aid, and the three of them were able to pry Dunne's hands away and subdue him. He sank to his knees, his shoulders sagging, all fight gone. "My son," he said again, in a bare whisper.

Several hours later, Jack Dunne was sitting on the deck of the boat house. The rescue crew had finished searching the pond. The diver had gone over every square inch and had not found a body. The search had continued through the tidal creeks and muddy banks. Gillian had called her husband to ask if he would help get the Coast Guard involved, and a helicopter had been dispatched to circle the island and make several passes over the tidal flats looking for any sign of the boy. So far, there had been nothing.

The rescue and police vehicles had now been joined by a half dozen white vans, parked along the causeway entrance to Serpent Point. Each van grew a long spiral horn which held the transmission antennas that were ready to beam live shots back to the studios in Boston and Hyannis and New Bedford when the searchers found the little boy's body. The well-coiffed reporters, both men and women, gathered around one of the vans, smoking cigarettes and swilling energy drinks, exchanging gossip and checking their phones for text messages. Missing boy from Senator Malcolm O'Malley's exclusive Cape

Cod neighborhood feared dead…that was a potential lead on the evening news, and each reporter silently rehearsed the stand-up, imagining the visage of earnest sadness they would adopt as they gave the world the tragic news.

Dunne had called Kathryn, probably the most difficult thing he had ever had to do. She had, of course, been frantic. Dunne had arranged for a company car to pick her up and bring her down to the Cape—he didn't want her driving in such an emotional state. Now, there was nothing he could do but wait. Wait for his worst fears to be realized. He knew, deep in his heart, that Tiger was gone.

His cell phone rang and he snatched it up quickly. "Yeah?" he said.

"Jack," came a familiar voice. "Tom here. I just heard. My God."

"Yeah," Dunne said. "I can't believe this is happening."

"Listen, I want you to come right over. We need to talk."

"Now?" Dunne said. "I don't think I'm in any shape to discuss business."

"No," Pyle said. "This may concern Tiger. Please. Right now."

Hearing that, Dunne agreed. He asked Gillian to stay in the boat house in case any further word came in, and told her he was going next door. He walked down the beach and entered the Pyle house through the rear door on the deck. The house was strangely quiet, all the lights out.

"Tom?" he called.

"In here, Jack," Pyle called back. "In my study."

Dunne entered the quiet, paneled room. Tom Pyle sat behind the large mahogany desk, a brass lamp with its green shade providing a pool of golden light, the only light in the room. A single tufted leather chair sat empty in front of the desk. There was a man standing against the wall to Dunne's right. He was dressed in a dark business suit, and his arms were folded across his chest. He looked to be about forty-five years old, with short brown hair and dark eyes which looked at Dunne with a kind of curiosity.

"Sit," Pyle said, indicating the empty chair.

"Tom, I really don't have the time right now," Dunne said.

"Sit down!" This time, Pyle barked his words in a sharp command. Dunne shrugged and sat down.

"This is Greg Greenfield, former FBI agent," Pyle said, nodded at the man against the wall. Dunne turned to look at him. "I hired him about a month ago to do some private investigation work for me. On someone in the company."

"Really?" Dunne said. "Who?"

"You," Pyle said, his gaze even, his chin thrusting at Dunne. "It was after Jason died. I had some questions. Michael had some questions. I asked Greg here to find out the answers."

Dunne was silent. He folded his hands in his lap quietly and waited.

"Two weeks ago, Greg's people managed to find the wreckage of Jason's plane," Pyle continued. "It was in twelve hundred feet of water. We hired the best marine salvage company in the world to help us get the plane to the surface. It probably cost Pyle Industries two million dollars. Best money I've ever spent." Pyle waited, watching the man sitting across the desk. But Dunne's face was implacable, calm.

"We hired the best criminologists money could buy to go over that plane with a fine-toothed comb. Do you know what they found?"

Dunne was immobile, a statue.

"Of course, you already know, don't you? They found the remains of two paper cups floating in the fuel tanks in the wings," Pyle said. "There were remnants of adhesive around the edges of both cups, and more adhesive inside the fuel chamber. There was also evidence that the fuel gauge had been tampered with. I've been told that this is an old saboteur's trick. You empty the fuel tanks, or don't fill them up, but instead you glue a container, like a paper cup, inside the fuelling pipe and fill that, so when the pilot sticks a finger in the pipe as part of the pre-flight check, he thinks the tanks are full. The only way a pilot could suspect something was wrong is if he rocked the plane itself back and forth and listened for the sloshing sound of the tanks full of fuel. But most pilots don't do that. Hell, most of them don't even stick their finger in the tank anymore. They see the receipt for a fill-up on the seat, they look at the fuel gauge and they figure they're good to go. Pretty neat trick, no?"

"I don't see what this has to do with me," Dunne said.

"Greg then checked with the maintenance department at the Winter Cove airport," Pyle continued. "They recalled a visit the afternoon of Jason's last flight by someone who said they were with Pyle's aviation department. Someone who showed them the paperwork that gave him access to the plane for the two or three hours while Jason and that poor girl were here with Margaret, having a picnic. Someone who looked a lot like you. And, after we showed them a photograph, that someone was identified as being, in fact, you."

Pyle stared across the desk. His hands were trembling with emotion. He fought to maintain control.

"While all that was going on, Greg also visited the homes and the offices of Jason and Michael overseas, and he found that all four places had been bugged," Pyle continued. "He traced the electronics back to the office of somebody, I forget the name, who reported directly to you."

"Is that all?" Dunne said, keeping his voice level.

"Not quite," Pyle said. "At my request, Greg began a 24-hour surveillance of you some three weeks ago. We've had people watching your every move, Dunne. We know where you got the blue sedan. We saw you run that poor woman, that reporter, down in Boston. We know where you stashed the car afterwards."

Pyle watched as Dunne absorbed that news. "I think the Globe will be pretty interested in finding out where that car is," he continued. "Not to mention the state police. Or, for that matter, Joe Bruno. He might be a little pissed that someone tried to frame him. You really don't want to piss a guy like Joe Bruno off. He tends to react, ummm, violently."

Pyle smiled. Dunne rocked back in his chair slightly. Then he set his shoulders straight again. "So what?" he said. "I don't give a shit anymore. I'm only thinking about Tiger right now. So do what you have to do."

Pyle continued to smile. "Ah, yes, young Tiger," he said. "It hurts, doesn't it? Losing a child? I know exactly what you're going through. Because I went through it myself just a few weeks ago, I knew exactly how to inflict the same kind of pain on you."

Dunne's eyes narrowed to near slits. "What are you saying?" he said, his voice now hoarse. "Did you have something to do with Tiger? What did you do? Where is he? Did you hurt him?"

"It's not a pleasant feeling, is it Jack?" Pyle said. "It's probably the worst feeling in the world. Losing a child. Knowing he is dead and isn't coming back. All the hopes and dreams you have for them… gone. Forever. I thought you ought to know what that feels like."

"You son-of-a-bitch," Dunne said. "You fucking son…"

He leapt forward, trying to crawl across the polished expanse of the big desk, trying to reach the throat of Pyle. His eyes were crazed, his mind empty of all thoughts except the one: kill this man.

A gun appeared in Pyle's hands, an Army-issue .45 revolver. He had been keeping it hidden in his lap, knowing that Dunne was likely to do something rash. The gun roared, and Dunne's forward motion stopped. Dunne shook his head, he snarled, reached out again. And again the gun barked, and this time, Dunne fell backwards, knocking the leather chair over and then he lay still. Greg Greenfield had drawn his gun as well, but he never had to use it.

The silvery smoke that had drifted from the barrel of the

gun swirled in the golden light in the room, drifting away to the ceiling. Tom Pyle picked up his phone and dialed a number. He waited while it rang, and then someone answered.

"OK, Margaret," he said. "Send the boy home."

THE REPORTERS WAITING IN THEIR TRUCKS double-parked on the causeway got a story. But it wasn't the one they expected. It was even better than that.

The sun had almost set when a small silver Nissan sedan turned onto the causeway leading to Serpent Point. It drove slowly down towards the entrance, where it had to pass the line of TV vans. One of the reporters waiting there noticed a small boy in the passenger seat. He looked about six years old. He was staring out the window at the trucks and pointing, his eyes wide.

The silver car stopped briefly at the entrance gate, where a police car from the Winter Cove department was parked. One of the officers bent his head down and spoke briefly to the driver, an older woman with graying hair. They exchanged a few words and the officer stood up and gestured to his partner. Then he reached up to his shoulder, pressed the button on his radio handset and began talking.

The reporter, a woman named Shelley Cranston, began to walk towards the silver car. "What is it?" she called out to the police officer? "It's him, isn't it? It's Tiger. He's come home, hasn't he?"

A huge grin broke out across the officer's face, and Shelley knew. Son of a bitch! she thought to herself. A happy ending! The kid is safe! This is gonna make me a star!

The officer waved the car through the gateway. Shelley Cranston motioned frantically to her cameraman and chased the car up the lane, her heels clicking on the road's hard surface. Within seconds, there was a line of television reporters, cameramen and sound engineers chasing the little silver car up the tree-shaded roadway onto Serpent Point. Microphone booms were extended, the bright lights clicked on, questions began to be shouted in the gathering dusk.

The silver car halted at the entrance to the boat house and the driver honked the horn, once. The gaggle of reporters caught up and surrounded the car. The boat house door opened, and Kathryn Dunne came out, her face streaked with tears. She stopped and her hands flew up to her face.

The passenger door to the car opened and a little boy climbed out.

"Mommy!" he shouted, his voice thin and high and clear. "Mommy, I'm back!"

He ran and Kathryn gathered him in her arms and hugged him tightly as if she would never, ever, let him go.

The cameras caught the entire scene. Shelley Cranston found herself weeping, uncontrollably. Her cameraman, after capturing long seconds of Tiger and his mother hugging and crying, turned to the reporter. She was unable to speak, but simply looked on at the scene as tears ran down her face. Later, the director back in Boston ran the tape as it had been shot. There really was nothing more to be said.

It was then that the police cars, sirens wailing in the lingering evening, began to approach on the causeway, and the story got even better. Five cars, two from Winter Cove and three from the local state police barracks, barreled down the lane, squealed past the emotional scene at the boathouse and pulled to a stop in front of the Pyle house next door. The word quickly went out that there had been a shooting. Tiger's father was dead.

Suddenly, Shelley Cranston, still weeping, realized that this lost-boy story had become much, much bigger. This was the stuff of national news. *Look out Couric, you bitch*, she thought. *I'm coming for you!*

For the next few days, Serpent Point was the dateline leading every newspaper in the country. The boy gone missing, the father shot dead, the boy miraculously returned…it was a story discussed at bus stops and water coolers across the country.

Margaret Anderson had taken the boy to a local fair that afternoon—she insisted that Jack Dunne had known about it and approved. "He must have forgotten," she said. They had spent an enjoyable afternoon riding the Ferris wheel, eating caramel-dipped apples on a stick, trying to win a stuffed tiger at the ring-toss game. She said she had no idea why Dunne would have thought the boy had disappeared. She was mortified to think of all the trouble that everyone had gone through.

The shooting of Jack Dunne had been described as self-defense; and an inquest that followed a week or so later concurred. Greg Greenfield, the former FBI agent, testified that Dunne and Tom Pyle had been having a business discussion when Dunne suddenly turned violent and attacked the older man. Everyone agreed that he must have snapped with the stress and believing his son was dead. A most unfortunate series of events. Of course, Tom Pyle had no choice but to defend himself. Justifiable homicide. Case closed. People talked about it for weeks.

Timothy Regan, for one, paid very little attention to the story. No longer did Regan enjoy lingering in bed with breakfast and the morning newspaper, followed by a leisurely soak in the hot bath and perhaps a rub-down from the skilled hands of Willie. Now he rose with the dawn, quickly showered and dressed himself, and brought himself down to the kitchen for a cup of coffee and a quick breakfast. He would then take another cup of coffee to his den, and sit behind the large desk, staring out the window at the awakening marshes, thinking and making occasional notes in a pad in front of him.

After several days of planning, he began to act. He picked up the telephone and began to place calls across the county. To Miami. Houston. Los Angeles. Chicago. St. Louis. Seattle. He talked to people he knew in music and show business. He talked to pimps and procurers. He even talked with several old tricks he had kept up with; they were certainly older now, although they had been young and compliant when Regan had known them, had played with them.

The word went out: Timothy Regan was looking for information, and for people to come forward and tell what they knew, from personal experience, about Malcolm O'Malley. He was offering a hundred thousand dollars for good information and twice that for someone who would agree to make a sworn statement. And he was negotiable. Regan had spoken the truth when he said money was no object. His net worth was over a billion dollars, and most of it was in blue chip securities. He could, and would, sell them as needed to aid The Project.

His goal was to have the first wave of former O'Malley conquests ready to go public by the first week in November. Regan had heard that O'Malley was planning to launch his presidential campaign with a big event at his home across the road on Serpent Point. The national press would certainly be in attendance. It would be the perfect time to begin the campaign to undermine O'Malley's bid for the presidency.

Regan kept in contact with Fat Peter, who had been successful, so far, in keeping Joe Bruno in the dark about his daughter's rape. Angela had agreed to go along with the plan, although she had been less than enthusiastic. She really wanted to forget the whole thing, not to have to think about it ever again; but she also understood that something had to be done. Fat Peter had explained that if her father ever found out what had happened to her, bloodshed would be the only possible outcome. O'Malley would die in a hail of bullets, the *Filibuster* would burn to the waterline and Joe Bruno would likely be sent to jail for the rest of his life. The family's honor would be restored, in Bruno's eyes at least, but forever after he would be considered an assassin, O'Malley would be the victim, and Angela herself would be notorious for the rest of her life. "That crazy old fart next door has another idea," Fat Peter had explained to the girl, speaking about Regan. "His plan will take away from O'Malley the one thing he wants more than anything else. It will hurt him more than any number of broken bones or bullets could. And then, maybe one day when he thinks it's safe to be seen in public again…well, maybe then I'll personally blow his fucking head off."

Angela had listened, her big brown eyes round and serious. She had conceded that Regan's plan made sense. She had agreed that she didn't want to lose her father. She understood that part. She didn't seem happy, of course. But Fat Peter and Timothy Regan believed that she understood what they were trying to accomplish. She went back to school after Labor Day and never said another word about it to either man.

Finally, Regan's offered bait began to attract some nibbles. And then some strong interest. And, finally, some results.

In Los Angeles, he found two girls who had recently graduated from Beverly Hills High School who had volunteered to work on an earlier O'Malley campaign in return for credit in their civics class. They thought they were going to stuff envelopes and help with the phone banks. But the senator had seen them and invited them both up to his hotel suite. They had been given alcohol and drugs and had been the central attraction in a boisterous evening of sex with the senator and several of his campaign aides. One of the girls, the next morning, had suffered a serious breakdown and had to be hospitalized for several months. Both of the girls had agreed to make an official statement of the facts of the event, and to file a suit—attorneys paid for by Timothy Regan—against Malcolm O'Malley and the state party.

In Miami, there was a teenaged Cuban boy who had been dramatically rescued by the Coast Guard when his rickety boat finally sank some two miles from the Florida coast. He had been slated for return to Havana under the current law, but there had been a hue and cry in public and Malcolm O'Malley had come to town and announced he would introduce special legislation in the Senate to make sure the boy, Justin Ruiz, would not be returned to Cuba against his will. O'Malley had met the boy, taken him to dinner and then forced him to fellate him in his hotel room. Ruiz was willing to go public; he had made a statement and turned it over to a lawyer that Regan had paid for.

Regan was still following up on some other possibilities: young girls that had been abused or raped in Houston and Seattle; boys who had been forced into sex in Denver and Portland, Maine. He had spoken to a number of high-class procurers he had known and dealt with over the years, men and women who worked with rock stars, show business people and others for whom discretion was mandatory. He had promised to keep the names of the procurers and arrangers secret—all he wanted was statements from the victims of O'Malley. Regan was certain that he could prove through this initial series of statements that Malcolm O'Malley was a dangerous pedophile. Regan believed that the exposure of these first cases would serve to disqualify O'Malley for the presidency, but he knew he would need more to make sure. O'Malley's political operation was one of the slickest and best-funded in American politics, and the senator would not give up without a fight. O'Malley and his people would try to attack the reputations and veracity of the victims. They would blame it all on some kind of conspiracy. They would blame the media for dwelling on the bad news. Regan wanted to be ready for all that and more. And then he wanted to roll out some more victims of O'Malley's rapacious appetites. He wanted the sheer weight of the numbers of victims to overcome any counterattack by O'Malley. He would not let his campaign get sidetracked; he would fight any attack from the O'Malley camp with more offensives. He would not rest until O'Malley had been humiliated from coast to coast. Or until O'Malley had finally withdrawn from the race.

ANGELA BRUNO WAS HAVING TROUBLE SLEEPING. Like most teenagers, this had never been a problem before—she was entirely capable of deep, undisturbed sleep for twelve to fourteen hours at a time. But now, she found herself tossing and turning at night, beset by thoughts of anger and revenge, violent dreams that left her sweaty and slightly nauseous. She wanted to forget what had happened to her that evening on O'Malley's yacht; indeed, she only had the foggiest memories of what actually had taken place. Most of the events of that night were hazy, lost in the cloud of drugs that he had slipped into her tea. But she remembered enough. And those memories kept her awake during the long hours of the night, and sometimes occupied her mind during the day.

She began to lose weight, enough that her mother had commented on it. She had laughed it off as stress from a new school year, saying that her teachers had loaded up the homework assignments and increased the pressure for making good grades to demonstrate to potential college admissions officers that she was worthy of consideration. But Rosa Bruno was not convinced it was that simple. She saw her daughter pushing her food around her plate at dinner, rather than eating it; she noted how Angela didn't snack much anymore; she saw the girl's hollow, tired eyes in the mornings. She knew something was wrong, but she didn't know what. It was worrisome.

Fat Peter had also noticed the change in Angel's personality. He saw the lack of energy, the disappearance of her usual buoyant nature, heard her frequent deep sighs. He knew what she was thinking about, and it killed him, again, that he couldn't do anything about it. Peter was used to dealing with problems in the most direct way. Guy owes money? Go pay him a call, get the money. One way or another. Somebody in the organization not doing what they're supposed to do? Fat Peter's job was to take care of it. And he knew how to do it.

But this was different. He didn't know how to fix Angela's mood, how to stop her from thinking about what she had been through. He knew, deep down, that his usual method of problem-solving—walking across the street to the O'Malley house and putting a couple of caps into the senator's head—wouldn't solve this problem, and would likely make it worse for the girl. But he was bothered by the fact that there was nothing he could do to help. He was a man of action and he had been rendered actionless.

Despite his frustration and concern, Peter had come to look forward to the afternoons when Angel came home from school. She would often spend an hour or two hanging out with him, out in the garage office, telling him about the events of her day at school. Fat Peter knew that Joe Bruno didn't like his kids hanging around "the office" where he was afraid they could get in the way or hear something they shouldn't, but he and Angel both enjoyed this time together. She could decompress a little from school before Rosa would pop her head in the door and gently suggest it was time to tackle the homework; and he could spend a good hour with the girl, trying his best to jolly her out of any moods. The other soldiers in the office, usually Benji and Angelo, had gotten used to her presence as well, and they carried on with their usual duties while she lolled around and chatted about her day.

Peter didn't know that Angela was hanging around the office for a reason. She waited and watched for the time when Benji was cleaning some of the guns that were kept under lock and key in a special closet. She watched carefully as he broke the guns down, carefully cleaned and oiled all the little metal parts and gizmos, and then put them back together again, making sure each part was oiled and polished. She watched to see where the key to the closet was kept, where the ammunition clips were stored, how the things worked. She watched, she waited. Angela Bruno also had a plan.

Ladies and gentlemen, it is my high honor to introduce to you the next President of the United States ... Senator Malcolm O'Malley! The people assembled on the sunny lawn next to O'Malley's Serpent Point home rose as one and began to cheer and applaud. Strobe lights from the gaggle of press photographers began to flash, sending brilliant white illuminations against the deep brown tan of O'Malley's smiling face as he mounted the dais and shook hands with the Governor who had just introduced him. His leonine shock of white-gray hair was swept back carelessly, and his eyes sparkled with proud excitement as he acknowledged the outpouring of affection from the crowd of friends and supporters. He pointed at several in the audience, mouthed some words of thanks, and waved. The cheers rolled on and on.

In the excitement of the moment, no one noticed the thin teenager who rose from her white plastic chair in the third row when everyone else stood to cheer. No one saw her reach into her leather school bag. No one saw her fingers wrap themselves around the cold steel handle of the revolver she had taken from Benji's desk earlier that morning. No one saw her raise her arm and point the gun straight at Malcolm O'Malley's tanned and grinning face.

No one saw her finger squeeze the trigger. But everyone heard the loud report of the gun. Everyone saw O'Malley's face disintegrate into a bloody pulp. Everyone saw him stagger and fall over backwards, blood geysering out of the hole in his forehead and spilling across the dais.

A woman screamed …

ANGELA BRUNO AWOKE FROM HER DREAM, drenched in cold sweat. She looked at her alarm clock. It was just before six in the morning. Her alarm hadn't gone off yet. But she was wide awake now. Today was the day. She closed her eyes and tried to recall the images of her dream. But it was over. The time for dreaming was done. It was now time to act.

She threw back the covers and leapt from her bed.

THE MORNING OF NOVEMBER 2 dawned clear and unusually warm. Gordon Congdon also woke just before six and peered outside the window at Nantucket Sound across the broad lawn of the O'Malley mansion. The sky was free of clouds. He heaved a sigh of relief. Maybe this campaign really was going to be kissed by the Gods, he thought, if they've sent us nice weather for the kickoff.

Everything was ready for Malcolm O'Malley's noon announcement that he was formally entering the race for President of the United States, the election due to be held exactly one year hence. It was hardly a secret, of course—the political world had known for at least the last year that O'Malley would be the candidate. No one else of importance in the party was even bothering to run. The primaries would be more coronations that contested elections, and O'Malley would be able to marshal his resources for the general election campaign. He already had hundreds of millions of dollars from the O'Malley family coffers stowed away in the campaign account, and Congdon could raise millions more whenever it was needed with just a couple of calls. It had been generations since one candidate had been so universally acknowledged as the favorite, and Congdon expected that O'Malley would be swept into office with one of the largest electoral mandates in American history.

Of course, there had been a few blips along the way. Just a few weeks ago, there had been a troubling report from Los Angeles about a young starlet who was currently appearing in a popular sitcom who had claimed that the Senator had once made some untoward advances. But Congdon had managed to keep the lid on that. Barely. Of course, the Senator had indeed molested the young actress at a boozy Hollywood dinner, but, well, so what? Congdon knew that nobody cared about things like that anymore. The surprise among the cognoscenti and the mainstream media would be if someone like Malcolm O'Malley didn't occasionally play a little grab-ass. Bimbo eruptions in politics were so last decade, he thought.

Congdon heaved himself out of bed and quickly checked his Blackberry. There were dozens of messages, as always. Congdon noted a few marked "Urgent:" from San Francisco, Miami, Houston and Portland, Maine. But he decided those could wait—he had more important things to do to get ready for the noon gala announcement. He knew that O'Malley would want to go over the text of the address one more time, making sure the message was clear and that the applause lines were emphatic enough.

Several hours later, the press began to arrive, shuttled in vans from the nearby Winter Cove Yacht Club. The camera crews began setting up their tripods and dragging cables across the lawn. Campaign staffers were setting out white folding chairs and a thin metal microphone was attached to the wooden riser on which O'Malley would make his address, with the sparkling blue of the ocean behind him. Congdon had decided against any kind of podium, which might detract from the view. O'Malley liked the informality of speaking without one, feeling it made him look closer to the people. His two TelePrompter screens were set up on either side, so he could move his head to the left and right, speaking to everyone in the audience in front of him.

Katrina Allberg, the political correspondent for CNN was standing next to her camera crew and smoking a cigarette when she saw Gordon Congdon surveying the scene, a cell phone glued to his ear. "Man of the people, huh Gordon?" she snarked. "What's this place worth, coupla hundred million?"

Congdon sneered back at her. "I hope you're not going to be a pain in the ass for the entire campaign, Katrina," he said. "Be too bad if your credentials got lost or something just before we all go out to California."

"Is the Senator going to see his little actress friend while he's out there?" Katrina asked with a smirk.

Gordon flipped the woman a bird. She laughed. *This campaign is going to be more fun than I thought*, she mused to herself.

The audience for the O'Malley speech was made to be up of campaign staffers, political friends, bigwigs from state and local government, and big donors to the campaign. Nothing but friendly faces. They began filtering in an hour before the appointed time. Gillian O'Malley, looking radiant in a pretty navy suit that offset her golden hair, was assigned to greet the VIP guests at the entrance to the lawn as the official hostess of the O'Malley estate on Serpent Point. Playing her role perfectly, she hugged or air-kissed almost everyone who came in through the arched white gates.

Security was tight, of course, and the front drive was full of Secret Service agents, dressed in their impeccable dark suits, wraparound dark glasses and ear pieces, with little trails of curled wires disappearing into their collars. All the guests, including the media, had walked through the metal detectors and been wanded back at the yacht club before boarding the vans that shuttled them to the O'Malley house.

"Miz O'Malley, Miz O'Malley!" a girlish voice penetrated through the hubbub and Gillian looked over and saw Angela Bruno waving at her. The girl was wearing her parochial school uniform: a blue blazer over a pressed white shirt and a gray wool skirt that fell down below her knees. She had a brown leather school bag draped over one shoulder. A Secret Service agent had stopped the girl, who didn't have a security pass. Gillian walked over and smiled at the agent.

"It's OK, Burt," she said to the agent. "She's a neighbor."

She turned and gave the girl a hug. "How are you, Angel?" she said.

"I'm fine," Angel said. "This is so exciting. I'm skipping school to be here, but I told my teacher I'd write a paper about it. Is it OK if I come in?"

"Of course, honey," Gillian said. "Let me make sure you get a good seat." She turned and grabbed one of the young campaign workers and told her to find Angel a seat near the front. The Governor and his wife arrived in a long black limousine, and Gillian went over to greet them.

Angel settled into her chair, next to the central aisle and four rows back from the riser where the Senator was going to make his address. She put the leather bag between her legs and reached inside to pull out a spiral notebook, which she placed on her lap. She then rooted around for a pen. Her fingers touched the cold metal of the small handgun that rested at the bottom of the bag.

Her parents had spent the night in their Boston apartment and Fat Peter was supposed to drive her to the school that morning, but she had told him she wasn't feeling well. She had insinuated that it was her monthlies, and he hadn't wanted to argue with her about that. She had stayed quietly in her room for the morning, and then snuck out of the house in plenty of time to cross the road and join the crowds of people coming from the buses and vans, streaming towards the O'Malley house.

And now all she had to do was wait. She grabbed a pen and pretended to scribble some notes in her notebook.

Malcolm O'Malley huddled inside his office with Gordon Congdon, waiting for just the right moment to make his appearance on the lawn. They had decided that he would dress informally today, in a sports coat, slacks, and an open-necked shirt. No tie, no formality. He wanted to project that "man of the people" look, since that was what his speech, what his campaign would emphasize. "Of course, you're about as much a 'man of the people' as I am a pussy-hound," said Congdon with a crude laugh. "But it's all about the image, the optics. If you look like one of them, sound like one of them, they'll buy it. They always have."

O'Malley was only half listening. He was going over the text of his speech one more time, reading again those lines that he wanted to punch. "A champion for the little guy." "Time for the average American's voice to be heard." "End the rule of the fat cats and the rich." He went over the lines in his head, imagined the applause that would follow. He stopped and looked into a gilt mirror, admiring the man he saw reflected there. This was it, he thought, the culmination of it all. The work that his family had begun, he, Malcolm O'Malley, was going to complete. This was the first step on his journey that would, a year hence, take him right into the Oval Office and the position of most powerful man in the world. He had been born for this. He had patiently waited his turn, and now it was his time.

"OK," he said, still looking into the mirror. "Let's go."

Shoulders back, head held high, Malcolm O'Malley strode out of his mansion and entered the side garden. The people who had gathered and were waiting there stood as one and began to cheer.

ACROSS THE STREET, BENJI MOTILLA stuck his head into the kitchen of Joe Bruno's house and caught the eye of Fat Peter, who was sitting at the table with a cup of coffee and the morning's Globe, reading all the excited anticipation of the beginning of the O'Malley campaign. Much of it made him chuckle. "If you only knew," Peter thought to himself. But he saw the look of concern in Benji's eyes and heaved himself out of his chair and followed Benji across the drive and into the garage office.

"Came in this morning and unlocked the closet," Benji said quickly. The door to the gun closet stood open. Fat Peter glanced inside and immediately saw that one of the snub-nosed .38s was missing, its peg empty. "I asked Rico, and he said he hasn't opened the closet since Tuesday. But he did say that he saw Angel in here early this morning. But what would she want with a gun?"

Fat Peter thought about that for a minute. Then he heard the public address system squawking from across the road, where the senator was about to make his announcement. Shit. He felt raw panic sweep into his body. He didn't bother to go look to see if Angel was upstairs in her bedroom. He knew that she wasn't. He knew where she was. With a speed that was surprising for a man of his bulk and raw size, Fat Peter bolted out of the garage and began to run towards the mansion of Timothy Regan.

He met the old man just coming out of his front door, heading across the street to watch the senator's speech. Regan, dressed in a dapper tweed suit with a matching pocket square, stared at Fat Peter's red and worried face.

"You gotta get the girl," Fat Peter said, his voice harsh and rasping. "She's got a gun. I think she's gonna try and take O'Malley out. Get her. Get her out of there. I can't get within a hundred yards of the place."

Regan reached over and patted the large man's arm. "I'll try," he said.

THE CAMERAS THAT HAD BEEN SET UP in a long line down one side of the lawn swung as one to follow the man as he waded into the crowd of well-wishers, shaking hands, kissing proffered cheeks. Flashbulbs went off in staccato fashion. Across the country, television screens showed the progress of the senator, flashing red LIVE boxes in the corners of the screens telling the world that this was happening right now, in real time.

O'Malley waded slowly through the throng, taking his time, enjoying their adulation. These were his people, his friends, his supporters. This was his time.

The Governor made his introduction and O'Malley rose to acknowledge the cheers of his people. The photographers' strobes flashed. The television cameras were beaming the announcement live to the country. Millions were watching as O'Malley waved and smiled and pointed as the people stood and cheered.

He nailed his speech. He spoke of the troubles facing the country, the need for strong leadership to guide America back to the future that the founding fathers had promised us. He promised to represent all the people when he was president, to make sure the poor and forgotten members of society were heard again. He promised better days for all, with equality, justice and opportunity for all. The crowd hung on his every word, entranced, excited about this new day in American politics, when the head of the leading political family of the era would take control of the government and finally fulfill the promise that had been waiting for so long.

The assembled crowd stood as one when he finished his speech and their cheers rang loudly across the green lawn and carried out into Nantucket Sound. O'Malley stepped down off the dais and waded into the people, shaking hands, accepting congratulations, kissing cheeks and grinning from ear to ear. The cameras flashed again and again and the television reporters began their stand-ups, recounting the main points of the speech while the candidate continued his slow progress through the adoring multitudes.

He had started to push his way up the central aisle, but the crowds had quickly choked off the narrow passage between the chairs, and one of the senator's Secret Service minders had whispered to him and pointed him towards the side aisle, which was more open. He veered off and continued working the crowd as he walked.

Angel Bruno watched carefully as her target got further and further away. Her hand was thrust into her leather satchel, her fingers curled around the cold metal handle of the gun. She frowned as the senator was guided to the side aisle, well away from where she was waiting. Then she turned and began to make her way against the crowds as she headed for the back of the lawn. The small girl flashed her brightest smile as she began to dodge and weave her way through the pushing crowd of people. She would have another chance. She would make sure she did.

Malcolm O'Malley finally made his way to the side porch that overlooked the broad lawn and climbed the stairs. He turned and waved again to the crowd, which responded with another loud roar of approval. Campaign aides began ushering in the national press reporters to an area in front of the porch railing. They would be able to ask a few questions of the new candidate before he went inside. The afternoon had been reserved for one-on-one interviews with the anchors from all three networks, which would dominate that night's newscasts. Gordon Congdon had pre-planned the entire event for the maximum coverage.

No one noticed when the slender teen slipped in beside some of the reporters. She managed to wiggle her way to the front, but off to one side. Still, she was no more than twenty feet from O'Malley. The senator, grinning broadly, spread his hands on the wooden railings and looked down on the press gaggle.

"I'll be happy to take any questions," he said.

Katrina Allberg stood up. "Senator O'Malley," she said. "We have heard this morning that there are several allegations being made that call your personal life into question. Do you have a comment?"

O'Malley smiled. "Allegations?" he said. "I don't know what you mean."

Allberg looked at her notebook. "Specifically," she said, "A teenaged actress in Los Angeles is claiming you molested her during a private dinner last year. There are also claims that you acted inappropriately from three other young women, one in Miami, one in Houston and one in Portland, all of whom were volunteers with your campaign. And finally, there is a high school boy in San Francisco who has claimed that you sexually abused him two months ago after a fund-raiser. Do you have a response?"

O'Malley glanced quickly at Gordon Congdon, who was standing with other campaign staffers at the back. Congdon looked stricken. O'Malley grinned and shook his head.

"Well," he said, "I had hoped that the opposition would wait at least one day before unleashing what is sure to be an ocean of mud in my direction. But I guess that hope for a clean campaign is running up against the realities of today's political climate. Obviously, I have no idea what you're referring to, and I just hope that you in the media will take all these bogus reports with an appropriate skepticism."

"So you deny that you have raped or molested five young people?" the reporter pressed.

"Of course I deny it," O'Malley snapped. "It's totally false and demeaning to even bring such a thing up. I am a happily married man, as my wife will tell you."

Everyone turned to look at Gillian O'Malley, who was standing next to Gordon Congdon. . She wore a glassy expression, her face frozen in shock. Several reporters rose to shout questions. O'Malley held his hands up as if to ward them off.

Angela Bruno had managed to snake her way to the front of the crowd standing in front of the porch. She could look up and almost reach across the railing to touch the senator. Now, she thought. This is close enough. Do it.

She reached into her satchel and her fingers closed around the handle of the small revolver. She began to take it out of the bag. Then she felt a hand closing around her arm. She started and looked up. The smiling, creased face of Timothy Regan bent in close and he whispered.

"There, there, dear heart," he said softly to her. "You don't want to do that. My plan is going to work. You'll see."

Tears formed in her eyes. "I am a Bruno," she said, her voice wavering. "I have to do something."

He looked into her eyes. "You have done something, child, just by coming here today," he said. "You are a brave, strong girl. But you have your entire life in front of you. I can't let you waste it on a scumbag like him." He nodded at the senator, answering another question from the porch. Angel looked at O'Malley too. Regan, his hand still holding the girl's arm, felt her relax. She began to weep softly. He put his arm around her, and gently led her away from the crowds and the flashing lights. She went with him, tears rolling down her cheeks.

The two of them walked down the driveway and headed back towards Regan's mansion across the road. No sooner had they left, two navy-blue sedans, unmarked but with federal license plates, pulled into the drive with a squeal of tires.

The passenger side door of the first car opened, and a tall, lanky man dressed in a dark blue suit, white dress shirt, neat rep tie and highly polished shoes unfolded himself from the front seat. He wore dark wraparound glasses and carried a leather folder. Moving with the slow, unhurried movements of a man who had a role to play and knew his part well, the man in the suit reached into his inside jacket pocket and pulled out a gold shield, which he tucked into his front pocket. He then slowly mounted the steps of the O'Malley's porch and strolled casually over to the side porch, where Malcolm O'Malley, his campaign staff and the assembled crowd of national and international press were watching as if mesmerized.

The man approached O'Malley, opened his folder and withdrew some official-looking documents, folded in several parts and wrapped in a light-blue cover. He then took off his dark glasses, revealing his icy gray eyes, which stared at the man standing before him.

"Malcolm O'Malley?" he said, his deep voice carrying out over the lawn so that everyone could now hear. "I am U.S. Marshall Devon Corrigan. I have been ordered by the Third Judicial Circuit sitting in Los Angeles, California, to serve you with these papers notifying you of a suit that has been filed against you by Jane Doe and June Doe, both aged 16, alleging that you knowingly enticed them into your campaign headquarters on May the 23rd this year, provided them illegally with alcohol and hallucinogenic narcotics, and committed acts of rape, sexual assault, and assault upon their persons."

Corrigan paused and the sound of a collective gasp rattled through the lawn. The press cameras began clicking again furiously. "I also have similar allegations that are being filed today in Federal District Courts in Miami, Houston and Portland, Maine. You are hereby requested to present yourself for arraignment in the Federal courthouse in Los Angeles one week from today, or the judge has ordered that you be arrested and brought to court to answer these and other charges." He handed the papers to the senator who, silent and white, dumbly accepted them. "You have been served, sir. Govern yourself accordingly. Have a nice day."

The marshall turned on his heel and ambled back across the porch the way he had come, descended the stairs and folded himself back into the front seat of his sedan.

The crowd of people watched all this in utter silence. Then, when the door of the sedan clunked shut and the engine cranked up, all heads turned back to the gray-haired senator standing on his porch overlooking the sea. He was looking down at the papers in his hand, staring at them without comprehension.

And then the questions shouted from the press began.

Epilogue

THREE DAYS LATER, MALCOLM O'MALLEY went outside his home for the first time since the disastrous launch to his short-lived presidential campaign. He had been in seclusion while the maelstrom of the news had swept across the country. More than a half-dozen victims had come forward to claim that O'Malley had drugged and sexually assaulted them, most of them when they had been young. Within twenty-four hours, that news had led to another dozen claimants who came forward with similar stories. This amazing news had crowded out everything else that was happening in the world, including a nuclear test in North Korea and another outbreak of brutal tribal warfare in a small and corrupt African nation.

Earlier that day, O'Malley had released a statement saying that he was temporarily suspending all campaign operations until such time as he could answer the charges against him and clear his name. It was universally accepted that this meant O'Malley knew that he was finished. It would take months, if not years, for the legal process to grind its way through the cases that had been brought, and were still being filed, and everyone knew that Malcolm O'Malley would not be elected to any office while the accusations that he was a child molester and rapist were still open. Malcolm O'Malley was not going to be elected President, next year, or any year.

O'Malley had just fired Gordon Congdon and had watched as Gillian O'Malley packed her things and left for Boston. She told him that she was going to file for divorce as soon as possible, news that did not affect him much one way or the other. Letting Congdon go was more difficult. They had been together for nearly thirty years. But someone had to take the fall for the collapse of O'Malley's political world. And that was Gordon Congdon.

His longtime chief of staff was philosophical. "Whatever," Congdon had said with a shrug that morning in the senator's plushly appointed office. "This will eventually blow over," he had said. "And then there will be someone else in Washington who'll want me to do for him what I did for you. You, on the other hand, are radioactive. You got caught fucking children, boys and girls. Lots of 'em. You've got no political career left. If you don't resign from the Senate, they'll impeach your ass. You're probably going to jail. You'll certainly be paying for the rest of your life for all those kids. Me? I'm just the chief of staff to a disgraced leader. Sooner or later, they'll forget my name, forget that I worked for someone like you. But they'll never forget Malcolm O'Malley. You're done. History. Woulda been better for you if that little Bruno girl had blown you away like she wanted. Then you'd be the hero instead of her. And you'd be dead, which is better than what you are now."

Better than what you are now. O'Malley thought about that as he walked on the beach in front of his Serpent Point home. That phrase echoed in his head, but O'Malley refused to believe it was true. He still had millions of dollars and could hire the best legal team money could buy. He still had some power and influence. He could fight this thing. Fight it hard, every step of the way. There was still a chance he could win, still a chance people would listen.

He sat down on the cold sand and stared out at the grey ocean. A chilly wind had come up out of the north and it foretold of the long weeks and months of winter that lay ahead. O'Malley replayed the scenes of the last few days over and over again in his mind. How could this have happened? How?

He felt a shadow and looked up.

"Oh," he said. "It's you. I was wondering when you'd show up."

"Sooner or later," Fat Peter said. "You knew that."

O'Malley nodded.

Fat Peter reached inside his jacket. O'Malley flinched. Fat Peter saw that and chuckled.

"Naw," he said, pulling a gun from out of his coat pocket. "Nothing in the world would give me more pleasure, Senator. Believe me. After what you did to Angela, I've dreamed of this moment. But I can't do it."

The Senator lifted his head and stared at the big man with a quizzical look on his face.

Fat Peter smiled down at him. "We still have a business," he said. "Anything that even hints at us blowing you away would not be good for our business. I can't think of a human being on this earth that more deserves to die a long, painful and ugly death than you, Senator. But it ain't going to be on us. That's why Joe Bruno wasn't told what you did to his little girl. If he knew, you wouldn't be sitting here on the beach. You'd be fuckin' feeding the crabs at the bottom of that ocean."

Fat Peter laid the gun down on the sand.

"So it's up to you, Senator," he said quietly. "You can do the right thing, or the next time you see me, it will be very unpleasant. For you, not for me."

He stood towering above the Senator for a moment, then turned and walked away.

O'Malley stared at the gun for a long time after Fat Peter had left. *Better than what you are now.*

Caleb Clarke is the pseudonym of a well-known journalist and editor, He currently resides in Little Compton, Rhode Island.

Check out these e-books from Yeoman House Books ...

$1.99 each!

Available now at amazon.Yeom